"The most brilliant woman Western taleteller since Mary Austin."
—New York Journal-American

"If you deem locale of prime importance in classifying stories, these are westerns, but calling them thus would be much like suggesting that Walter Van Tilburg Clark's *The Oxbow Incident* is merely a western. Miss Johnson is concerned with the responses of men and women to the whiplash of adversity. She tempers her characters in a crucible often of their own making and from the torment evolves conclusions that are sometimes ironical but invariably 'right.' Of the stories, the longest and, I think, best is the title story. It is a novelette of a doctor who had failed, ironically renamed himself Joe Frail, came to dominate a roaring mining town and then, in a stroke that redeemed his entire life, found himself under the hanging tree with a rope around his neck . . . As in her "Indian Country," Miss Johnson has produced a collection of stories worthy of the most discerning of readers."
—*Chicago Sunday Tribune*

Also included in this collection are ten of Dorothy Johnson's finest stories—among them, "Lost Sister," which won the Western Writers' Award for the best short story of the year.

THE HANGING TREE

Dorothy M. Johnson

BALLANTINE BOOKS • NEW YORK

"Blanket Squaw," Copyright 1942 by
The Curtis Publishing Company

Copyright © 1951, 1954, 1955, 1956, 1957, by
Dorothy M. Johnson

Library of Congress Catalog Card Number: 57-9141

SBN 345-23663-7-095

First U.S. Printing: November, 1958
Second U.S. Printing: March, 1959
Third U.S. Printing: January, 1960
Fourth U.S. Printing: August, 1964
Fifth U.S. Printing: September, 1970
Sixth U.S. Printing: December, 1973

First Canadian Printing: December, 1958
Second Canadian Printing: October, 1964
Third Canadian Printing: March, 1970

Printed in the United States of America

Cover art by Norman Adams

BALLANTINE BOOKS, INC.
201 East 50th Street, New York, N.Y. 10022

Contents

THE HANGING TREE

Lost Sister

OUR HOUSEHOLD was full of women, who overwhelmed my Uncle Charlie and sometimes confused me with their bustle and chatter. We were the only men on the place. I was nine years old when still another woman came— Aunt Bessie, who had been living with the Indians.

When my mother told me about her, I couldn't believe it. The savages had killed my father, a cavalry lieutenant, two years before. I hated Indians and looked forward to wiping them out when I got older. (But when I was grown, they were no menace any more.)

"What did she live with the hostiles for?" I demanded.

"They captured her when she was a little girl," Ma said. "She was three years younger than you are. Now she's coming home."

High time she came home, I thought. I said so, promising, "If they was ever to get me, I wouldn't stay with 'em long."

Ma put her arms around me. "Don't talk like that. They won't get you. They'll never get you."

I was my mother's only real tie with her husband's family. She was not happy with those masterful women, my Aunts Margaret, Hannah and Sabina, but she would not go back East where she came from. Uncle Charlie managed the store the aunts owned, but he wasn't really a member of the family—he was just Aunt Margaret's husband. The only man who had belonged was my father, the aunts' younger brother. And I belonged, and someday the store would be mine. My mother stayed to protect my heritage.

None of the three sisters, my aunts, had ever seen Aunt Bessie. She had been taken by the Indians before they were born. Aunt Mary had known her—Aunt Mary was two years older—but she lived a thousand miles away now and was not well.

There was no picture of the little girl who had become a legend. When the family had first settled here, there was enough struggle to feed and clothe the children without having pictures made of them.

Even after Army officers had come to our house several times and there had been many letters about Aunt Bessie's delivery from the savages, it was a long time before she came. Major Harris, who made the final arrangements, warned my aunts that they would have problems, that Aunt Bessie might not be able to settle down easily into family life.

This was only a challenge to Aunt Margaret, who welcomed challenges. "She's our own flesh and blood," Aunt Margaret trumpeted. "Of course she must come to us. My poor, dear sister Bessie, torn from her home forty years ago!"

The major was earnest but not tactful. "She's been with the savages all those years," he insisted. "And she was only a little girl when she was taken. I haven't seen her myself, but it's reasonable to assume that she'll be like an Indian woman."

My stately Aunt Margaret arose to show that the audience was ended. "Major Harris," she intoned, "I cannot permit anyone to criticize my own dear sister. She will live in my home, and if I do not receive official word that she is coming within a month, I shall take steps."

Aunt Bessie came before the month was up.

The aunts in residence made valiant preparations. They bustled and swept and mopped and polished. They moved me from my own room to my mother's—as she had been begging them to do because I was troubled with nightmares. They prepared my old room for Aunt Bessie with many small comforts—fresh doilies everywhere, hairpins, a matching pitcher and bowl, the best towels and two new nightgowns in case hers might be old. (The fact was that she didn't have any.)

"Perhaps we should have some dresses made," Hannah suggested. "We don't know what she'll have with her."

"We don't know what size she'll take, either," Margaret pointed out. "There'll be time enough for her to go to the store after she settles down and rests for a day or two. Then she can shop to her heart's content."

Ladies of the town came to call almost every afternoon while the preparations were going on. Margaret promised them that, as soon as Bessie had recovered sufficiently from her ordeal, they should all meet her at tea.

Margaret warned her anxious sisters, "Now, girls, we mustn't ask her too many questions at first. She must rest for a while. She's been through a terrible experience." Margaret's voice dropped way down with those last two words, as if only she could be expected to understand.

Indeed Bessie had been through a terrible experience, but it wasn't what the sisters thought. The experience from which she was suffering, when she arrived, was that she had been wrenched from her people, the Indians, and turned over to strangers. She had not been freed. She had been made a captive.

Aunt Bessie came with Major Harris and an interpreter, a half-blood with greasy black hair hanging down to his shoulders. His costume was half Army and half primitive. Aunt Margaret swung the door open wide when she saw them coming. She ran out with her sisters following, while my mother and I watched from a window. Margaret's arms were outstretched, but when she saw the woman closer, her arms dropped and her glad cry died.

She did not cringe, my Aunt Bessie who had been an Indian for forty years, but she stopped walking and stood staring, helpless among her captors.

The sisters had described her often as a little girl. Not that they had ever seen her, but she was a legend, the captive child. Beautiful blonde curls, they said she had, and big blue eyes—she was a fairy child, a pale-haired little angel who ran on dancing feet.

The Bessie who came back was an aging woman who plodded in moccasins, whose dark dress did not belong on her bulging body. Her brown hair hung just below her ears. It was growing out; when she was first taken from the Indians, her hair had been cut short to clean out the vermin.

Aunt Margaret recovered herself and, instead of embracing this silent stolid woman, satisfied herself by patting an arm and crying, "Poor dear Bessie, I am your sister Margaret. And here are our sisters Hannah and Sabina. We do hope you're not all tired out from your journey!"

Aunt Margaret was all graciousness, because she had been assured beyond doubt that this was truly a member of the family. She must have believed—Aunt Margaret could believe anything—that all Bessie needed was to have a nice nap and wash her face. Then she would be as talkative as any of them.

The other aunts were quick-moving and sharp of tongue. But this one moved as if her sorrows were a burden on her bowed shoulders, and when she spoke briefly in answer to the interpreter, you could not understand a word of it.

Aunt Margaret ignored these peculiarities. She took the party into the front parlor—even the interpreter, when she understood there was no avoiding it. She might have gone on battling with the major about him, but she was in a hurry to talk to her lost sister.

"You won't be able to converse with her unless the interpreter is present," Major Harris said. "Not," he explained hastily, "because of any regulation, but because she has forgotten English."

Aunt Margaret gave the half-blood interpreter a look of frowning doubt and let him enter. She coaxed Bessie. "Come, dear, sit down."

The interpreter mumbled, and my Indian aunt sat cautiously on a needlepoint chair. For most of her life she had been living with people who sat comfortably on the ground.

The visit in the parlor was brief. Bessie had had her instructions before she came. But Major Harris had a few warnings for the family. "Technically, your sister is still a prisoner," he explained, ignoring Margaret's start of horror. "She will be in your custody. She may walk in your fenced yard, but she must not leave it without official permission.

"Mrs. Raleigh, this may be a heavy burden for you all. But she has been told all this and has expressed willingness to conform to these restrictions. I don't think you will have any trouble keeping her here." Major Harris hesitated, remembered that he was a soldier and a brave man, and added, "If I did, I wouldn't have brought her."

There was the making of a sharp little battle, but Aunt Margaret chose to overlook the challenge. She could not overlook the fact that Bessie was not what she had expected.

Bessie certainly knew that this was her lost white family, but she didn't seem to care. She was infinitely sad, infinitely removed. She asked one question: "Mary?" and Aunt Margaret almost wept with joy.

"Sister Mary lives a long way from here," she explained, "and she isn't well, but she will come as soon as she's able. Dear sister Mary!"

The interpreter translated this, and Bessie had no more to say. That was the only understandable word she ever did say in our house, the remembered name of her older sister.

When the aunts, all chattering, took Bessie to her room, one of them asked, "But where are her things?"

Bessie had no things, no baggage. She had nothing at all but the clothes she stood in. While the sisters scurried to bring a comb and other oddments, she stood like a stooped monument, silent and watchful. This was her prison. Very well, she would endure it.

"Maybe tomorrow we can take her to the store and see what she would like," Aunt Hannah suggested.

"There's no hurry," Aunt Margaret declared thoughtfully. She was getting the idea that this sister was going to be a problem. But I don't think Aunt Margaret ever really stopped hoping that one day Bessie would cease to be different, that she would end her stubborn silence and begin to relate the events of her life among the savages, in the parlor over a cup of tea.

My Indian aunt accustomed herself, finally, to sitting on the chair in her room. She seldom came out, which was a relief to her sisters. She preferred to stand, hour after hour, looking out the window—which was open only about a foot, in spite of all Uncle Charlie's efforts to budge it higher. And she always wore moccasins. She was never able to wear shoes from the store, but seemed to treasure the shoes brought to her.

The aunts did not, of course, take her shopping after

all. They made her a couple of dresses; and when they told her, with signs and voluble explanations, to change her dress, she did.

After I found that she was usually at the window, looking across the flat land to the blue mountains, I played in the yard so I could stare at her. She never smiled, as an aunt should, but she looked at me sometimes, thoughtfully, as if measuring my worth. By performing athletic feats, such as walking on my hands, I could get her attention. For some reason, I valued it.

She didn't often change expression, but twice I saw her scowl with disapproval. Once was when one of the aunts slapped me in a casual way. I had earned the slap, but the Indians did not punish children with blows. Aunt Bessie was shocked, I think, to see that white people did. The other time was when I talked back to someone with spoiled, small-boy insolence—and that time the scowl was for me.

The sisters and my mother took turns, as was their Christian duty, in visiting her for half an hour each day. Bessie didn't eat at the table with us—not after the first meal.

The first time my mother took her turn, it was under protest. "I'm afraid I'd start crying in front of her," she argued, but Aunt Margaret insisted.

I was lurking in the hall when Ma went in. Bessie said something, then said it again, peremptorily, until my mother guessed what she wanted. She called me and put her arm around me as I stood beside her chair. Aunt Bessie nodded, and that was all there was to it.

Afterward, my mother said, "She likes you. And so do I." She kissed me.

"I don't like her," I complained. "She's queer."

"She's a sad old lady," my mother explained. "She had a little boy once, you know."

"What happened to him?"

"He grew up and became a warrior. I suppose she was proud of him. Now the Army has him in prison somewhere. He's half Indian. He was a dangerous man."

He was indeed a dangerous man, and a proud man, a chief, a bird of prey whose wings the Army had clipped after bitter years of trying.

However, my mother and my Indian aunt had that one thing in common: they both had sons. The other aunts were childless.

There was a great to-do about having Aunt Bessie's photograph taken. The aunts who were stubbornly and valiantly trying to make her one of the family wanted a picture of her for the family album. The government wanted one too, for some reason—perhaps because someone realized that a thing of historic importance had been accomplished by recovering the captive child.

Major Harris sent a young lieutenant with the greasy-haired interpreter to discuss the matter in the parlor. (Margaret, with great foresight, put a clean towel on a chair and saw to it the interpreter sat there.) Bessie spoke very little during that meeting, and of course we understood only what the half-blood *said* she was saying.

No, she did not want her picture made. No.

But your son had his picture made. Do you want to see it? They teased her with that offer, and she nodded.

If we let you see his picture, then will you have yours made?

She nodded doubtfully. Then she demanded more than had been offered: If you let me keep his picture, then you can make mine.

No, you can only look at it. We have to keep his picture. It belongs to us.

My Indian aunt gambled for high stakes. She shrugged and spoke and the interpreter said, "She not want to look. She will keep or nothing."

My mother shivered, understanding as the aunts could not understand what Bessie was gambling—all or nothing.

Bessie won. Perhaps they had intended that she should. She was allowed to keep the photograph that had been made of her son. It has been in history books many times —the half-white chief, the valiant leader who was not quite great enough to keep his Indian people free.

His photograph was taken after he was captured, but you would never guess it. His head is high, his eyes stare with boldness but not with scorn, his long hair is arranged with care—dark hair braided on one side and

with a tendency to curl where the other side hangs loose
—and his hands hold the pipe like a royal scepter.

That photograph of the captive but unconquered warrior had its effect on me. Remembering him, I began to
control my temper and my tongue, to cultivate reserve as
I grew older, to stare with boldness but not scorn at people who annoyed or offended me. I never met him, but I
took silent pride in him—Eagle Head, my Indian cousin.

Bessie kept his picture on her dresser when she was
not holding it in her hands. And she went like a docile,
silent child to the photograph studio, in a carriage with
Aunt Margaret early one morning, when there would be
few people on the street to stare.

Bessie's photograph is not proud but pitiful. She looks
out with no expression. There is no emotion there, no
challenge, only the face of an aging woman with short
hair, only endurance and patience. The aunts put a copy
in the family album.

But they were nearing the end of their tether. The Indian aunt was a solid ghost in the house. She did nothing
because there was nothing for her to do. Her gnarled
hands must have been skilled at squaws' work, at butcher-
ing meat and scraping and tanning hides, at making tepees and beading ceremonial clothes. But her skills were
useless and unwanted in a civilized home. She did not
even sew when my mother gave her cloth and needles and
thread. She kept the sewing things beside her son's picture.

She ate (in her room) and slept (on the floor) and
stood looking out the window. That was all, and it could
not go on. But it had to go on, at least until my sick Aunt
Mary was well enough to travel—Aunt Mary who was
her older sister, the only one who had known her when
they were children.

The sisters' duty visits to Aunt Bessie became less and
less visits and more and more duty. They settled into a
bearable routine. Margaret had taken upon herself the responsibility of trying to make Bessie talk. Make, I said,
not teach. She firmly believed that her stubborn and un-
fortunate sister needed only encouragement from a
strong-willed person. So Margaret talked, as to a child,
when she bustled in:

"Now there you stand, just looking, dear. What in the world is there to see out there? The birds—are you watching the birds? Why don't you try sewing? Or you could go for a little walk in the yard. Don't you want to go out for a nice little walk?"

Bessie listened and blinked.

Margaret could have understood an Indian woman's not being able to converse in a civilized tongue, but her own sister was not an Indian. Bessie was white, therefore she should talk the language her sisters did—the language she had not heard since early childhood.

Hannah, the put-upon aunt, talked to Bessie too, but she was delighted not to get any answers and not to be interrupted. She bent over her embroidery when it was her turn to sit with Bessie and told her troubles in an unending flow. Bessie stood looking out the window the whole time.

Sabina, who had just as many troubles, most of them emanating from Margaret and Hannah, went in like a martyr, firmly clutching her Bible, and read aloud from it until her time was up. She took a small clock along so that she would not, because of annoyance, be tempted to cheat.

After several weeks Aunt Mary came, white and trembling and exhausted from her illness and the long, hard journey. The sisters tried to get the interpreter in but were not successful. (Aunt Margaret took that failure pretty hard.) They briefed Aunt Mary, after she had rested, so the shock of seeing Bessie, would not be too terrible. I saw them meet, those two.

Margaret went to the Indian woman's door and explained volubly who had come, a useless but brave attempt. Then she stood aside, and Aunt Mary was there, her lined white face aglow, her arms outstretched. "Bessie! Sister Bessie!" she cried.

And after one brief moment's hesitation, Bessie went into her arms and Mary kissed her sun-dark, weathered cheek. Bessie spoke. "Ma-ry," she said. "Ma-ry." She stood with tears running down her face and her mouth working. So much to tell, so much suffering and fear—and joy and triumph, too—and the sister there at last who might legitimately hear it all and understand.

But the only English word that Bessie remembered was "Mary," and she had not cared to learn any others. She turned to the dresser, took her son's picture in her work-hardened hands, reverently, and held it so her sister could see. Her eyes pleaded.

Mary looked on the calm, noble, savage face of her half-blood nephew and said the right thing: "My, isn't he handsome!" She put her head on one side and then the other. "A fine boy, sister," she approved. "You must"—she stopped, but she finished—"be awfully proud of him, dear!"

Bessie understood the tone if not the words. The tone was admiration. Her son was accepted by the sister who mattered. Bessie looked at the picture and nodded, murmuring. Then she put it back on the dresser.

Aunt Mary did not try to make Bessie talk. She sat with her every day for hours and Bessie did talk—but not in English. They sat holding hands for mutual comfort while the captive child, grown old and a grandmother, told what had happened in forty years. Aunt Mary said that was what Bessie was talking about. But she didn't understand a word of it and didn't need to.

"There is time enough for her to learn English again," Aunt Mary said. "I think she understands more than she lets on. I asked her if she'd like to come and live with me, and she nodded. We'll have the rest of our lives for her to learn English. But what she has been telling me—she can't wait to tell that. About her life, and her son."

"Are you sure, Mary dear, that you should take the responsibility of having her?" Margaret asked dutifully, no doubt shaking in her shoes for fear Mary would change her mind now that deliverance was in sight. "I do believe she'd be happier with you, though we've done all we could."

Margaret and the other sisters would certainly be happier with Bessie somewhere else. And so, it developed, would the United States government.

Major Harris came with the interpreter to discuss details, and they told Bessie she could go, if she wished, to live with Mary a thousand miles away. Bessie was patient and willing, stolidly agreeable. She talked a great deal more to the interpreter than she had ever done before. He answered at length and then explained to the others that she wanted to know how she and Mary would travel to this far country. It was hard, he said, for her to understand just how far they were going.

Later we knew that the interpreter and Bessie had talked about much more than that.

Next morning, when Sabina took breakfast to Bessie's room, we heard a cry of dismay. Sabina stood holding the tray, repeating, "She's gone out the window! She's gone out the window!"

And so she had. The window that had always stuck so that it would not raise more than a foot was open wider now. And the photograph of Bessie's son was gone from the dresser. Nothing else was missing except Bessie and the decent dark dress she had worn the day before.

My Uncle Charlie got no breakfast that morning. With Margaret shrieking orders, he leaped on a horse and rode to the telegraph station.

Before Major Harris got there with half a dozen cavalrymen, civilian scouts were out searching for the missing woman. They were expert trackers. Their lives had depended, at various times, on their ability to read the meaning of a turned stone, a broken twig, a bruised leaf. They found that Bessie had gone south. They tracked her for ten miles. And then they lost the trail, for Bessie was as skilled as they were. Her life had sometimes depended on leaving no stone or twig or leaf marked by her passage. She traveled fast at first. Then, with time to be careful, she evaded the followers she knew would come.

The aunts were stricken with grief—at least Aunt Mary was—and bowed with humiliation about what Bessie had done. The blinds were drawn, and voices were low in the house. We had been pitied because of Bessie's tragic folly in having let the Indians make a savage of her. But now we were traitors because we had let her get away.

Aunt Mary kept saying pitifully, "Oh, why did she go? I thought she would be contented with me!"

The others said that it was, perhaps, all for the best.

Aunt Margaret proclaimed, "She has gone back to her own." That was what they honestly believed, and so did Major Harris.

My mother told me why she had gone. "You know that picture she had of the Indian chief, her son? He's escaped from the jail he was in. The fort got word of it, and they think Bessie may be going to where he's hiding. That's why they're trying so hard to find her. They think," my mother explained, "that she knew of his escape before they did. They think the interpreter told her when he was here. There was no other way she could have found out."

They scoured the mountains to the south for Eagle Head and Bessie. They never found her, and they did not get him until a year later, far to the north. They could not capture him that time. He died fighting.

After I grew up, I operated the family store, disliking storekeeping a little more every day. When I was free to sell it, I did, and went to raising cattle. And one day, riding in a canyon after strayed steers, I found—I think— Aunt Bessie. A cowboy who worked for me was along, or I would never have let anybody know.

We found weathered bones near a little spring. They had a mystery on them, those nameless human bones suddenly come upon. I could feel old death brushing my back.

"Some prospector," suggested my riding partner.

I thought so too until I found, protected by a log, sodden scraps of fabric that might have been a dark, respectable dress. And wrapped in them was a sodden something that might have once been a picture.

The man with me was young, but he had heard the story of the captive child. He had been telling me about it, in fact. In the passing years it had acquired some details that surprised me. Aunt Bessie had become once more a fair-haired beauty, in this legend that he had heard, but utterly sad and silent. Well, sad and silent she really was.

I tried to push the sodden scrap of fabric back under the log, but he was too quick for me. "That ain't no shirt, that's a dress!" he announced. "This here was no prospector—it was a woman!" He paused and then announced with awe, "I bet you it was your Indian aunt!"

I scowled and said, "Nonsense. It could be anybody."

He got all worked up about it. "If it was *my* aunt," he declared, "I'd bury her in the family plot."

"No," I said, and shook my head.

We left the bones there in the canyon, where they had been for forty-odd years if they were Aunt Bessie's. And I think they were. But I would not make her a captive again. She's in the family album. She doesn't need to be in the family plot.

If my guess about why she left us is wrong, nobody can prove it. She never intended to join her son in hiding. She went in the opposite direction to lure pursuit away.

What happened to her in the canyon doesn't concern me, or anyone. My Aunt Bessie accomplished what she set out to do. It was not her life that mattered, but his. She bought him another year.

The Last Boast

WHEN THE TIME CAME for them to die, Pete Gossard cursed and Knife Hilton cried, but Wolfer Joe Kennedy yawned in the face of the hangman.

What he wanted to do was spit, to show he was not afraid, because he knew men would talk about him later and describe the end he made. But even Wolfer Joe could not raise enough saliva for spitting when he had a noose around his neck. The yawn was the next best thing.

Barney Gallagher, the United States deputy marshal, finished adjusting the rope and asked half-admiringly, "Are we keeping you up?"

"Hanging me up, they told me," Wolfer Joe answered.

On a packing box between his companions, he stood glaring out at the crowd of miners, with his lips pulled back from his teeth in the grin that was his trade-mark. He had foreseen the hour of his death, but not the way of it. He had felt the jar of the bullet, heard the Cheyenne arrow whir, gone down screaming under a grizzly's claws —all these were probabilities for a man who had lived as he had lived, and a man had to die sometime.

But he had always seen himself fighting to the end. He had not dreamed of an end by hanging, helpless, with his hands tied behind him. He would not give his executioners the satisfaction of knowing he was astonished. They were going to get satisfaction enough without that.

Knife Hilton stopped crying and stood drooping on his packing box, snuffling like a baby. Pete Gossard stopped yelling curses, and thinking he had figured out a way to delay the performance, shouted earnestly, "I want a preacher! You wouldn't deny a man a preacher, would you?"

The Vigilanters had thought of that, too, and had a

preacher there. They knew, by this time, about all the tricks a man could think of to make delay. Pete Gossard had nothing to say to the preacher, after all, except the frantic plea: "Tell 'em to give me a good drop."

"They will, Pete," the preacher promised. He shivered and added, "They always have. May God have mercy!"

There was still a lot of noise from the crowd of miners —the seven or eight hundred of them who had constituted the jury and had filed solemnly between two wagons to vote. Fourteen men had voted for acquittal, and after four hundred voted "guilty," the Vigilanters had stopped the farce of tallying. The noise was far out on the edge of the crowd, where those who could not see clearly were milling around, but in the center, at the hanging place, there was hardly any sound. Here death was, and the men who would beckon to it had nothing much to say.

The three packing boxes were sturdy; each had a rope tied to it by which it would be pulled away at the signal; the nooses were soundly wound. The Vigilanters, Wolfer Joe recollected, had had plenty of practice.

He felt a shudder coming over him, and to disguise it, he threw back his head and laughed.

He had few illusions about himself. Once he had said, grinning, "Reckon I was born bad." More accurately, he might have said, "I was born outside the law, and mostly I've stayed outside it." He had kept moving westward to places where the law was not. And what caught up with him at last was not law but anger. The angry men at the diggings could not wait for the law to catch up; they set up the Vigilance Committee to enforce ruthless justice.

Barney Gallagher frowned at that laugh. He stepped down from the box, wiping his hands on his pants, and said reflectively, "I was wondering—did you ever do one good thing in your life?"

Wolfer Joe looked into his eyes and answered with his lips pulled back from his teeth, "Yeah. Once. I betrayed a woman."

At the hangman's signal, men pulled the ropes on the packing box.

The word love was in the language he used with women, but its meaning was not in his understanding when he met Annie. Even when he left her, he was not sure he knew the meaning, and after that he never had much chance to find out.

She stood with her arms outspread, her hands touching the barn wall, trembling, withdrawing not so much from Wolfer Joe as from life itself pressing toward her.

"You don't really like me," he insisted. "Bet you don't."

"Maybe I do," Annie answered, breathless. "I got to go in now." She could have ducked under his arm, but she only glanced up at him with a scared smile. She was seventeen years old. Wolfer Joe was twenty-nine.

"You go in now," he said, "and I'll know you don't love me." He said the word lightly; he had said it before. The shape of it was easy in his mouth.

She looked away desperately, and the color rose on her neck. "I do so l-love you," she said. "You could just as well stay here, instead of going on."

Oh, no. not at twenty-nine. He could not stay in the settlements for long at a time. The law was creeping westward too fast. He was not sure what the law was, but he knew that he and his like had better keep ahead of it.

"Nothing here to keep me," he said. The words hurt her as he had meant them to hurt, and she drew back. "I got to go on," he said. He added boldly, suddenly seeing a dream, "Going to move on and settle down somewheres. Where I'm going, a girl like you wouldn't go. You wouldn't go with me."

She was pressed tight against the barn wall. "Maybe I would, if I wanted to."

"Your pa wouldn't let you," he scoffed.

"Pa couldn't stop me. Now let me be—let me go!" She struggled against him, but his arms were an iron cage, and his heart pounded against hers.

"Tonight, at the fork of the trail," he said when he let her go, when he loosed her arms from their clinging. "Wait for me there.—But you won't come."

"I will!" she said. "Because I l-love you."

That was the last thing she ever said to him.

"I believe you mean it," he answered, and found his voice was hushed with wonder. "I guess you really do," he said, trying to laugh.

The wonder was still on him when he waited where the trail forked But Doubt hovered there too, and roosting on his shoulder, Suspicion watched the trail with cold, yellow eyes.

If she came, he could take her west and build a soddy, get a bunch of cattle started—he knew how to swing a long loop on someone else's beef. He had done it before, for pay.

'What makes you think she'll come?" hooted Doubt, circling over him.

"What reason would she have if she did?" croaked Suspicion, with claws sharp in his shoulder.

"There's no reward out for me around here," argued Wolfer Joe "Supposing she does come, her reason's her own business It's her I want, not her reasons. I'll settle down somewheres If she comes."

He watched the trail from up above, belly-down on a flat rock He jerked when he saw her ride to the meeting place and look anxiously around She had a little bundle of clothing tied to the saddle He saw her dismount and look around again. But she didn't call out or say a word. She simply sat down to wait.

He was furious, with an unreasoning anger. "Damn little fool!" he whispered. "Running off with a man she don't hardly know! What she'll get is no more'n she's got coming."

He remembered that he himself was the man, and he lay there grinning at his own nonsense.

He would wait a while. When she gave up, he would appear and accuse her: "I knowed it was just a notion. You never meant what you said. You start but you can't finish."

Then he would let her go home weeping—or on with him, to do her crying later, when she knew what a fool she was.

But she did not give up. When darkness came, she built a little fire to keep the night away. With his heart pounding, with his lips pulled back from his teeth Wolfer Joe lay on the flat rock, watching her. She had come so far; she had been so faithful How long would she wait there for him? How far could he trust her?

Suspicion whispered, "There'll come a day when she'll

go crying to the law and say, 'I know where Wolfer Joe is if you want him.' "

He answered, "You don't know my Annie."

He watched her head bend forward on her knees as she waited and dozed. He saw it snap up again when a night sound scared her. After a while the fire burned low, and he knew she was sleeping. She awoke and fed it, and it blazed.

Then he knew he wasn't going down there. He saw not the girl, but her patience. He saw not the red glow of the fire, but faith abiding.

He saw love by the fire, and he could not endure looking for fear he might see it end, during that night or some year to come.

He crept back off the rock and slid silently into the darkness to where his horse was waiting.

He lived for fourteen years after that. He was said to have seventeen notches on his gun, but that wasn't true. He never notched his gun butt for anything he did.

He was justly sentenced to hang for helping to murder two miners whom he and Pete Gossard and Knife Hilton had dry-gulched when the miners tried to take their gold out.

Wolfer Joe made an ending that earned him grim respect, and he left Barney Gallagher puzzling about how betraying a woman could be a thing a man might boast of with the last words he ever had a chance to speak.

I Woke Up Wicked

I USED TO RIDE with the Rough String, but not any more. They were tough outlaws, the Rough String; and the lawmen that chased them—from a safe distance—were hard cases too. In fact, everybody around was plumb dangerous except me.

I was just a poor innocent cowboy, broke but not otherwise wicked. I didn't want to join them outlaws, but I was running away from justice—the crookedest justice a man ever did see.

I was twenty-two years old when I rode into Durkee, a cow town in Montana, after helping eight other fellows deliver a trail herd of steers.

"Meet me at the bank in an hour, boys," says the wagon boss. "I'll pay you off there."

We scattered and started strutting the streets, all ragged and dusty. We was too broke to do anything but strut. Anyhow, while I was strutting, I see this fellow behind a lawman's badge; he's leaning against a wall and looking at me with his eyes narrow. It made me kind of mad, and my heart was pure, so I says, "See anything green? Well, by gosh, if it ain't Cousin Cuthbert! Cuthbert, you shouldn't of ever run off. Your ma's been real upset. . . ."

This fellow's eyes got so narrow I doubt if he could see out of 'em. "I am Buck Sanderson, deputy sheriff of this county, stranger," he says. And then, looking around, he whispers, "How are you, Willie?"

"My name is Duke Jackson," I says, huffy. "Seems like I made a mistake."

"You are a likely-looking young fellow," he says, "and you remind me of somebody." He grinned, and I knew

27

that he had got the idea—when I mentioned a mistake—
that I meant I was on the run. But I wasn't, not then.

"You got any plans?" he says.

"The crew is gonna get paid off at the bank pretty
quick," I says. "After that, I don't know what I'm going
to do."

"Well, come have a drink," Cuthbert says. I should
have known better than to drink with Cuthbert; he'd been
a mean one as far back as anyone could remember. But I
had a beer and he had red-eye, and then he says, "I'll
mosey along with you to the bank."

"I can find it," I says, but he come anyway.

On the way, he stopped by a hitch rack and squinted at
a sorrel gelding with a fancy saddle on it. "Now what's
the sheriff's horse doing there?" Cuthbert says. "It was
supposed to be took to the livery stable, but I guess the
hostler forgot. Here, you lead him. I got to keep my gun
hand free. This is a tough town."

So I led the sheriff's horse, rather than argue with him.
There was some fellers standing in front of the bank, but
none of them was from our crew, and there was some
horses standing around.

"I'll go see if they're paying off yet," Cuthbert says.
"You hold the horse."

"You hold him," I says. "It's me that's getting paid
off."

"Hold the horse," he says, and walked into the bank.

So I was standing there, getting mad, when three or
four shots blasted out. And then men came boiling out of
the bank like hornets and leaped onto those horses that
were waiting. Cuthbert came running out with them and
after he'd let the men get a start, he began shooting after
them but up in the air. Well, I saw that Cuthbert hadn't
changed any, and so I did the obvious thing. I jumped on
the sheriff's horse and galloped him out of town.

Ten miles out, I stopped to see if any bullets had hit
me. They hadn't.

There I was, a refugee from justice. I'd stolen the sheriff's horse and the bank had been robbed with me standing there looking like I was part of the gang; and I was a
witness to the fact that Cuthbert was in on the holdup.

I sat down in some bushes and wished for a smoke and

thought what a perfidious villain Cuthbert was. I decided to go back and tell the sheriff so, but not just then. Some other year would do. If I went riding back to Durkee that day, on the sheriff's horse, people might misunderstand.

So I rode another ten miles farther away. It was getting dark then, so I unsaddled and went to bed in the brush, wishing I could eat grass like the sorrel.

I woke up in the dark, only it wasn't as dark as it should have been. Somebody had a fire going, and I could hear voices. Couldn't even get a good night's sleep. I sat up, and somebody says, "That you, Larry?"

"Never heard of him," I says, "and can't you guys shut up?" That just goes to show what a pure heart I had, and how little brains. All of a sudden I recalled that I was a wanted man.

"Got a rifle on you, mister," a man says. "Come into the light with your hands up."

Well, I didn't even stop to pull my boots on.

"How long you been there?" says a man with a black mustache. There was four of them, all with guns.

"How long don't matter," says a man with a beard. "Either he's on our side or he's dead."

"I'm on your side," I says. "Which side is it?"

The man with the beard scowled. "You ever drive cattle on shares?"

"Just for wages," I says. "I'm a hard-working cowpuncher looking for an opportunity."

"It has found you," he says. "What name do you go by?"

"Duke," I says.

"No you don't," he says. "I'm Duke." He glared at me in the firelight and says, "You're Leather."

"Why, no such thing," I says. "I'm just ordinary skin like anybody else." Then it dawned on me who Duke was. Everybody knew the name Duke—he was one of the head men of the Rough String. Fact was, I took the name Duke not long before just because a reputation went with it. "If you say so," I says politely, "I'm Leather."

"Go bring Leather his boots," says Duke. "Give Leather a cup of coffee."

So that was how my name changed to Leather. And that was how I turned outlaw. No trouble at all. Went to bed honest and broke, woke up wicked and still broke, and misunderstood by everybody.

"We'll use you in our cattle business," Duke says. I didn't have to make any decisions at all. Seemed like I was cut out to be an outlaw.

You might think driving stolen cattle was exciting, but it wasn't. They didn't look any different, viewed from the dust of the drags, than they had when I pushed 'em along as a law-abiding citizen. Why should they look any different? They were some of the very same cattle.

After they became rustled cattle, they were easier to move. When they were an honest herd, the trail crew was always running into officious lawmen and nesters that said, "You can't bring that herd through here," or "You can't cross this line." But when the Rough String moved them steers, the lawmen were somewheres else on urgent business, and the nesters waited for the Rough String with open arms.

This is the life, I began to think. It's safer and quieter than being an honest cowboy. Nobody gets close enough to point a gun at you.

I could even have enjoyed it, if all them outlaws hadn't made me so nervous. Duke and the boys looked like cowboys anywhere, dusty and needing a shave, and red-eyed because with a trail herd you never get enough sleep. But just knowing they were the Rough String made me shiver. I tried being real polite and they glared at me. So I glared back and showed my teeth, and after that we got along pretty good. Being an outlaw is awful tiring on your facial muscles.

We moved them cattle right along because the former owner had men on our trail. When the men got too close, they slowed up and waited for a prudent length of time. Their boss was even safer—he was home on the ranch.

One day we pushed them cattle up to the top of a ridge of rimrock, and Duke says with a happy sigh, "Well, there it is. Eagle Nest."

The boys sat their horses and we looked down into the prettiest green valley I ever saw. The steers went snorting down the trail to water and that good green grass, and most of the boys went "Yippee!" and spurred their horses down that way too.

"Got girls waiting down there," says Duke, explaining to me. "Now there is a settlement no lawman ever laid eyes on, boy. Eagle Nest. Not that they don't know where it is." He chuckled fondly. "We got a nice layout there. Families, kids. Even had a school till the teacher got married."

Then he yelled, "Yippee!" and off he went.

"I am Leather Jackson," I says out loud to myself. "One of the Rough String. I am a real bad fellow." But I wished my teeth wouldn't chatter.

I yelled, "Yippee!" and spurred my horse down the trail to Eagle Nest. Down there they would protect me. I flung out of the saddle in front of a log building with a hitch rack. I started to swagger in. A dark-skinned girl with long earrings came out, grinned at me.

"You are Leath-air Jackson," she says to me.

I swept off my hat and says, "Yes, ma'am, I sure am, and what might your name be?" Not that I gave a hang, but it occurred to me that the Rough String's womenfolks might be even more dangerous than the outlaws themselves, and one thing you can always do when you meet a strange woman, dangerous or not, is be awful polite.

"My name ees Carmen," she says. She would have been kind of pretty if she hadn't had a front tooth missing.

Just then Duke came out, glaring at me and her, so I says, "Pleased to meet you, ma'am," and "Boss, where do I bunk? Because it's a long, long time since I had a solid night's sleep."

"The big cabin is for the single men," Duke says. "The little shacks is for those of us that's got our own housekeeping arrangements. Carmen, you git along home and don't dally."

She dallied long enough to wave her eyelashes at me, and that raised a chill along the back of my neck.

"Your credit's good at the store here," Duke says, motioning.

That was a relief, because being an outlaw hadn't made me any more prosperous than I was while honest.

The storekeeper squinted at me and says, "I reckon you're Leather Jackson. What'll you have?"

"Soap to get the dust off the outside," I says. "And a can of peaches to cut it on the inside, and some smoking tobacco to relax with before I go to sleep for four or five days." I was a real tough rustler, I was. Still wanted the same old comforts.

While I was drinking the peach juice, my eyes got used to the dim light and I see there was a woman about ten feet away. I put a little more distance between us, and she says in a ladylike voice, "Mr. Frasier, would you introduce us?"

"Oh, gosh, excuse me," the storekeeper says. "Miz Pickett, meet Leather Jackson, the new man."

I grabbed off my hat and bowed, and she says, "How do you do."

She was a pretty lady, real young, had all her teeth too, but she looked prim and wore a black dress. Now if there was anything you didn't expect to see in Eagle Nest, it was a prim lady.

"I hope we shall become better acquainted," she says, and went out.

"Yes, sir," I says, baffled. "Yes, ma'am, I do too."

Mr. Frasier leaned on the counter and says, "The widow there, she came in here to teach school and married Ed Pickett. He got shot a while back. The other women say she's a snob because she keeps her marriage certificate up on the wall. They're just jealous."

"A very nice lady," I says.

"You bet she is," says Mr. Frasier. "And if you ever find out whether she really did ride with the String when they took the express car at Middle Fork, I sure wish you'd tell me."

I didn't say anything. My teeth were chattering on the rim of the peach can.

Then I could see it all—the poor orphan girl with no folks, lured into that nest of thieves to teach school, falling in love with this bandit, Pickett, then widowed when he was shot. Poor girl.

I put down the empty peach can and throwed my shoulders back and says, "If you want trouble with Leather Jackson, mister, just let me hear you say one evil word about that little lady."

He cringed. "I wouldn't, Leather, I sure wouldn't! I bet it's all a vicious rumor, about her riding with the—"

"That's the kind of evil word I mean," I grated at him, getting my gun out after only one fumble.

He backed off with his hands hovering level with his shoulders. "Just a vicious rumor," he repeated, "and to show you my heart's in the right place, I won't even charge you for that merchandise you just bought."

"I'll let the slander pass this time," I says through my teeth.

I found the bunkhouse, swaggered in like I owned it, growled at the boys, and laid down in a bunk. I slept thirty-six hours and would have stretched it longer except I got hungry.

I woke up mad—and scared—and laid there with my eyes shut, figuring. William Jackson, I says to myself. Duke Jackson. Leather Jackson—now I know you, boy. What you going to do about the jam you're in? You're not the best shot in the world, and your hide's not made of cast iron.

Then I figured out why I was mad, and I was ashamed of being so selfish when there was that unprotected little widow marooned among that bunch of outlaws.

She dassent leave, I figured, because probably the hard-hearted lawmen would get her on account of her associations. She wouldn't have no money to live on if she could escape. And them saying she held up a train!

Well, I worked up such a mad that I wasn't scared no more. I marched out of there in a towering rage, clean forgetting to put on my gun belt, which was in my war sack. Outside I met two or three of the Rough String and glared 'em down. They glanced at my hip—no holster there—and my murderous expression, and they seen a cold-blooded killer who didn't need firearms. Why, Leather Jackson was the type that would throttle an innocent grizzly bear with his raw hands.

They stepped aside for me, they did, and made me welcome.

I never did so much loafing since I got out of my cradle. There was nothing to do but lounge around and gossip and play cards and get drunk. But I didn't wish to drink in that company and was scared to win at cards and was not willing to lose, even if I'd had any money. So I listened, and that got monotonous too. My face got tired from keeping that tough look on it, just waiting for somebody to drop an evil word about poor little Miz Pickett.

They gabbed about old holdups till hell wouldn't have it. Miz Pickett's late husband was horse-holder when they robbed a bank, I learned, and some kid shot him from an upstairs window when they came out with the money.

About once an hour somebody would say with a long face, "I never did believe that nonsense about the widow riding with the boys when they took that train, though," and the rest of them, carefully not looking my way, would chime in, "No, no!" like the Ladies Aid fighting off the idea that the preacher had been seen staggering out of a saloon.

After three or four days, one of Duke's boys gave me the word I was on guard duty that night.

"Take your rifle up to the rim," he says, "and keep it ready. Nobody's tried to bust into Eagle Nest yet, but some lawman out to make a reputation might try it.

"One shot from up there, and we'll all be with you. But don't go shooting just to hear the echo. There's few things make the boys madder than to get routed out of a quiet night's sleep because some green guard gets jumpy and shoots the blazes out of a friendly juniper.

"In fact," he says, "one fellow that done it ain't been seen since."

There was even a password. It was Twenty Dollars.

Night-herding rimrock and juniper trees is even duller than riding around bedded-down cattle. I hummed and whistled and sang and practiced cussing. Then I dozed, setting on a rock with the rifle on my knees.

I woke up with an awful start, hearing horses coming up the trail from the outside. I rolled down behind the rock and yelped, "Who's there?"

A deep voice says, "Who the hell do you think it is? And who are you?"

See, no password. So if he didn't want to give in, I was willing. Nobody told me who was supposed to deal.

"For twenty dollars I'd bore a hole clean through you," I says, big and rough, but protected by that rock. Anyhow I hoped I was.

He says, "Oh, hell, I forgot that. We got lots more than twenty dollars on a led horse here."

So we got acquainted. There was five of them, and they had eighteen thousand dollars in gold coin on a pack horse. We shook hands and had a smoke and then they went on down to Eagle Nest.

I set there shaking like a leaf, because I found out, hiding behind that rock, that I wasn't going to shoot nobody no matter how big I talked about it. Even if they'd all been Cuthbert, I wouldn't have fired. I'd shot lots of game and butchered yearlings that wasn't mine, like any cowboy when the grub's short. I'd even shot a horse once. But I never had shot any people. And damned if I was going to start then, just to protect that bunch of bandits down in Eagle Nest.

It was quite a surprise to find that out, let me tell you. Made me stop and think.

Well, I wasn't hobbled on that rimrock. What's to stop me, I says to myself, from getting on my horse and going down over the side to where the rest of the world is?

Several things stopped me. The Rough String wouldn't like it, though I hadn't taken no blood oath or anything. The law might not like it too well because I still had the sheriff's horse. And if I left, who was going to look out for Miz Pickett? No, I wasn't hobbled. But I was sure ground-tied.

So there I was, a stout young fellow with no bad habits, stuck with them outlaws and helpless to protect the lady. Rustling cattle was no habit with me. I never did drink much, I'd quit gambling and I was scared of the girls in Eagle Nest—they carried little knives in their garters. All in all, I was a nicer fellow since turning badman. I was way too good for Eagle Nest, but I was scared to pull out.

When I rode down at sunup, Miz Pickett was lugging a couple buckets of water to her cabin, so I stopped to help. Delicate-looking little thing, she was.

"I'd ask you in to breakfast," she says, "but you know how people talk."

"Ma'am, I would gladly go hungry to protect your good name," I says gallantly, setting down the buckets on her doorsill.

She gave me an approving look, and I noticed something funny. She was such a prim little lady, and she looked at me like my aunt used to, over her glasses. But Miz Pickett didn't have any glasses on.

"Leather," says she, "have you ever thought of quitting this life of banditry?"

Of course I hadn't thought of much else since I got into it, but I was cautious. Anyhow, if she wanted to reform me, I wanted to give her the satisfaction of having a job to do. "A fellow thinks about a lot of things," I says.

"Crime brings nobody any good. There was my husband, shot down in a bank robbery. Are you any better off since you joined the Rough String?"

"Well, yes," I says. "I've got credit at Mr. Frasier's store."

"But no cash. Not until those steers you brought in are fattened up and sold. And what if the nesters who usually buy them get cold feet? The price on stolen beef goes pretty low."

"Was you thinking of getting out of here, ma'am?" I asked in a whisper. "Not that I want to inquire into your private business."

She looked droopy and pitiful. "I could go back to teaching. But would the Rough String dare to let me leave?"

"Any time you want help, ma'am." I says, big and bold. "Any time you want to go. . . ."

She smiled, sad and sweet. "Thank you, Leather. Thank you for carrying the water."

Less than a week later, Duke said it was my turn on guard again. For a minute—or less, probably—I thought of asking him what those other lazy loafers were going to do with their time and why should I get night duty so soon, but it seemed smarter to show my teeth and answer, "Fine. Maybe a posse will try coming in tonight."

So I went up there again on the rimrock, but this time it was some different. Miz Pickett had fixed up a nice lunch for me. I ate away at it in the dark, mourning my misspent past and cloudy future, and yawning and fretting. Then I sat up with a jerk.

There was the sound of a horse down below, on the Eagle Nest side of the rim. No horse in his right mind would be up there in the rocks and brush of his own choice. The Rough String prided itself on good horses; there wasn't a halfwit in the lot. So that horse wasn't there by accident.

Maybe Duke or somebody was testing me out, I thought. I hollered, "Who's there? Come up and lemme look at you or I shoot!" My, I sounded mean. Even scared myself.

A woman's voice says, "Oh, please don't!"

If there was anything I didn't want up there, it was a visit from one of those Eagle Nest girls. I grabbed the sheriff's horse's reins, ready to ride down to the outside into the arms of the law, if I could find any.

Then the voice said, "Leather, please help me. Can you change twenty dollars?" and I went plunging through the brush toward it, because it was Miz Pickett. For her, I wouldn't even have needed the password.

She had a saddle horse and a pack horse, and one of them had a hoof caught between two logs. She had come up through the brush instead of on the trail. I yanked him out. I felt so big and strong I could have picked him up and lifted him out if necessary.

"This is the night I'm leaving," Miz Pickett says. "The String is having a big meeting down in the saloon, planning something."

"Let's ride," I says, with my chest puffed up like a balloon. And that was how I left Eagle Nest. Easy enough, once somebody gave me a push.

We could have gone faster if she hadn't brought so much stuff on that pack horse. I didn't even have my war sack, what cowboys used to call their forty years' gatherings, but Miz Pickett had everything—grub and blankets and a couple of wooden boxes roped on. A neater job of packing stuff on a horse I never saw.

"Those are my books in there," she explained when I glanced at the boxes at our first camp stop.

But when I stepped toward the pack horse to start unloading, she says, "Never mind. Get the fire going."

"Sure, I'll get the fire going," I says, "but I wouldn't want you to lift that heavy stuff off the pack saddle."

"Leather," she says, and I turned around. She still looked prim, in a black dress with a divided skirt for riding, but do you know what? She had a gun in her hand, pointed right at me.

"There's some good firewood over there to the left," I says, marching that way in a hurry. Right then I got a strong suspicion there was mighty few books in them boxes.

Officially, we took turns sleeping, with one awake staying on guard, not necessarily against wandering lawmen. The Eagle Nest boys were going to miss that gold any minute. But Miz Pickett didn't seem to sleep at all. We camped four nights, and every time I moved a muscle while I was on guard, I could feel that she was watching me from where she was supposed to be asleep.

One morning she says, "Another forty miles to the railroad."

"Fine," I says, wondering if she'd dry-gulch me before we got there.

"Ever been in the cattle business on your own?" she asks, drinking coffee by the breakfast fire.

"Never have," I says.

"I think I'll give up schoolteaching," she says, "and raise beef instead. I'll need a foreman."

That girl didn't need a foreman. Everything she needed she already had. But I was in no position to refuse.

"Expect you will, ma'am," I says, and she nodded as if it was all settled.

"I'm going to take the train," she says. "You can come along a week later. I'm your sister, Mary Smith."

"Pleased to meet you, sis," I says. "And where should I meet you later?" Not that I was going to, but it seemed wise to act interested.

She wrote down the address, and I put the paper in my shirt pocket.

She smiled her prim little smile and says, "We're going to get along all right in the cattle business, Leather."

I hoped we were, with a thousand miles between us as soon as I could arrange it.

"You'd better hide out," she suggested. "The Rough String must be getting pretty close by now."

"Reckon so," I agreed. She didn't recommend any place for me to hide. With the law ahead, and the String hot on the trail behind, what was a poor cowboy to do that was wanted for bank robbery, cattle rustling and stealing the sheriff's sorrel horse?

"By the way," I says, "where do you figure to catch your train?"

"Durkee," she says.

I jumped a foot. "Durkee! Hell—excuse me, ma'am—shucks, I can't go to Durkee! That's where the bank was held up while I was holding this horse right in front of it, and this horse belongs to the sheriff."

She looked annoyed. I sure hated to annoy Miz Pickett.

"Durkee is where I intend to get the train," she says. "My goodness, do you think you're so outstanding that anybody's going to recognize you?"

She had a sound argument there. I did look like an ordinary feller, now I'd stopped scowling at the Rough String and let my face hang loose. And if Cuthbert was around, was he going to identify me? He certainly was not. I'd identify him right back.

"There's a man in Durkee I'd like to meet sometime," she says thoughtfully. "I don't know for sure who he is, but he's a cunning wretch. He engineered a bank holdup there that the Rough String got the blame for. The String didn't hold up that bank."

"No, ma'am, they didn't," I says. "They were rustling cattle."

We made it to the depot just ahead of the train. As I was snatching at the ropes on the pack saddle, I glanced at the loafers by the depot, and cold chills went up my spine, because there was Cuthbert behind his nickelplated star. But I preferred his company to Miz Pickett's. Also to the Rough String, and they might catch up with me any time, now she was going to leave me with no protection but my own wits.

"Good-by, Harry, take care of yourself," says Little Rattlesnake, and I histed her boxes on the train.

"My books," I heard her tell the conductor.

The train started chugging, and I heard my second cousin say behind me, "Hello, Duke."

Cuthbert has got a nice safe jail, I says to myself. That's one place the Rough String won't come looking for me. I says, "Hello, Buck."

"Who's the girl?" he says.

"My sister," I says.

"I know your sisters, Willie, and she ain't one of 'em," he says. "You always were a liar."

So I hit him, but not very hard. He grappled me and I fought just a bit.

"Resisting an officer, eh?" he says, yanking his gun out and relieving me of mine. "March right along, Willie, and if you tell anyone we're related, I'll shoot you."

"I'd rather be shot than admit it," I says, marching so fast he had to trot to keep up with me.

I was sure glad to get in that jail.

"Now we'll see what you got in your pockets," says Cuthbert. "H'm, broke, of course. What's this piece of paper here in your shirt pocket? I bet that's the address of the girl you put on the train."

"Don't take that!" I says. "I'll never remember where I'm to meet her."

He backed off, grinning, with the paper in his hand. "And why should she want you to meet her?" he says.

"Don't know as she does," I says, "but she's my golden future. She's not only pretty, she's also rich and wants a foreman for her ranch."

"Shouldn't be hard to find her a good man," says Cuthbert, tilting his hat.

"She said she'd sure like to meet you," I says, "but if you was to go climb on that train, it would be just plain dirty of you, because I seen her first." The train tooted and Cuthbert grinned.

"Stay here, Willie boy," he says.

He plumb forgot to lock the door, but I stayed in the cell. I stayed and stayed and stayed.

Around suppertime an older man came in. "What you doing here?"

"Was put here by a fellow with a star on," I says.

"Ain't nothing wrote down in the book," he says. "What you in for?"

"Hitting him, I guess," I says.

"Often wanted to do it myself," says the man. "You can go, for all I care."

Was there no refuge for Willie Jackson, the reformed outlaw?

"I'm wanted in nine states and some territories," I

says. "Robbing banks, rustling cattle, forgery, arson—and stealing horses! Why, I've got a horse that belongs to the sheriff right now!"

"You have!" be says, grinning. "Why, boy, I'm so glad to find that horse, you know what I'm going to do? I'm going to make you a deputy. Somebody said they seen Buck get on the train, so I'm going to need a new deputy. We got some big game coming in here. You know who's coming? Eight members of the Rough String, that's who. Got fourteen more of 'em divided up among two other counties, and we get the overflow. Telegram just came in about how they run into a posse that was looking for somebody else. You want to work for me?"

"My health ain't good," I says. "I get the leaping flitters."

He yelled down the street after me, "Hey, you forgot your gun and your hat," so I had to delay long enough to go back and get them.

"Yes, sir," the sheriff says, "they got just about all the Rough String except the little lady that was boss of the whole shebang. Five thousand dollars' reward for her, but nobody outside the outlaws knows what she looks like."

"Five feet two," I says, "dark hair, looks like the president of the Ladies Aid. She took the same train out as your deputy. That's why he was on it."

"Whoof!" says the sheriff and left without warning. I was right behind him, but I passed him when he swung into the telegraph office. His horse was ten yards farther on.

It was a year or so, I guess, before they stopped looking for me, the unidentified cowboy riding the sheriff's horse who set the law on Miz Pickett and perfidious Cuthbert. If I'd turned myself in to be a witness, I could have been a hero. But I always felt kind of guilty about Cuthbert, and anyhow you never knew which ones of the Rough String would break out of the penitentiary next.

Miz Pickett broke out and got away to South America. I was sure relieved to read about it in a newspaper, though I never had nothing against the South Americans. But they saved me from having to run off to some heathen place like China to stay clear of Miz Pickett. I went home to Pennsylvania and took up plowing.

The Man Who Knew the Buckskin Kid

NOBODY KNOWS for sure what became of the Buckskin Kid. You can read in books about Western badmen that he killed himself with a pistol shot after he was wounded in a gun battle in Colorado and so avoided capture. Or that a doctor in Wyoming attended a fatally wounded man in his last hours and was pretty sure it was the Buckskin Kid who died then. You can read that he got clean out of the country and went to live in South America. It doesn't matter any more.

Legends grew up along the trails that he had ridden, and as the years slipped by, people who remembered him found that their scanty recollections were of interest to a new generation. An old man can take pride now in having seen the Kid top off a mean bronc on a cold morning half a century ago. Not that he was a better rider than others, but they weren't chiefs of outlaw bands.

Men who were young when the Kid was young grew old in obscurity and now, in their last days, have something to boast about because they saw him once.

John Rossum is one of those obscure old men, but he has never boasted about knowing the Buckskin Kid. A reporter cornered John Rossum at a church social last summer. John didn't know he was a reporter. He just saw this stranger talking to Bill Parker and writing something down.

Bill Parker can't talk without flinging his hands around, and John knew from the hand motions that Bill was telling about the Kid's last train robbery, fifty years ago.

You wouldn't have guessed that John Rossum was amused. His craggy face didn't move a muscle. But he planned what he would tell his wife on the way home:

"There was Bill, telling every detail like he'd been there, and the young feller writing it all down for an eye-witness account."

Mary would snort, "I declare, and Bill didn't come out from Iowa 'til a good ten years later!" and they would chuckle together.

After fifty years, he knew just about what Mary would answer to anything he said. He looked with accustomed admiration toward her; she was bustling with the other women behind the long tables where the bountiful food was set out buffet style.

The stranger was getting restless, listening to Bill Parker go on and on. John Rossum, seeing Bill motion his way, turned quietly toward the door, but half a dozen ranchers blocked the way, talking weather and the price of beef. Courtesy kept him from pushing, so Bill and the young fellow managed to catch him there.

"I was telling him," Bill said importantly, "that you knew the Buckskin Kid."

"I knowed him," John Rossum answered. "Lots of people did."

The young man said, "Well, thanks," to Bill Parker, dismissing him. "How do you spell your name, Mr. Rossum?"

"I wouldn't care for you to use my name no way," John said gently. "I haven't done nothing to get it wrote down for. Traveling by yourself, are you?"

But the young sprout wouldn't have the subject changed.

"This Buckskin Kid Jackson, or Harris, whichever he went by—he hid out around here, I understand. Did you know him then?"

The Kid had been a killer four times over, and, in John Rossum's opinion, knowing him was nothing to boast about, but there was such a thing as truth. And the memory of even the Buckskin Kid deserved justice. John Rossum spoke for truth and justice:

"He wasn't one to hide from nobody. Take any old broken-down cabin, and somebody'll tell you that was the Kid's hideout. But he didn't have to hide. He wasn't afraid of nobody."

The reporter looked pleased. "You were here then?" he insisted.

Unable to avoid answering, unwilling to lie, John Rossum said, "I was here."

He glanced over at Mary, behind the long tables, and knew that she was aware he was in mild trouble. But she couldn't leave there; she was ladling out baked beans.

"What did the Kid look like?" the reporter asked.

John Rossum tried to remember. "Just ordinary, far as I recall. His brother Ben was skinny, but the Kid just looked ordinary."

"Bill Parker was telling me somebody put a fence around Ben's grave," the reporter remarked. "Thought I'd go get a picture of it tomorrow. I'd like to have you in the picture, Mr. Rossum. Okay with you?"

"I wouldn't wish to have my picture made," John Rossum said firmly.

"Do you think the Kid went to South America?" the reporter demanded. "Mr. Parker says he knows people who say they got postcards from him there."

"I always thought he went there," John Rossum said. Meticulously honest, he added, "I never got no postcards."

"I met a man yesterday who said Pinkerton's Detective Agency was still looking for the Kid in 1914, when he was supposed to be long dead."

"I don't know what become of him," John Rossum said. "I suppose he'd be dead by this time. He'd be prid-near eighty now."

The reporter got a sly grin on his face as he asked, "You knew his girl friend, I suppose?"

"I seen her once or twice. Never could see why she took up with the Kid." (Couldn't understand why he took up with her, either, John Rossum thought; she was real plain. But gallantry did not permit him to say that.)

"She lit out about the same time he did, I heard."

"I heard the same," John Rossum agreed.

He wished the reporter was willing to talk about something important, like Russia or how Jet planes worked. The problems of the present concerned John Rossum mightily. But this young fellow was interested only in some old-time outlaws.

Mary was getting away from the beans. Nobody was in line any more. She patted her hair as she came toward him, and he noted with relief that she had on her managing expression.

She managed fine, too. She nodded at the young man and dismissed him with a motherly smile.

John nodded politely to the reporter, who said with a grin, "I don't suppose you ever rode with the Kid, Mr. Rossum?"

"No," John Rossum answered. "I never did." He added without rancor, "Not so long ago, you could have got in trouble for asking a question like that." Then he went with Mary and ate pie he didn't want at all.

"The other ladies will clear things away," she said. "We can go now, unless you want to stay."

"Got nothing to stay for, unless you do," John answered. He thought she wanted to, but she said not. That was Mary for you—willing to leave early because she knew he would like to get away. There never was a woman like Mary. Or if there was, he hoped she had a man who deserved her.

Driving home in the old pickup, steering along rutted roads, his conscience hurt with an ache to which he was long accustomed. He and Mary didn't talk, because there was no need for it. Mary understood that he wished to think.

He remembered the Buckskin Kid, after Ben was dead and after the Kid came back and killed Ben's killer. The Kid was at his peak then. He owned the world, or anyway he roamed free in a piece of Montana about a hundred miles across.

And in those days John Rossum didn't own a thing but a bay horse and a saddle.

Johnny Rossum was young then and unsure, just a drifting cowboy, didn't know what he wanted of the world and wouldn't have known how to get it anyway. The Buckskin Kid told him once, "By damn, Johnny, the trouble with you is you think too much."

Young John Rossum answered, "Guess you're right, Kid, but how's a man going to stop?"

"Here's one way," the Kid said, grinning, and pushed a bottle along the bar.

"That won't stop a man from thinking for very long, though," Johnny commented. "And anyway, there's so many things to think about."

"Besides women and money, what is there?" the Kid challenged, so seriously that Johnny laughed out loud and said, "See, you're doing it, too."

Women and money—the Buckskin Kid was partly right. Johnny did a lot of thinking about them, or to be exact, he thought about one young woman and how he had no money. Mary Browning had other admirers, but Johnny thought—when he was feeling optimistic—that she sort of favored him. His rivals had what Johnny lacked: some land, some cattle, a roof, even if the roof was only sod on a shack.

Mary was better off at home with her pa than she would be with Johnny Rossum. But she was nineteen, old enough to marry, and she was not indispensable to her pa, for she had a sister two years younger who could cook. Somebody would sure enough stake a claim to Mary Browning before very long.

Johnny Rossum wasn't exactly courting her. He just stopped by her pa's place whenever he was in the neighborhood—say twenty miles away. Sometimes she favored him by going for a walk with him along the river.

"Do we always have to have your horse along?" she demanded once.

Johnny glanced back in some surprise at the horse he was leading.

"Shucks, no. Could leave him in your pa's yard. You don't like having the horse along, huh?" That seemed important to him.

Mary thought his feelings were hurt. She reached up and scratched around the horse's ears.

"He's a nice horse. I don't mind if he comes along. I just wonder why you bring him when we're only out for a few minutes on foot."

There was something for Johnny to think about, and he thought hard. When he got the answer, it was so silly it embarrassed him.

"I'm not used to going afoot, that's all, I guess. If my boss was to order me to, I'd ask for my time. But as long as a man's leading his horse, he ain't afoot, really. Now ain't that silly! But it's true," said honest Johnny Rossum.

"And now I made a fool of myself admitting that," he suggested. "Maybe you'll say why you don't like the horse's company?"

Mary Browning giggled. "I always think if I made a quick move you'd swing up on him and ride for your life, that's all," she said.

"Quick move? You think I'm scared you'll make a quick move?" John Rossum said triumphantly. "I'll show you what a quick move is!" and grabbed her and kissed her good while she struggled and laughed and her hair came loose, pretty Mary Browning.

She had no cause for struggle, having invited that kissing, but it was part of the game, and they both knew it. Johnny knew, too, that it was only a game. That was the kind of kissing a man could give a girl at a party, laughing and funning, even with her folks and her relatives and the preacher looking on.

Riding back to the ranch where he worked, he dreamed idly of the kiss he had never given Mary Browning and maybe never would, the solemn, earnest kind, with sighing but no laughter. Mary couldn't afford to take a serious kiss from a man who was only a cowboy. Cowboys did not marry.

We got no homes, Johnny told himself.

He had a roof over his head when he was at the headquarters ranch. He slept with two other cowboys in a sod bunkhouse. Mostly the roof kept the rain off.

"But it ain't my roof, damn it," he said out loud.

A week later, he didn't even have another man's roof, because the boss insulted him and he had to quit the job. Even making allowances for the fact that the boss was a tenderfoot, an Eastern fellow who had inherited the cattle, what he did could not be overlooked or excused. He did it right in front of the other hands, too.

The boss asked, "Johnny, did you look for the new bulls over beyond the red butte?"

Johnny had been told to find those bulls and move them, and he had done so. If he had failed, he would have said so. To be asked about it was to be insulted, although Johnny was not unduly sensitive. So he did what unwritten law required.

"I carried out your orders, Mr. Smith," he said gently. "Now I'll have to ask for my time."

So he collected the pay he had coming, packed up his war sack with what every cowboy called his "forty years' gatherings" whether he had lived forty years or not, and headed sadly for town.

It was only ten miles out of his way to stop at Mary's, so he did, but he didn't stay long. She had company, a rancher named Tip Warren, who spoke politely but then ignored Johnny Rossum, as much as to say, "With Mary Browning I've got the inside track. You count so little that I won't even waste time cutting you out."

And Mary paid much attention to Tip Warren. It never dawned on Johnny that she might be trying to make him jealous. He didn't feel jealous. He just felt as if something he hadn't expected to get anyway had been moved a little farther out of reach.

Tip Warren remarked while they were sitting around, "I'm short-handed. One man broke his leg, another one lit out ahead of the sheriff. Guess I can pick up a couple hands in town though."

That was Johnny's cue to say Tip didn't need to go into town, but he didn't say it. He wasn't figuring to work for a man who was courting his girl. Not if he starved, he wouldn't do that.

So he went on into Fork City right after supper, turned his horse into the small pasture back of the livery stable, and bedded himself down on the hay by permission of the hostler.

It was pure accident, next morning, that he ran into the Buckskin Kid. The Kid was affable except when he was roaring drunk, and when he was in Fork City he didn't get drunk. He watched his step there and usually didn't come in unless he was pretty sure the sheriff was at the other end of the county. And when the sheriff had an idea the Kid might come in, he found business to take him to the other end of the county. That was how they got along, with a kind of truce that nobody talked about or maybe even thought about.

Johnny Rossum wasn't afraid of the Kid, but didn't like him much. He had an idea he might glimpse blood on the Kid's hands if he stared long enough, but he never stared at the Buckskin Kid, and neither did anyone else. In brief, Johnny's attitude was just about normal—he respected the Kid as a successful man and steered clear when he could do so without being conspicuous.

But the Kid liked Johnny Rossum, as most people did, and admired his brains, which other people ignored.

So in the saloon that morning, where Johnny was hanging around in the hope that some cattleman would come in who wanted to hire a hand, the Kid friendlied up to him. Johnny valued his health, so he friendlied back.

"I been thinking about you," the Kid said,. "since I seen you last. A man that can think is kind of useful sometimes, know what I mean?"

"Sure," agreed Johnny.

The Kid saw that he hadn't got the point. "A thinking man could be useful to me, I mean," he hinted.

Johnny got the idea and answered, "I ain't very useful to anybody."

The Kid set down his glass. "I'll be out at Mamie's this evening with some of the boys, if you was to come by."

There it was, a direct invitation to a man who could think, an invitation to join up with a man of action. And Johnny had nothing to lose, the way he looked at his life right then.

So that evening he rode out to Mamie's, thinking hard. Once he pulled up his horse and thought hard while sitting in the saddle, with half a mind to turn back toward obscure respectability. What moved him on toward the meeting with the Kid was not any final decision of his own but the restlessness of the horse. When the horse started ahead in a tentative kind of way, Johnny growled, "Well, all right, if you're so anxious."

He hollered cautiously in Mamie's yard and didn't dismount until the door opened. It wasn't the Kid in the lighted doorway. But the man said, "Git down, we're waiting," and as Johnny came up to him he saw it was Windy Witherspoon. The others in there were Deaf Parker and Gus Graves, and, of course, Mamie was there.

Afterward, it struck Johnny as funny that while he sat with the Kid's gang, planning a train robbery, Mamie tiptoed around with a plate of layer cake and glasses of lemonade. The Kid finally told her to stop it and go on with her packing if she intended to get out of the country while the getting was good.

"She's going to go visit her brother's folks in Minneapolis," the Kid told Johnny with a wink. So Johnny always supposed that wherever she did go, certainly not Minneapolis, the Kid met her there later.

The Kid said, with cake frosting on his mustache, "There's a currency shipment coming through, Johnny. You want to throw in with us?"

The other men stared at Johnny Rossum through the smoke of good cigars. Deaf Parker died of gunshot wounds in Wyoming. Windy died of the same in Nevada, Gus of old age in prison, and nobody knows for sure how the Kid ended, or where. But that night, none of them knowing how they'd finish up, those famous outlaws sat in Mamie's cabin, waiting for Johnny Rossum to say something.

"I come, didn't I?" he growled. Then his conscience hurt him. "Whose money is it?"

The Kid shrugged. "Who cares? The bank's getting it —or they think they are. Maybe the railroad gets held responsible. You got a soft spot in your heart for banks and railroads?"

"Guess not," Johnny admitted. He had had little contact with either of them. "It ain't like robbing folks. Where are we going to do it?"

Gus grunted, "That's what you're supposed to help figure out, Mr. Brains."

Johnny stuck his chin out and demanded, "You willing I should?" and Gus nodded.

The Kid said, "Not very far from here. We never pulled a train job around here, so they won't expect it. Means we can't hang around here afterwards, of course, because we'd get the credit even if somebody else done it. But you could stay if you want to take the chance. If everything goes all right."

Johnny Rossum drew in a deep breath. Get me some cattle with my share of the take, maybe get my girl too, settle down and never do another wicked thing. Where'll I tell her the money came from? Figure that out after I get it. Got brains, ain't I?

"The boys and me, we don't want to be seen investigating along the railroad," the Kid explained. "But I got two, three places in mind. You go look, make plans, come back and tell me, and we'll all work out the details, if you're still game."

"All right," Johnny said, "Go ahead and talk."

He was a jobless cowboy; nobody cared where he went. If anyone saw him go for a swim under a certain bridge, nobody connected it with the train robbery that became history. He had himself a good bath in the river and lazied around for a while, all alone. He took some rough measurements, by eye, of how far away the cottonwood grove was and just where the brush was thick, and he noted where there were some railroad ties that would come in handy.

He loafed around on the prairie for a couple of days, sizing things up at the places the Kid had mentioned, and one night he went out to Mamie's to talk to the boys.

He drew a diagram. "Put the ties on the track right there. Not so's to wreck the train, but so the engineer will see 'em and stop. That'll bring the express car to right about here. The man that's going to cover the engine crew can hide under the bridge till the time comes. Others behind the tie pile on the north. Horses can be waiting in them cottonwoods, handy for the getaway. The conductor'll come running when the train stops, and the man at the head end can get a gun on him right away."

The boys argued every foot of the layout to make sure the plan was solid. The Kid asked them, "Sound all right to you?"

They nodded, and Johnny saw they were grinning.

"That's the exact place we picked out ourselves," the Kid told Johnny. "We wasn't so ignorant as we let on."

Johnny wasn't mad when he learned they had just been testing him out. He began to think maybe he had talent.

"You're going to hold the horses," the Buckskin Kid told him. "This ain't like a bank job, where the horse holder is liable to get shot at. Nobody's going to see you in the cottonwoods, and we might need some covering fire from there. Got a rifle, boy?"

Johnny nodded. He had never hit a human being with

his rifle, though he had tried once when an Indian was trying to steal a cow.

"When I find out the day," the Kid said, "I'll send you word. Just hang around town."

In the next few days, while the Kid was waiting to find out when the currency would be coming through, Johnny tried to get the feel of being an outlaw. He couldn't tell yet what it would be like, but he decided one thing: no dirty outlaw was good enough for Mary Browning.

A man's got to say good-by to his girl, he told himself. Without letting her know it's good-by. Got to have one last look at her, to remember; got to hint that he's going away for a while. She'll catch on, finally, that it's forever. And likely she won't care much anyway.

So he went to see Mary one last time.

"Leaving the country pretty soon," he said casually. "Man might want me to drive some horses to Canada. Wants me to work for him there anyway."

"Canada?" Mary repeated, as if the border were a thousand miles away instead of fifty. She didn't talk much, seemed mad at him when he left. He was sorry about that but thought it was probably for the best.

As he rode back to Fork City, he felt bad enough to cry.

One day the Kid sent him word, and they met secretly.

"Monday afternoon," the Kid told him. "We'll be away from here before that. Separately. You go before daylight Monday. Looking for a job somewhere, something like that. It don't matter what your reason is as long as it sounds good."

"Nobody'll care," Johnny admitted. "I'll grouch and gab to the hostler about going to Canada."

"All right with me," The Kid hesitated. "I'm giving you the easy part. You know that, don't you?"

"I didn't ask for no favors," Johnny reminded him. "But I'm grateful. I thought maybe you were making me horse holder because I'm green and might get in the way doing anything else."

The Kid barked a laugh. "Yessir, you got brains. My brother Ben, now, I used to have him hold the horses because he wasn't smart enough for anything else. But for you it's a kind of apprenticeship. And you get the same split the other boys do."

He slapped Johnny on the shoulder when they parted, and Johnny kept imagining he felt the mark of the outlaw's hand on him for quite a while afterward. When he was out on the street, he wondered if it showed.

Sunday, he grouched and gabbed to the hostler, who agreed things were pretty quiet and a man might have a better chance to get work if he hit north. So Johnny put his forty years' gatherings in his war sack before he went to bed in the hay.

He got up while it was still dark and walked out carrying his saddle. Nobody saw him, and if anybody had, they would not have guessed that he was scared or that he wished he wasn't going to rob a train.

He never did rob it, either.

The Buckskin Kid's gang got $40,000 out of the express car safe, but Johnny Rossum wasn't with them, because he couldn't find his horse in the pasture.

The horse just wasn't there. Someone had opened the gate.

He squinted all around in the darkness and searched over every foot of the ground, but there was no horse in there.

A man couldn't rent a horse if he said he was taking it across the border. And if he just took one, he'd be a horse thief, beneath contempt. Money belonged to banks, but horses belonged to people. A man had to draw the line somewhere.

That was a bad day for Johnny, because he thought a lot of that horse. He was glooming around town when the train robbery took place miles away.

Word of the robbery came about suppertime. It spread along the telegraph wires and caught up with the sheriff. He came tearing back and began organizing posses, cussing a blue streak at the Buckskin Kid, and paid no attention when Johnny tried to report that his horse was strayed.

So when the sheriff said a few minutes later, "I want you in a posse, young feller," Johnny told him to go to hell and take the posse with him.

Somebody picked up the stray horse on Tuesday in

time for the sheriff to requisition it, along with every
other four-legged animal big enough to cinch a saddle on,
for the posses that went riding out in every direction.

They never got the Buckskin Kid, though, and Johnny
Rossum never saw him or heard from him again.

While the posses were riding around hell for leather,
chasing bandits, Johnny went out to see Mary Browning.
Having no horse to ride, he walked all ten miles of it.
When she came out to meet him, she had the most startled look on her face.

"You mean to say you came all the way on foot?" she
demanded. "Just to see me? Oh, Johnny!"

That was the time he first kissed her the solemn, earnest way, with sighing and no laughter, right there in
front of her pa's house with her sister peeking out the
window. Then he pulled away and shook his head.

"A while back," he said, "I didn't have a thing but my
horse and saddle. Right now, I ain't even got the horse.
But I come to tell you . . ."

"Yes?" she whispered, trying to snuggle into his arms
again. "Say it, Johnny, say it."

"I come to tell you," he finished lamely, "that I wish I
was rich!"

She knew, miraculously, exactly what he meant, but he
always regretted he hadn't said it fancier.

There wasn't any serious problem after that, really.
They built a shack on her pa's place, and Johnny worked
for him, and after a few years he and Mary had cattle of
their own and four children and a mighty good life.

Fifty years later, the evil he had meant to do still
plagued him. He hadn't earned that good life at all.

The lane to the home place was half a mile ahead
when he said urgently, "I got to tell you something," and
the woman who had been his wife for half a century answered, "Hmm?"

He hated to do it, hated to have her know, even now,
how weak he had been, how wicked he had meant to be.

"That fellow talking about the Buckskin Kid," he said
hurriedly. "I got to thinking there's something I have to
tell you. I almost—that is, I would have—well, that last
big holdup the Kid pulled, I would have been in it if my
horse hadn't strayed."

Mary sounded as shocked as he had expected.

"John Rossum," she said, "I can hardly believe it!"

"It's true," he sighed.

"I never suspected that," she said, and was silent for a while. "Now I can tell you something *you* never knew. You were acting so mysterious in those days, I thought you had another girl on the string, in Canada, maybe, or that Mamie."

"Mamie!" John Rossum gulped.

"I thought there was some girl, anyway," his wife told him. "So I rode into town and let down that gate and spooked your horse out of that pasture myself, if you want to know it, so's you couldn't get away easy!"

He felt a wild chuckle welling up inside him, but before he could answer, Mary said something else:

"You know, I was bound and determined to have you. If you had gone off with those bandits, and if you'd asked me—well, I'd have gone along."

He said, "Why, Mary Rossum!" and took a quick, horrified glance at this woman whom he suddenly felt he didn't know at all.

The Gift by the Wagon

AFTER A WHILE, Caleb understood that he was sick, that he had been sick quite a long time. The simmering pain in his shoulder had been a boiling pain, he remembered dimly. So he must be getting better. And someone had been looking after him, but he did not know who it was or why they should be doing it or how he was going to pay for it.

There was a medicine smell, but that was on himself. Beyond it was the smell of horses, and he was bedded down on hay. He worried for a while and then wavered dizzily back to sleep.

Later he heard a girl's voice: "I could look after him if you'd move him to the house."

And a man's: "It wouldn't be fitting. Anyhow he's too sick to be moved yet."

"Did he say anything about who he is or who shot him?"

"I don't know any more than you do. A ragged stranger without a dollar in his pocket."

Ragged, yes. But rich, too. The shock of realization made Caleb start and hurt his shoulder. Then the gentle warmth of knowledge crept over him: I've got $15,000 banked with Wells Fargo. That's why I was dry-gulched back there somewhere. The men figured I was taking the gold out myself.

When the man came again and put a hand on Caleb's forehead to test the fever, Caleb asked, "Where is this place?"

"Livery stable in Fenton," the man answered. "Fort Fenton, it used to be. My boys found you in the pasture. Thought you were dead."

56

Caleb murmured, "I came a long way, then, after I was shot."

A long way I rode—must be ninety miles—with the fever blazing. And what brought me this direction in the first place? I wanted to go back ten years and prove to somebody that I amounted to something after all. Somebody who probably isn't here any more, and I hated her anyway because I was a coward and she wasn't.

He wanted to call out to the man, You needn't think you have to give me charity. I can pay you well.

But he knew that was not true. You cannot balance a debt of kindness with a poke of gold any more than you can subtract three pigs from five apples. He was in debt to this man whose name he did not know, and the thought angered him.

The man did not know him, either; the man looked after him, that was all. Charity, Caleb, thought. It's a burden to me.

He found out the man's name, Pete Wilson; he ran the livery stable. He had two half-grown sons who hung around sometimes. The girl's name was Fortune.

When she came with a pitcher of lemonade (pretending she did not know Pete was away just then), Caleb said, "You don't look old enough to have boys as big as they are," and she answered with a laugh, "They're not mine, except I'm raising them. I'm Pete's sister."

She was a pretty girl, calm and easy to talk to.

When Caleb was well enough, he moved to the hotel. But first he called on the local banker and made some arrangements and paid the doctor. After that, the hotel keeper was cordial, although Caleb wore the same clothes he had come in. They were clean now, and no longer ragged but nicely mended by Fortune. Even when Caleb lived at the hotel, he spent much time at the livery stable, talking to Pete or anybody, because he wasn't yet able to do anything else.

Pete asked no questions, but he was willing to answer them.

"How long you been here?" Caleb inquired, just passing time.

"Came right after the war. Some of my folks was here before me."

"I came by here once, to the old fort, with a wagon train on the way west," Caleb volunteered, hating to remember that but having a need to mention it. "Things have changed."

And with me they've changed, he assured himself. Gold banked with Wells Fargo now. I can have just about anything—but what do I want? Why, just to prove to somebody that was here once that I amount to something. A fool reason for heading this way, but a man's got to head somewhere.

Pete's boys went into the house across the road, and Caleb asked lazily, "What makes the younger one limp?"

"Got hurt when he was a baby. Don't mention it to him—he hates that limp."

"How old is he?"

"Twelve. Wesley's fourteen. . . . What you shivering for? Got a chill?"

"Goose walked over my grave. I'm all right."

But they could be the same boys who had howled with fear ten years ago. Fortune could be the little girl he remembered with envy and distaste, the little girl he wanted to prove something to and still wanted never to see again.

But they can't be, Caleb decided. Those folks must have moved on.

When he had been at the hotel for a week, he got up courage enough to ask if he might accompany Fortune to church.

"Why, I'd be pleased," she answered, looking as if she meant it. "There's preaching next Sunday. The circuit rider comes once a month."

"I figure to dress up a little better than I am now," Caleb promised.

"A person can go to church in whatever clothes they've got," Fortune said stoutly.

He bought new clothes and a black scarf to make a decent, inconspicuous sling for his left arm, which couldn't stand being moved much.

Sunday morning lasted about a month, he calculated, until it was time to call for Fortune at the house across from the livery table.

Fortune's nephew Basil, who walked with a limp, said,

"She ain't ready yet," and Fortune called from some-where, "I am so!" but didn't come for a few minutes.

Basil and his brother Wesley had found Caleb in a field, face down and bloody, with his horse standing over him because he had tied the reins to his good arm before he fainted. They took it for granted he was dead, but Basil had dared to touch him so as to boast that he had touched a dead man. Basil was still a little edgy with Caleb because of that.

Fortune came into the kitchen, walking rapidly with small steps, neatly slim in a gray dress. She said, "Good morning, Caleb," in businesslike fashion, and he an-swered "Good morning, Miss Fortune," and wished he hadn't, because she dimpled and young Basil haw-hawed.

"I mean, Miss Wilson," he corrected, embarrassed. He had not called her anything before that day.

"You may call me by my first name," she said, "with-out any Miss on it."

Basil remarked, "She says it's a misfortune to be Miss Fortune."

"It is my good fortune to take her to church," replied Caleb, feeling better about everything.

This is a more important day, he thought, than any day there ever was. More important than the day I found col-ors in the pan at Greasy Gulch or the day I sold my mine.

And he thought—he hoped—it was important for her too. She seemed breathless, as he was. It was a wonderful thing that had happened. One day he was a sick stranger lying in a stable, and another day he was almost well and Fortune was glad of his company.

My life is twisted with hers for good now, he realized. Forever, even if we part forever. For no reason except that we have met and she likes me.

In church she made sure nobody bumped his arm, and he wanted to protect her from dragons. But there were no dragons, unless you counted the inquisitive good women, and they attacked Caleb, not Fortune, with their ques-tions.

"You're getting better, I see. Just how did it happen?"

"Three men dry-gulched me, ma'am, and thought they finished me off."

"At Greasy Gulch, we heard?"

"A little this side of there, ma'am. I didn't aim to go back there and run into the same robbers, so I rode this way."

Ninety miles of pain and horror, of increasing fever and increasing fear that he wasn't going to make it.

"And Pete Wilson's boys found you. How fortunate!"

"Yes ma'am. It was indeed."

They eyed him closely, pretending not to. If he could wear good clothes now and stay at the hotel, why had he come in rags?

He had headed out of Greasy Gulch silently, by night, alone, but the road agents guessed it and ambushed him. They got maybe a hundred dollars in dust for their trouble. The rest of it had gone out on Wells Fargo's treasure coach and was safe. But all that was none of the good ladies' business.

"You were prospecting?" one of the women inquired.

"Lately I was mining, ma'am," he answered, and the woman didn't know the difference between seeking for gold and digging it out after you'd found where it was.

Someone asked, "Do you plan to stay here for a while?" but Fortune interrupted that they'd have to go now to see whether the boys had put the potatoes on as instructed. So he didn't have to answer that question.

On the way to the Wilson house they were breathless again—"It's a lovely day, isn't it? . . . A fine day indeed. Sun's bright but not too warm. . . . How pretty the light is on the cottonwoods! . . . Sure is pretty. Yes, it is."

Being together was so splendid, so important, that they could not speak of anything that mattered.

The boy had put the potatoes on and kept the fire going. Fortune tied on a starched apron and busied herself with Sunday dinner while Caleb watched. Watching Fortune mash the potatoes was as fine a sight as he'd ever seen, he thought. As pretty as flake gold showing yellow in a pan of gravel.

Fortune told the boys, "Now go get your father. We'll be ready soon as he washes up."

When Pete Wilson sat down with them at the table, he

guessed the situation, and Caleb saw his face change, sag into weariness.

Fine way I'm treating the man who saved my life, Caleb thought. He's got two motherless boys to raise, and now he figures to lose his sister that's raising them. Maybe, on account of that, she wouldn't go away with me if I asked her. Fortune is a girl that wouldn't shirk her duty.

But we needn't go away! he realized. A man that's got fifteen thousand dollars put away with Wells Fargo can live anywhere he wants to.

Caleb was so recently rich that the idea still shocked him. He hadn't yet got any pleasure out of it to speak of, except buying a fine chestnut horse in Greasy Gulch and now he had new clothes.

"Shall I cut your meat, Caleb?" Fortune asked. "With your sore arm, you can't."

"You cooked it so tender it don't need a knife," he said, and she looked pleased.

"Wouldn't be interested in selling your horse?" Fortune's brother suggested. "A man was in, asking."

Caleb shook his head. "If you had a real good horse for the first time in your life, would you sell him?"

"Not if I didn't have to."

"I don't have to. I never had any luck till lately," Caleb explained. "Worked at one thing and another since I was a young kid. I struck pay dirt at Greasy Gulch. Enough so the road agents figured I was worth robbing."

Fortune was not startled at the news that he had found gold. She beamed approval, because she was sure that so remarkable a man as Caleb naturally would find what he was looking for.

Her brother commented without jealousy, "Struck it rich. Well, I'm glad to hear it."

"And all the gold in the gulch wouldn't have helped me if you hadn't taken me in," Caleb reminded him. Then he made a mistake. He added, "I aim to pay you for what you did."

"No," Pete said, offended. "I make out all right with my business."

One of the boys yelled from the yard, "Hey, Pa, Mr. Hendrickson wants the sorrel."

Pete got up, grumbling, "He can't have it when it's out, can he?" and went across the road to his place of business.

So Caleb and Fortune were in the kitchen by themselves, and Caleb longed to say something memorable, but Fortune became very housewifely just then.

"Just you sit," she advised, "while I pick up the dishes."

"Please," he said, "I'd like to help with them."

She glanced at his arm in its sling and answered, with the sweetest smile he had ever seen, "Some other time you can."

And he knew that she had said something memorable, if he hadn't. It was a hint of a promise. There would be other times. He wanted to yell with jubilation, but he only smiled instead and they understood each other perfectly.

"Smoke if you want to," Fortune invited, so he lighted a cigar and admired her domesticity.

There was quick movement outside—he only glimpsed it, without understanding. But Fortune said, "I declare!" and ran out, dropping her dish towel. Caleb waited, puzzled, for it seemed to him that nothing had happened except that one of the boys had run past, and why should that upset her?

She mothers those kids, he thought. She mothers everybody.

He remembered a little girl of whom he had thought the same thing, a gaunt, serene child who had once been near this fort.

It can't be the same, he told himself. They surely didn't stay. She had two little brothers—or were they her brothers? They could have been nephews. He hadn't been concerned with relationships that day ten years before when he himself was fourteen.

He did not want Fortune to be that little girl grown up. He remembered the time and the girl with horror. He was so disturbed that he got up and walked back and forth across the floor while he waited for Fortune to come back.

"What's wrong?" he demanded.

Something certainly was wrong. He thought she had been crying.

"It's Basil. Some new boys teased him because he's lame. It's a terrible thing; it happens too often. And he gets mad and cries, and that makes him madder."

"But you made him feel better."

She shook her head. "Not unless it helped him to take his mad out on me. He said it's my fault he's lame, and it is. I—I hurt him when he was two years old."

Then she was crying, with her hands over her face, and Caleb yearned toward her, wanting to touch her but aware that he had no right.

"It wasn't your fault," he insisted. "It couldn't have been. You wouldn't hurt anybody."

"But I broke his leg," she sobbed. "I should have managed better."

Caleb put his good hand on her arm firmly, whether he had any right or not.

"Look at me, Fortune, and stop crying."

He knew now that she was that little girl he remembered.

"Was it when the Indians came and you hid the children in a tree?" he demanded.

She gasped and stared at him, trembling. She didn't say yes. She didn't have to.

So Caleb would be no hero to Fortune now. He would kill no dragons for her. Because he had been a coward when he was fourteen years old, and she had kept her head in the midst of danger—and remembered, when it was over with, to come and comfort him.

Caleb thought bleakly, Well, I can partly pay Pete back. Pete's charity and mine can sort of balance out.

"Call Basil in here," he commanded. "I want to tell him something. What have you been telling him all these years?"

"Why, what could I tell him? I never meant to hurt him, but I did, and he's lame for life."

There was, Caleb thought, a dragon he could kill for Basil at least, and then he would ride on somewhere away from the old fort that was called a settlement now. Maybe the truth would help Fortune too, but it would do no good for Caleb.

She didn't have to call the boy. He limped in and went to the kitchen pump for a drink.

"Go tell your pa I want a rig and a horse," Caleb ordered. "Mine's not broke to harness. You and I and Fortune are going for a drive."

"What for?" the boy challenged, snuffling.

"I want to show you a place and tell you what happened there." Caleb turned to Fortune. "How far is it? Ten, eleven miles?"

She was trembling. "I won't go. I've never been back there. I won't go."

"Yes, you'll go," he said gently. "Because you have to."

She would not sit next to him in the buggy but put Basil between them. Caleb talked about the sun and the trees, but nobody answered.

It was a long drive to the place, and ten years since he had seen it, but he found the overgrown wagon road. He had gone that way on foot the other time—first, mile by slow mile with the wagon train westward, and then alone into a meadow, looking for a lost cow. He could have recognized now any landmark in the hundreds of miles he had trudged ten years before.

"We'll leave the horse here," he said when he found the old wagon track. "From here we'll walk."

Basil whined, "I don't want to. This is where the Indians came."

Caleb tied the horse to a tree. "Do you remember anything about it?"

The boy shook his head. "I was only two."

"Did you ever stop to think you're lucky not to remember it?" Caleb asked.

He led the way along the traces of a rough road.

I am fourteen years old, he thought, and I am looking for Mr. Forsyth's cow. Not that his lost cow is any concern of mine, but I want the people in the wagon train to know how useful I am. Maybe some of them will take me in when we get to Idaho. Because my sister Elsie is going to marry that man Hankins, and he doesn't like me. There'll be no place for me in their house when they get one.

Fortune spoke piteously behind him: "Why do we have to go to—this place?"

"To see that it is only a little meadow with nothing in it. And to tell Basil some things he doesn't know."

There was no menace there. No menace had whispered the first time he walked that wagon track, either. But he had smelled smoke that other time and had seen the charred, ruined cabin and a dead man, bloody, lying on the ground.

Caleb turned to Fortune and asked, "Will you tell your nephew what happened here, or shall I do it?"

She would not answer except to shake her head.

"All right. I will, as far I can. Basil, see that old broken snag to the right of the cabin. She hid inside that snag with you boys. There's a window at the back of the cabin. You can't see it from here. I guess she went out that window while the Indians were busy with the man out in front.

"I never found out who he was," Caleb said, feeling faintly surprised. "I never asked." Or cared, either, he admitted to himself. The man was dead and didn't matter.

Fortune said in a strained voice, "My father's brother. He went out and they killed him. It gave me time to go out the back window with the boys."

She looked at the ground before her feet, but she did not turn her back on the place of horror.

"She could have run and saved herself," Caleb told the boy. "But she took the two of you out with her, and she put you both in that hollow snag before she climbed in to hide. Remember that, boy. When the Indians were killing a man not twenty feet away, she didn't run and save herself and leave you. And she wasn't more than twelve years old, I judge."

Basil's head was bent, but he kept stealing glances at the ruined cabin and the hollow snag, crumbling now with rot.

I've given him something to think about, Caleb told himself. Something nobody bothered about before. They never talked about all this any more than they had to. It was something they would rather not think about at all.

Basil demanded, "And where were you?"

"Way on beyond by the river with a wagon train when this happened. Nobody knew it was happening. We were stopped for Sunday by the river so the women could do their washing and we could go on to the fort next day. I was traveling with my older sister and her kids. I came this way on foot, looking for a lost cow.

"First I smelled smoke. Then I saw the meadow with the cabin in it. And a man lying there."

Basil was seeing those things too, identifying himself with that other boy who had become a man named Caleb Stark.

Basil asked in a hushed voice, "Why didn't you run?"

"Why, because—" Why didn't I? Caleb wondered. "I guess because I didn't believe it, what I was seeing. The meadow was so quiet, so peaceful, not even a bee buzzing. It was as quiet as—death. You know," he said earnestly, "you can't believe death either, first time you see it close."

The boy blinked. "Like I saw you, lying in the field. I thought you were dead."

"And you touched me so you could boast you had touched a dead man. You didn't want to. You were afraid. But you did it. It didn't matter one way or another. Except then you saw the dead man was breathing, and you went for your pa."

Basil nodded, feeling himself something of a hero.

"It was something like that with me here at the edge of the meadow. After I could believe what had happened, then I was scared. I wanted to run, I was going to run and get out of here. But there was a little sound from over to the right there, a faint little sound in the deathly quiet. I thought it was a wounded Indian, and I thought if he was wounded I could kill him. And have something to boast about back at the wagon camp.

"Because God knows," Caleb burst out, "I never had had anything to boast about or be proud of, and it was time I did. So I yelled something, some kind of challenge. I don't know what it was."

Fortune spoke quietly, "You said, 'Damn you, I'll shoot!' and I couldn't hold my hand over Basil's mouth any longer because he'd bitten me, and he screamed and then you came and got us out of the hollow snag."

Caleb said to the boy, "How many hours did she stay in there, cramped in there with you two kids, holding your mouths so you couldn't scream and bring the Indians back to kill the lot of you? She was so cramped she couldn't climb out.

"I found an axe with the handle half burned off and chopped out the side of the snag before any of you could get out. I was so scared I couldn't even see good. It's a wonder I didn't chop you with that axe."

He felt bathed with shame, as always, remembering how scared he had been, how witless. And how cool and sensible that little girl was, telling him what to do as she lay on the ground where she had fallen out of the snag. She was trying to move her cramped legs, and her face was contorted with the pain, but she wasn't crying, she never cried once. And she thought of everything.

Caleb said, "First thing she said was, 'Get the kids some water.' I didn't want to stop for that. I wanted to get out of this place to where it was safer. But she said, 'Get the kids some water,' and told me where the spring was, so I carried water in my hat, and she didn't drink till after you boys did."

Every step of the way, he remembered, I hated her for delaying me. I hunched my muscles, expecting a bullet from somewhere in the brush, or an Indian yell and death right behind it.

"And I wanted to go then, just grab one of you kids and run for it—or leave you there, for that matter. I didn't care. But she said, 'Basil's hurt,' and I saw your leg looked crooked. You were trying to crawl but couldn't, and you and your brother were howling blue murder. I thought you'd bring the Indians for sure.

"She said, 'You'll have to brace his leg someway to carry him. Get a stick or something and tie onto it.' She thought of that, even, and told me, while she was still working the cramps out of her legs. So I got a straight stick and then couldn't think of anything to tie it with, but she tore the shirt off your brother and we tied the splint that way. She got blood on the cloth, you'd bitten that deep into her hand.

"When she could walk, she dragged your brother by the hand and I carried you and my rifle, and we went as fast as we could along the wagon track to get out of here."

Fortune whispered, "Then we had to hide."

That was another thing that Caleb hated to remember
—and to have her remember.

"I was so scared," he said slowly. "We heard men's
voices ahead of us on the wagon track and I couldn't
move any more. I was so big a coward I couldn't move or
think. I just stood there, hanging onto you and waiting
for someone to kill me."

Fortune said sharply, "Nonsense! I was the scared one.
I said, 'Let's hide,' and we did, in the brush. But it wasn't
Indians, it was men from the wagons."

"I was a coward," Caleb repeated. "But after that it
didn't matter much because they hustled us out of there.

"That's all, kid. You can be glad you don't remember
anything about it."

Caleb turned abruptly and led the way back along the
grass-grown ruts, away from the quiet meadow where
death and terror had been a long time ago.

On the way back to the old fort, Fortune was willing to
sit beside him in the rig, with her hands in her lap. After
a while she said, "That wasn't all. You gave me your
coat. And I think it was the only one you had."

Caleb shrugged. "My sister fixed me another one."

He remembered that makeshift coat with shame. It was
made of a torn patchwork quilt. He wore it when he had
to, the rest of the way to Idaho, and many a time he shivered in the cold rather than put it on. Some of the people
laughed and some tried to comfort him, which was worse.
They called it Caleb's coat of many colors; they said the
lilies of the field were not arrayed like Caleb.

I've got fifteen thousand dollars banked with Wells
Fargo, he reminded himself. But that did not erase the
bitter memory of the gaudy coat that took the place of
the one he gave away.

Fortune said suddenly, "Basil, he didn't tell you the
straight of it. That boy that rescued us—I never knew
his name till today—he was no coward. He was the brav-
est boy I ever knew. He could have run away. Nobody
would have known. Nobody but him, anyway. But he
stayed and got us out.

"Some people took us in their wagon for overnight,
and a man who did some doctoring fixed your leg as well
as he could, and they fed us. My father was coming from

the fort; we met him on the way. He and Uncle Will used to sell hay there. That's why we were at the meadow.

"Just before the wagon train moved on to the fort, Caleb saw I was cold, and he gave me his coat.

"I still have it."

Caleb said, "What!"

"I wore it out, because we didn't have much in those days. But I've still got it, what there is left. It was something—to remember you by."

Caleb said gently, "Why, Fortune!"

And then nobody said anything the rest of the way to the settlement that had once been a fort.

That chilly morning long ago, cold before the sun came up, he wore his ragged brown coat while he harnessed the horses. The whole camp was stirring, getting ready to move on, and he felt that everybody stared at him. He was no hero, he was only an unwanted boy who had brought in some other unwanted, desperate children that somebody had to look after, at least temporarily.

The people felt that he had just about brought the Indians down on them. Men had been on guard all night, and nobody got much sleep.

Mr. Forsyth slouched up to him and asked with a long face, "I don't suppose you found my cow?"

"Never saw her," Caleb admitted.

Forsyth sighed and slouched away, not saying thanks for your trouble, just giving the impression that nobody expected Caleb to succeed even at a simple thing like that.

Caleb wondered, as he worked, what he would do in Idaho. There would be no place for him in his sister's home, and Caleb had a poor opinion of his own abilities. Nobody had ever suggested that he had any abilities. He was small for his age, hadn't got his growth, and that would handicap him in getting work.

He was as miserable as he had ever been in his life when the little girl came to him from behind a wagon. Her face was clean, and her hair was combed and braided, but she wore the same stained, torn dress, and she shivered, hugging herself with her arms but not saying anything about being cold. Someone had tied a clean rag on her hand, the hand the baby had bitten.

Caleb looked at her with distaste. The people in the wagons blamed him because they were worried about Indians. He had nobody to blame but the girl whose name he didn't know and didn't want to know.

She said politely, "I wanted to say thank you."

He shrugged, not knowing any better answer. He detested her because her need was so great and her future so bleak and she wasn't afraid of anything.

In the growing light of dawn she stepped toward him. Before he could guess her intention, she took his scowling face between her hands and lightly kissed his cheek.

He jumped back, angrily, scrubbing at his face, and demanded, "What's that for?"

"I don't know," she said, and turned away.

That was when he couldn't stand her shivering any more. He shucked off his old brown coat and threw it at her.

"Put that on," he growled.

She nodded and kept on walking away while she thrust her thin arms into the sleeves.

"I'll show you!" he muttered. "I'll come back some time and show you!"

Show her what? Why, that he amounted to something, even if she didn't think so, even if she had come and kissed him as if he were a baby to be pitied.

In the settlement that was a fort no longer, Caleb pulled up in front of the Wilson house. He helped Fortune down and ordered, "Basil, take the outfit back to your pa."

Then he stood looking into Fortune's quiet face.

"Why," he asked, "did you kiss me long ago?"

"It was all I had to give you," she replied. "Like the coat was all you had to give me."

Caleb nodded. He should have understood that all along.

"The years gone by were bad ones," he said. "The years to come will be better."

He was almost sure of that, but he was completely certain when she put both her hands into his outstretched hand and answered, "Why, yes, Caleb. Of course they will."

A Time Of Greatness

I WAS TEN YEARS OLD the summer I worked for old Cal
Crawford. For years afterward I remembered it as a time
of terror. I had grown up before I understood it had been
a time of greatness, too.

Cal Crawford did not hire me and probably did not
know I was working for him. He never remembered my
name—he called me "Boy" when he noticed me at all—
and at the end, he got the idea that through some misfortune he had to look after me, instead of the other way
around.

But I was hired to look after him, because he was blind
and very old. If my father hadn't needed the money
desperately, he would not have let me go to the Crawford
place. Old Cal's daughter, who hired me, was half Indian.
White people didn't work for Indians. It was unthinkable.

She looked immensely old, older than Cal Crawford
himself, for he was tall and straight while she was short
and stooped. I never knew her name but got around it by
calling her "Missus." What most people called her was
"Monkeyface."

She wore her purple silk dress the day she came to our
place. My sister Geraldine saw her through the window
and said, "The old squaw's coming this way. Aren't we
being honored, though! And all dressed up in silk. *I*
haven't got a silk dress."

Geraldine snickered at the sight. She had little enough
to make her laugh those days. Her young man had gone
West without her, because she had to stay home and look
after Pa. She didn't think she would ever see her man
again.

I laughed, too, at the old Indian woman, and was sorry
later. If I hadn't laughed at Monkeyface, then maybe I

wouldn't have had to go away with her that day. Maybe it was a punishment. But she did look ridiculous in the purple silk dress, astride an old white horse and slumped like a sack of meal. Her gray hair hung in frowzy braids from under a red kerchief. When she got close enough, you saw the dress was grease-spotted and dull with dirt.

Monkeyface had little English, but she kept saying, "Mistah? Mistah?" and making the Indian sign for "man."

"She wants to see Pa," I explained to Geraldine. I answered the old woman with the sign for "sick," and added, "He's got a broken leg."

She still wanted to see him, so Geraldine took her into the bedroom. Any visitor broke the monotony.

Pa and Monkeyface had quite a talk, in her mangled English and sign language, and I shivered because she kept motioning toward me.

A boy of ten does not expect his own father will give him away, but that was how it looked. And dreadful things not expected had happened lately in our cabin, like the way my sister cried at night because she had to stay home instead of go West with her man. It wasn't Pa that made her stay, though. It was her conscience.

"You want a summer job, Buck?" my father asked.

I took heart. "Sure." Herding cows, maybe. I wasn't big enough for much else.

"She wants you to look after her father," Pa explained. "Cal Crawford, the old mountain man."

"Look after him how?" I demanded, getting suspicious. I had few skills and little ability, nothing to be proud of. If I had been big enough to amount to anything, I could have been taking care of Pa so Geraldine wouldn't have had to stay home. She sometimes told me so.

"Just see he don't stray off," Pa explained. "He's blind, and he wanders. She don't want him to get hurt or lost." He added, "They'll give you your keep and a dollar a month wages."

I had no choice, really. It was a big thing to relieve the folks of feeding me, and a bigger one to earn that much money.

So I went to Cal Crawford's place, twenty miles away, on a pinto pony, trailing behind Cal's half-Indian daughter. I was scared all the way, and all summer.

That was before he became a legend, and after he had stopped being one, you might say. He was like a deposed god. He had gloried and drunk deep with his peers, had dared much and suffered much, had gained and lost. But all his peers were dead. Conestoga wagons had swayed westward along trails he had unwittingly helped mark, and as the frontier crept forward, settlements nestled where his campfires had starred the vast and silent night.

After he was gone, historians resurrected the legends and found most of them were true. He had trapped beaver and traded furs with the Indians, had lived with Indians and fought against them. He had traveled the wild Missouri and the Roche Jaune, or Yellowstone, had seen a mountain of black glass and the place where hell broke through the earth's surface to spout boiling water toward the sky. He had sat in council with chiefs, had taken scalps and never lost his own. But when I worked for him, nobody was left who had known him when he was young and strong and in his glory.

In that last summer of his life, he was only a blind old man, looked after by his Indian daughter.

She never gave me any orders. She showed me a pallet on the floor by his bunk and signed, "You sleep there." The cabin had two rooms. She slept in the other one, the kitchen.

Cal Crawford rode into the yard on a tired old white horse, herded by a tired old black dog. Monkeyface made a gesture toward him as if to say, This is what you are here for, to help the horse and the dog keep him from getting lost.

So I went outside and stood around while he dismounted. I cleared my throat and asked, "Want me to take the saddle off, Mr. Crawford?"

He looked over my head with his blazing blue blind eyes, scowling, his defiant chin held high, and said, "No!" He didn't want me there, and if I had to be there, he didn't care to be reminded.

There was no conversation at supper. Monkeyface had changed from her silk dress to a faded gray one, such as any farm woman might wear. She cut up his meat and murmured to him, but he didn't answer.

He would not stay in the house or near it, and rain

didn't matter, except that he would turn his face up to catch it. And sometimes he would get off his horse and kneel down in a field, reaching with his hands to see how high the grain had grown.

Uncounted miles of tipped mountains and rolling prairie had passed beneath his moccasin-clad feet when he was young and had his sight. He had been at home in tepees and brush shelters, and fifteen years had passed in one stretch without his ever setting foot in a house. When he was old, he did not like houses but wandered on horseback, with the old dog to herd him home.

When he was not riding, he walked around the yard, prodding ahead with a long stick. I kept quiet and out of his way, and when he saddled his old horse, I scrambled bareback onto the pinto.

Cal knew I was there, but he acted as if I had never been born. Once or twice he asked irritably, "Boy, you there?" but most of the time he preferred to forget me.

Once, when he was walking to the house, he prodded me with his pole by accident—I hadn't jumped fast enough when he turned around—but he wasn't sorry. He challenged, "Well?" while I rubbed my shin.

I said apologetically, "Sorry I got in the way, Mr. Crawford," and was mad at myself for being such a ninny.

Then came the morning when he whistled as usual for the dog but the dog did not come stiffly out of the shed. He whistled again, scowling, and seemed lost in his darkness. For the first time, I was sorry enough for him to forget being scared.

"I'll get him," I offered.

The dog was too tired to get up. I went out of the shed and reported, "Dog's sick, Mr. Crawford."

The old man prodded in with his stick and was not grateful when I touched his arm and said, "He's to your right."

He hunkered down, and the dog inched himself over and put his head on the old man's groping hand, wagging his tail feebly. After a while, Cal Crawford stopped petting him and grumbled, "Well, he's dead."

When Monkeyface found out, she handed me a shovel and I dug a grave for the dog. Cal didn't pay any atten-

tion except that he was impatient because his daughter
wouldn't let him ride anywhere while I was busy.

When the dog was gone, I felt more useful, but I never
bossed old Cal. I followed him and warned when he came
to a fence or a creek.

I was desperately lonesome and homesick, with nobody
to tell about it. The Indian woman never talked to me,
and the tall, stiff-jointed mountain man usually would not
admit I was there. I suppose each of them was lonely,
too. The old man looked blindly through me or over my
head, and Monkeyface sometimes glanced at me with no
expression—wondering, I think now, whether this boy
who was her last hope would stay while she needed him.

Back home, my sister would be crying for her lost love
or shouting angrily at my father, and he would be helpless and melancholy, as dependent as Cal Crawford but
lacking his defense of arrogance. Nevertheless, it was
home, and I wanted to be there.

Homesickness was bad enough, but something worse
happened. One day, old Cal began to talk to people I
could not see. We were riding along beside a grove. I was
watching so as to warn him when we came to a creek
with a steep bank. Suddenly he chuckled.

He pointed ahead and said, "Good beaver there last
year. Plenty Blackfeet, too. Waugh!"

"Did you want to go back now, Mr. Crawford?" I
asked.

He swung around, scowling, and said something in a
language that was not English. Then he ignored the interruption and went on talking loudly in some tongue unknown to me, gesturing, telling a story. Along with the
spoken language, he used the sign talk of the prairie
tribes, but more gracefully, more swiftly, than I had ever
seen it. I got a few of the signs—men riding, an evil person, somebody dead. To the rider on his left he spoke,
and to the rider on his right. I was on his right, but it was
not to me he told his story. It was to someone I could not
see, someone who wasn't there.

And the comrades of long ago must have answered,
because once in a while he laughed. He pointed off toward the place where prairie met sky, and kicked his
horse into a faster walk.

I was afraid to warn him of the creek. He sat easy in his battered saddle as his horse slid down the bank, waded across, and lunged up the other side. I kept behind him, shivering.

Long afterward, when historians revived the legend of Cal Crawford, I knew in what company I had ridden that day. The ghosts were bearded trappers in fringed buckskin, long-haired men with shapeless headgear of fur, moccasined men who rode like wary kings, who had forgotten fear but not caution. And Indians, too, rode with us, half-naked, curious, cruel, with paint stripes on their dark faces and hair in long black locks like snakes.

It was I who was invisible. Cal Crawford was young again in a time long years before I was born.

I did not guide him home that day. His horse turned and headed back to the cabin with him. But I did not desert him. I rode with him all the way, and did not know when we lost those other riders only he could see and hear.

I was going to tell his daughter at first, but what was the use? There comes a time when you have to look out for yourself, and I figured it had come. I decided to leave that night, sneak out of the cabin and walk the twenty miles back home.

But he slept poorly. He mumbled and tossed, and when he groaned, how could I leave?

He cried out, "Arrowhead under my shoulder, boy. Dig it out! Dig it out!"

With some hazy conviction that it would be cowardly for me to leave him wounded, I went over to him and said firmly, "It's all right, Mr. Crawford. Everything's all right."

He turned toward me and threw out his hand, groping, and I took hold of it.

"Don't leave me, boy," he whispered. He was not speaking to those lost, unseen comrades. I was the one he called "Boy."

"I won't leave you," I promised.

The next morning he pretended as usual that I wasn't there. He may not have remembered my promise, but I did. It worried me. How could I stay there, being scared all the time? Well, I hadn't said I would never leave him.

Any day I was free to go, I thought. That was how I endured staying, just one day at a time, always knowing I could go.

One day he told me a story—or maybe he told it to someone else, but I could hear it, and he talked English.

"My little girl," he said, chuckling. "Right smart young one, she is. I got her at a mission school, where they can bring her up right. Wouldn't have been there if I hadn't went to a lot of trouble. Her mother died, you know."

I made a sound indicating I was listening.

"Shoshone woman, her mother was. Died when we was camped on Little Muddy. If I'd knowed how sick she was, I'd have gotten her back to her people some way, but we was all alone. And the baby only three months old.

"Well, now, how was I going to feed a baby? No other woman around to give her to. Had to get out to someplace there'd be milk. But we was five hundred miles from a settlement. So I rode for Buffalo country.

"I fed the young one on juice from chewed-up meat, but she cried all the time, getting weaker so she sounded like a sick kitten. The first buffalo I seen was a dry cow, didn't do me no good. Then I come on a little herd of 'em, and there was milk to be had."

He laughed, remembering.

"You can't make no buffalo cow stand still to be milked. I had to shoot 'em. A dead cow you can get milk from. I fixed up a buckskin sack to nurse her with, and you should have seen her light into that milk! Every time she yelled for dinner and the sack was dry, I'd kill another buffalo cow.

"And did I ride! The last two days she got awful hungry, because the closer I come to the settlement, the scarcer the buffaloes was. But we made it through. I saved her. The Sisters at the mission took her.

"That girl baby was more darned trouble! I got me boys, too—Cheyenne, Sioux, Crow, Nez Percé—lots of boys, but darned if I know what become of 'em. They wasn't no trouble to me, and I wasn't no trouble to them. It's that little girl that was all the trouble."

He went back into silence then, and after a while he talked to someone not present.

Seldom did anyone come to the Crawford place. A distant neighbor sometimes, looking for strayed stock, would ride in and stare with curiosity, nodding a brief greeting at Monkeyface and perhaps shouting, "Hello there, Cal, how are you?"

The old man might answer angrily, "Think I'm deaf as well as blind?" or he might stare with those blazing blue eyes and not answer at all.

The few visitors were curious about me, but beyond asking whether I was any relation, they seldom bothered to speak. A lordly boy of fifteen or so did condescend to conversation. He asked, grinning, "The old man been fighting any Injuns lately?"

Cal's wandering mind was known to him, apparently, but a burst of loyalty prevented me from admitting anything.

I said stiffly, "You crazy! No Injun fighting around here."

"The old squaw's man been around this summer?" he asked. "Long-hair Injun, comes to see her once in a long while."

"Nobody's been here. I don't know who you mean."

"He's her man. Wants her to go back to the tribe, but she stays with her pa," the boy explained. "She's waiting to inherit all his property. She don't want to live with the savages anyhow, not when she can have everything good like white folks, silk dress and all."

He rode on after a while. He was the only boy I saw all that summer, and I used to wish he would come again.

The tax collector came one day when Cal and I had just got back from riding and the old man was lying on his bunk, tired out. I was in the yard, throwing chips at the chickens, when a rig turned in from the road. I went to tell Monkeyface, and she seemed disturbed. She woke up her father, and he was angry.

He shouted at her and groped out with his long stick to face the enemy. Monkeyface scowled at me and ordered, "You stay!"—the only time she ever gave me a direct order. This was private business, humiliating, not for me to know.

But even in the house I could hear the conversation, because the tax collector was one of the people who took it for granted that Cal Crawford, being blind, must be deaf as well.

"This ain't no place for you, Cal," he pleaded. "Come winter, what you going to do? We got a county farm. You'd be well took care of there, wouldn't have to worry about nothing."

"I got nothing to worry about now," Cal roared.

"But this place is going to be sold for taxes, I tell you. You could keep it, did you have the tax money."

Monkeyface snatched the purple silk dress from its nail by the door and put it on over her other dress and walked out to stand by her father, glaring at the visitor.

I saw a thing then that struck me with pity, young as I was and lacking in understanding. Cal put out his hand and touched the silk of the dress and took new strength from it. He expected it to be there, and it was.

"I look after my own," he boasted. "Bought my daughter a nice white-woman dress. You think I ain't got money? I can pay them taxes any time I please to!"

"Then pay me now, Cal, and save trouble," the tax collector pleaded. "It's not that anybody wants to put you off. But you don't need this place. You'd be better took care of on the county farm."

"Hundred and sixty acres," muttered Cal Crawford. "And he says I don't need all that." He stared blindly at the man in the rig and said with pride, "Young feller, once I owned half the continent. Me and a few others, we shared it and all that was in it. I ain't got much room to spread out in any more, but what I got, I need. And I'm going to keep it till I go under."

The man in the rig looked as if he might cry. "It's only what I'm supposed to do," he defended.

Cal lifted his stick in a vast, threatening gesture. "I'm going to keep what I got as long as I need it," he said, spacing the words. "I'll kill the man that tries to put me off."

The tax collector swatted his team with the whip and drove out fast.

At that moment, I loved old Cal. For the ring of truth was in his voice. *I'll kill him, that's what I'll do.* When other men said that, the threat was a crutch for weakness.

But old Cal had killed, he could kill. If necessary, he would.

He turned toward the house, probing out ahead with his stick. Walking behind him, I straightened my shoulders. I was still afraid of him, but I was not lonely any more.

Cal lay down in his bunk again, one arm across his eyes. I hunkered on the floor, willing to wait as long as need be. Where was he then? In that Kansas cabin, maybe, thinking about the tax collector. Or maybe he was behind the log walls of a trading post far to the westward, planning defense against painted savages.

Wherever he was, he knew I was there, too. Because after a while he said, "Bring my gun."

I was honored to be so commanded, but I didn't know which gun he wanted. He had four, hanging on the wall of the kitchen. I had not touched them but had admired them from a distance. I was ignorant, but how could I confess it? Guns belonged to men, so a man naturally knew all about guns. But only one of Cal's looked like the rifle we had at home.

Cal Crawford's life had spanned two great developments in firearms. Flintlocks had been his weapons in his younger days. As civilization crept westward, he had used percussion arms. Before his sight went dim, metal cartridges and breech-loading rifles were available. So he had three kinds on the wall. One of them was a flintlock, with the stock scarred and set with brass-headed tacks.

I climbed on a chair and reached for the flintlock because it was the strangest. Monkeyface objected, "Uh! Uh!" and I told her, "He wants his gun."

She did not try again to stop me. I carried the strange, long old rifle carefully to the other room and put it in Cal's hands.

He knew it by touch and smiled. "Not that one, boy." He fondled it. "I took that off Bull Back in forty-three, lost it twice, and got it again. See this here, boy?" He fingered a bit of the long black hair on a scrap of leather, attached to the trigger guard. "That there is Bull Back's scalp lock."

Shrinking, I touched it and thought, Now I have

touched an Indian scalp, and I know the man who took it.

"Bring me the rest, boy. And the ammunition."

I carried the guns in one at a time, with more journeys for the dirty beaded and quill-worked bags for lead balls and percussion caps, two powder horns so thin you could see light through them, a couple of metal powder containers, and a box of cartridges.

"Lay 'em down here," Cal Crawford ordered. "And git out."

When I came back, half an hour later, I was disappointed. The old man was sleeping, and Monkeyface had put the weapons back where they belonged.

After that day, Cal never went riding any more. He stayed to defend the last vestige of his empire, the little hundred and sixty acres. And for the first time, he fretted. A couple of times he whistled for the dog, and I was afraid to remind him the dog couldn't answer his signal any more. He stayed in the cabin for hours at a time, going over the logs with his hands, measuring the windows, getting his bearings.

His Indian daughter fretted, too, but silently. Sometimes she stood looking to the west, always looking west, as if waiting for somebody. Cal Crawford was waiting, too, but not for the same person.

But someone came for me before anyone came for either of them. A man from town, on his way out to our home place with a wagonload of lumber, drove in to say, "Your pa said I might's well pick you up and carry you home, Buck, seeing's I'm going right by there."

He got down from the wagon and walked around, loosening up his muscles, looking things over. Monkeyface came out, but she didn't say anything. She only looked at me.

"This here's a friend of Pa's," I explained. "Pa says I'm to come home now."

She didn't answer. She turned to the house to get the pay I had coming, the three silver dollars.

"I'll get my stuff," I told the driver. "Be with you in a minute."

Getting my possessions didn't take long. But my extra shirt was in the room where Cal lay on his bunk, and it was only decent to tell him I was going.

"G'by, Mr. Crawford," I said politely. "A man's come for me, going to give me a lift home."

He was silent for a while, with one arm over his eyes. Then he said bitterly, "All right. You don't need to stay. I'll stand 'em off."

So something was going to happen, and if I went home then, I might never get the straight of it. That wasn't the important thing, though. What mattered was that I mattered to Cal Crawford.

"Shucks, I needn't go yet," I told him. "There's no hurry. I'll tell him I'm going to stay around a while more."

"Whatever you want to do," Cal Crawford answered. He would not beg. He gave me pride I had never had before. I could afford to stay.

When I explained to the driver, he thought I was crazy and said so.

Neither Cal nor Monkeyface said anything about how I was a good boy and thank you. They just went on waiting.

One morning before dawn, the way Cal was fighting for breath woke me out of a sound sleep, or maybe it was his daughter's presence that woke me. She held an oil lamp high and was looking at Cal, speaking to him in her own language. She put a gnarled brown hand on his forehead and he shook it off angrily.

She looked at me with pleading. When she went outside, I saw in the dim light that she had a rope to catch up a horse with, so I guessed she was going for a doctor. I was more afraid than ever before in my life. I guessed what was coming for Cal Crawford.

He had faced it often before, stared it down, fought it off, conquered it, got away. Now he was going to fight it again, or maybe he thought it was some other enemy.

"Get my gun, boy," he gasped. "Help me sit up."

The breech-loading cartridge rifle was the one he had preferred before, so I brought that, but he disdained it.

"What's this thing?" he demanded. "Give me one a man can shoot with! And see the flint's sharp and the powder's dry."

So I got the old long flintlock with the bit of Bull Back's scalp dangling from the trigger guard. His hands claimed and caressed it.

" 'Tain't Old Fury," he muttered, "but it'll do. Look around the rocks, boy, and tell me what you see. Keep your head down."

My voice wasn't above a whisper. "Nothing coming yet, Mr. Crawford."

"Stay clear and give me room, that's all I ask," he said. His breathing was full and fast by then. "And listen, boy, if I go under, you run and hide. Don't worry none. If they take you, likely they'll raise you like one of their own." He managed a grating chuckle. "There's worse ways to live than like an Injun."

I wanted to run, not from the Indians but from Cal Crawford and the enemy. I had not reckoned on staying alone with him while Monkeyface rode for a doctor. I still wonder why she did it. Probably because he was proud he maintained her in the style of a white woman and she wanted to go on to the end doing, for his sake, what a white woman would try to do.

Cal loaded the battered old flintlock. He didn't need to see. He put the lead ball in his cupped hand and spilled powder so the ball was almost covered. Getting the right amount of powder into the pan was harder, and he spilled some.

When he had the charge rammed home, he was tired out. He lay back, commanding, "Watch for 'em, boy, and let me know when they come up over the hill."

I never saw them come, and he never spoke again.

It was near noon when Monkeyface came with the doctor. I was crouching in a corner with my face turned away from the bunk. But I had not retreated.

Maybe it was not an enemy who came for Cal Crawford. Maybe it was the mountain men, riding in to guide him on a journey through a country of wonders even he had never glimpsed.

His daughter let me go home that day on the pinto pony.

It was good to be home, better than if I had gone scared and retreating. I went as one who had earned the right because the job was finished and the duty done. I didn't tell them much, only that the old man was dead.

Pa was better, he could walk with a cane. Geraldine went around with a look on her face as if she had seen angels. She had a letter from her man, the first one since he went West without her. She wouldn't let us read it. But she hummed at her work and her steps were light.

About a week after I went home, Geraldine said, "Some old Injun is riding in with a squaw following. Now, what would they want?"

The Indian man stayed mounted, but when the squaw got down, I saw it was Cal's daughter. She was not wearing the purple silk dress. She had a striped shawl over an old cotton dress, and a kerchief on her head, squaw-fashion.

"It's Monkeyface," I said. "And that must be her husband, come to take her back to the tribe."

"She waited long enough," Geraldine said, "to get what old Cal left her. She earned it."

I suddenly understood something. "That wasn't why she stayed with him. She ain't got much of a pack on that horse. He didn't have anything to leave. She was just looking after her old pa because he needed her."

"Faithful," Geraldine whispered softly. "Faithful. That's what John says I am. He said it in the letter." She began to cry in a happy, sparkling way, and ran out to make a fuss over Monkeyface.

They had come for the pinto, so I went out and roped it. And Monkeyface gave me something for a remembrance of her pa.

Then they rode on, the man ahead and Cal Crawford's daughter following, leading the pinto, going home, wherever that was. Somewhere west, in the direction she used to look.

"There *is* faith and trust," my sister said softly. "She knew her man would wait till she could leave her pa. I wonder what she did with her purple dress."

We heard later. She left it hanging on a nail in the cabin. She left almost everything there. She had no use for anything white women treasured.

I don't know what happened to Cal Crawford's things, except that his daughter brought me the flintlock rifle he had held when he made his last stand.

Journal of Adventure

WHEN HE HAD DONE everything he could to prepare the shallow cave under the roots of the fallen pine for winter, when he had made every effort to save his own life, he faced the fact that he might fail. But he could not bear the thought that he might be only unnamed bones when someone found him, years hence. A man has identity, and he would save *that* even if he could not save his life.

He had set and splinted his broken leg as best he could; he had shot his crippled horse and salvaged as much meat as he could carry while crawling. He had even hung a part of the horse's hide to dry and stiffen where he could reach it. Anyway, he could reach it if he did not become completely helpless.

He had dragged tree branches for firewood close to his shallow shelter; and he had planned how, after snow came, he would burn a part of the tree so as to make the cave deeper.

But he was not at all sure he could live through the winter.

So he got out the blank book that, with higher spirits, he had entitled Journal of Adventure. If the book was found with his body or his bones by some Indian—who would think it was medicine or magic—it would be left to rot. But if a wandering white man came upon the book, he would read it, or else take it to someone who could. The book would let it be known that the man who had died there had had a name and once had had a future.

He propped himself up and wrote on a blank page:

November—1868. I am Edward Morgan, age twenty. Was traveling with a party of friendly Crows when attacked by Cheyenne. Got separated and in crossing this

*creek my horse fell on me, breaking his leg and mine. I
have done the best I could. Please notify . . .*

He crossed out the last two words. They were too bru-
tal. He had been about to write: Please notify Miss Victoria Willis that Edward Morgan will not return to marry
her because he died of starvation and cold under the
roots of a tree somewhere in Montana Territory. No, he
could be gentler than that. He thought for a time with his
eyes closed, and then he wrote:

*I, Edward Morgan, being sound in mind but in danger
of death, do hereby give, devise and bequeath to Victoria
Willis, East Waterford, Vermont, all the goods and property, real and personal, of which I die possessed, including my books. There being no witnesses because I am
alone in the mountains, I sign myself, Edward Morgan.
This is my last will and testament.*

If someone found the book with the will in it, perhaps
the book would go to Vicky with his property. Then she
could read the journal that began with his departure for
the West and mentioned every letter he had received from
her in the year and a half he had been away. So there
was no reason for writing that he loved her. There was no
need for a message like that, to be seen by strangers.

He leafed through the journal. So much of it was still
blank pages, like his life. He had expected to fill many
pages. He had expected to finish his college education
and to become a teacher of Latin and Greek, and he had
expected to marry Vicky.

If he ever got home again, he would be content to
chronicle the small events of tranquillity. But now he
wrote what he thought would be the last entry in the
Journal of Adventure: *Farewell, Adventure! Thou'rt a
fickle jade.*

That was a gallant flourish, he thought, though he realized that it did not sound much like Edward Morgan. Yet
while he was dying, if he did die, he was not going to
keep a record of horror for Vicky to read if she ever saw
the book.

But before he closed the journal, he had to send her
one more message: *Vicky, I tried to come back to you.*
Then he leaned back with his eyes closed. There was

nothing now to write. Henceforth he had only to endure. . . .

He had found adventure in three or four gold camps, though he reached them a little too late for the gold. It was planned adventure and he preferred to stay on the side lines—an observer, not a partaker.

He joined a village of Crow Indians because he wanted to see how Indians lived and the Crows were friendly. He had money enough to buy impressive presents for them, so they were willing to have his company. He was hardy and adaptable, but theirs was not a life he would have cared to live for very long. Many of their customs shocked him, and he did not learn their language well enough to talk just for the pleasure of conversation.

His curiosity satisfied, he had decided to leave the Indians and he was riding with half a dozen of the men toward the nearest trading post when his whole life changed. The party of Crows was ambushed and attacked by a larger party of Cheyenne. The Crows and Edward Morgan rode for their lives. He was separated from them in broken, wooded country.

This will be something to tell Vicky! he thought, just as his horse, plunging across a creek, fell.

His horse lunged half a dozen times before it got up. Each time the animal fell back on him, Edward Morgan groaned and thought he might faint. When the horse at last staggered to its feet, trembling and blowing, Morgan pulled himself out of the icy water and knew that his left leg was broken.

At first, he thought that in spite of the pain he might manage to mount and ride to find the Crows. But the horse had a broken leg too. Neither of them could travel. He immediately faced the fact he would have to spend the winter in that place.

There was a shallow shelter, a crumbling cave, under the roots of a great fallen pine. He stared at the shelter and recalled a Bible quotation: Man goeth to his long home, and the mourners go about the streets. There might never be any mourners for Edward Morgan.

He did the best he could for his injured leg; for splints he used straight branches that he had padded with moss and creeping vines, and then he had tied them snugly with a rope he had carried on his saddle. Night was falling then, so he built a frugal fire, not daring to waste wood, for what he could reach must last a long time.

He warmed himself and ate some pemmican from his saddlebags. After making sure the horse could not hobble away, he slept fitfully in the cave until dawn came.

That day he had a great deal of work to do. He crawled to where the horse stood and with great effort he got the saddle off. Then he shot the horse in the head and set about skinning as much of it as possible. He would need the hide to hang in front of the shelter; it would keep out some of the snow that would come later. Some of the hide he cut into smaller pieces, which he might need for purposes he had not yet figured out.

All this he did hastily, awkwardly, in pain. The hide would be useful, but the meat would be life itself to him. He cut some meat into strips as he had seen Indian women do, and he hung it up, hoping it would dry and be preserved. He ate cooked meat that night beside his small fire.

He awoke from restless, pain-shot sleep in the dark night, hearing some animal eating on the horse carcass, and he fired a shot that scared it away.

He did not sleep any more, and at dawn the animal was there again—a mountain lion. He waited with patience and cunning until there was daylight enough and then shot the big cat.

That day had been the worst of all, because his leg hurt so much as a result of the crawling he had done and had to do. He skinned the mountain lion and hauled himself wearily back to the shelter, where he laid the hide, fur upward, on the cold, damp earth. He gnawed some raw horsemeat for supper because he was too exhausted to build a fire.

In the morning he awoke to the sound of groaning and found he was making the sound himself. Without moving, he looked up at the dirt roof of his shelter, his long home. Was there reflected light? He turned his head and saw pale sunshine on new snow within arm's reach.

So he need not go thirsty if he became unable to crawl the few feet to the creek. He could eat snow. If winter cold came soon enough, it would make his meat supply last longer—but cold might kill him as he lay there. The air was not really cold that morning, and he noticed, sniffing, that the carcass of the horse was beginning to stink.

He was the loneliest man in the world. He was primitive man in savage wilderness. But primitive man was not alone, he remembered. The Indians lived among unseen beings and told long, frightening stories about them. Most of the spirit beings were cruel; only a few meant well.

Feeling ashamed, but comforting himself with the assurance that nobody would ever know his shame, he made a little sacrifice to the heathen spirits the next time he ate. When he roasted horsemeat on a stick over his small fire, he dropped a bit of the meat into the flames.

That night the cold was cruel. He dreamed of being lost, of trying to escape from danger—wolves, grizzly bears, painted Cheyenne—and of being too slow. Even in sleep he was surrounded by enemies, as waking he was tormented by cold and pain and terror. Sometimes in a dream he moved just fast enough to take refuge in his shelter under the tree roots, only to find that he was trapped there.

When he awoke, it was true. He was too stiff and pain-racked to move.

He began to think his message to Vicky in the journal was a lie. *I did the best I could.* That was brave enough when he wrote it, but an injured man did not have to go on being valiant while slow death approached, not while he had a gun and ammunition.

If whoever came upon his bones found a bullet hole in the skull, Edward Morgan thought, he would have the decency not to mention it in sending the journal on to Vicky. But he was not ready to use a bullet yet. . . .

Four or five days later he was ready, but by that time he was too sick. His chest was torn with coughing, he was very feverish, and he was quite sure he had pneumonia. He realized that he must be delirious, because once he opened his eyes and saw a horse standing by the creek. A horse that was dead and skinned and partly eaten should not be standing there with its hide on. Edward Morgan was weakly angry at the unreasonable horse.

"Get along, there!" he shouted, and fell back, cough-ing.

Then Vicky was there. Vicky? Who else would have come? She murmured and reached out, kneeling, to put her hand on his forehead. She built a fire. He peered be-tween his eyelids to see her moving about it.

She gave him soup to drink from a cup of some kind. She tried to make his injured leg more comfortable, but she hurt him and he shouted in anger, trying to strike her away.

Fevered and vastly bewildered, he passed the night in periods of cold and warmth. When he was warm, it was because she was lying beside him, protecting him from winter and death.

Uncounted days later, he knew she was not Vicky. She was a Crow Indian girl whose name he could not even remember. The horse he sometimes saw was the one she had ridden in her search for him after the returning riders told how they had lost him.

He wanted to ask why she had come, but until he got well of his fever he did not dare for fear she might van-ish. During his worst sickness, he often woke, panting, trembling like a cobweb, and cried hoarsely for her and reached out—and found her there.

When the pneumonia was mercifully gone, he dared to ask her. He was weak and stinking with sweat; he lay in the shallow cave with the fire roaring in front of it—how many miles had she trudged through snow with loads of firewood on her bent back!—but his head was clear. He could not remember the Crow words for "Why did you come?" so he asked in English.

She murmured something, smiling, and went on with her endless toil. She had even moved the carcasses of the horse and lion off into the woods, salvaging some of the smaller bones for tools and dishes.

In midwinter, they came close to starvation, but the In-dian girl set ingenious traps and caught enough small ani-mals to keep life in their bodies. He had learned her name by that time—Blue Wind Woman—and why she had come to save him. He knew why, but for a long time he did not want to face the fact of the debt he had incurred. For her, a white man meant prestige. She was willing to gamble. She had staked her life on him.

In early spring—he guessed it was March—he could walk, though he limped badly. He would always limp, but he had not died.

Blue Wind Woman then announced, "Tomorrow we will go to look for my people."

For the first time since he had written his will, he took out the Journal of Adventure to make another entry. The girl huddled in her blanket and pressed against his shoulder, watching with admiration as he wrote. Sometime, he thought, I will read this, or my children will. There must be no bitterness. He smiled wryly at a recollection of something his grandmother used to say in admonition when he was too noisy as a little boy: "Edward, let us comport ourselves with dignity."

And so he wrote not what he wished to say, but what he would wish someone else to read:

March—, 1869, cave by the creek. A few days after the last entry in this journal, I became desperately ill and would surely have died had it not been for the arrival of a young woman of the Crow tribe.

She came, with great danger to herself, expressly to find the white man who her tribesmen said had been lost in their retreat.

She has worked unceasingly through these winter months to save my life. We have been near to starving, and that we did not starve is entirely owing to her constant efforts. Her patience and fortitude never falter. She is unfailingly good-humored, no matter how cold or tired or hungry. I owe her a debt that only my lifelong devotion can repay. Her name means Blue Wind Woman, but I call her Jane. Tomorrow we start from this place to find her people. The horse she brought has fared ill through the winter and is no more than bones held together with hide. But she says he is strong enough to carry me (for I can as yet walk only short distances), and she will travel on foot, carrying a pack of our necessities on her back. Until this winter, I never really understood the meaning of that word necessities.

When he stopped writing, she pointed at the page,

looked up into his face with an eager, inquiring expression, and laughed.

He smiled and said, "It's about you." Then he kissed her.

"We will go where you want to go," he promised. "We will be married by a preacher." He took her rough, cold hand in both his hands, and said solemnly, "I will be good to you and true to you so long as we both shall live, so help me God."

So Vicky was only a faraway sweet memory and a name that would appear no more in the Journal of Adventure.

They stayed for a few weeks with the Crows so that Blue Wind Woman could show her man to her people. But she had seen from a distance how white men's women lived in settlements, and she wished for that grandeur. Edward Morgan did not think that he could endure the Crow camp much longer anyway.

He rented a cabin on the edge of a town and went with his wife to a store where furniture could be bought. She was overwhelmed beyond speech, and at first would not point or touch but hide her face in her blanket.

Their cabin was furnished with real chairs, a painted table, an iron cooking stove and a brass bedstead. And then Edward Morgan made another entry in his journal:

July 3, 1869. This morning, I, Edward Morgan, and Jane or Blue Wind Woman, daughter of High Elk of the Crow tribe, were united in holy matrimony by the Rev. Walter Wickersham, a Methodist circuit rider. My bride wore a black satin dress that the wife of a departing citizen kindly sold me. I intend to do all in my power to make her life a contented one. Brother Wickersham baptized us both.

The baptism—Edward Morgan's second—made him feel better. His conscience had irked him about that pagan sacrifice he had made to the heathen spirits.

I am looking for a business connection in this region, he wrote. *A partnership is available in a mule freight business. I am now twenty-one years of age and can claim the money that is waiting for me in a Philadelphia bank.*

So Edward Morgan became a mule skinner and a boss

of mule skinners, instead of being a professor of Latin and Greek.

His wife was proud of her house, though she had no interest in keeping it clean as Edward urged. She sat more easily on the floor than on a chair. She built a brush shelter outside the door and did her cooking there over a fire rather than on the stove indoors. Sometimes he thought she was lonely, but she never said so.

He wrote seldom in the journal except to note business transactions he wanted to record. But in May, 1871, he made a jubilant entry:

At four o'clock this morning a daughter was born to my wife Jane. She is a perfect baby but finds this world less than perfect, I judge by her loud objections to it. We will name her Elizabeth for my mother. Jane is agreeable to this name and is practicing the pronunciation. My wife is in good health and spirits, though she wished for a baby boy. May God shower blessings on my little Elizabeth.

They were in another settlement, a hundred miles south, when he entered another birth two years later:

A son, who will be named for me, was born this morning to my wife, Jane Morgan. Edward Morgan the younger objects less strenuously to his new surroundings than his sister Elizabeth did. He is a beautiful baby, and I trust we will rear him to be an admirable citizen.

But they did not. Edward Morgan the younger, half-blooded son of Edward Morgan, was not yet two years old when he died with his mother. This was so harsh a tragedy that it was not entered in the battered Journal of Adventure until some three weeks later.

Elizabeth Morgan, not quite four years old, slept sweetly after she had said her Now I Lay Me. Her father moved quietly about the cabin, packing the belongings he would take when he left it. When he came upon his journal on a dusty shelf, he held it for a while, unopened, and then sat down at the table where a kerosene lamp gave light for reading. *My wife and son are dead,* he wrote and for a few minutes could go no further.

She was a fearless woman and impetuous. Six years ago these traits of hers saved my life, but now they have lost two others. Wishing to visit her own people, who had

*been camped some miles from this settlement, she took
the boy and set out on horseback, but they were caught
in a sudden blizzard and did not survive.*

*My little Elizabeth is spared to me, having been left
behind with a neighbor. A search party of which I was a
member found the two bodies in a snowdrift after my
wife's horse came back to our cabin.*

Let us comport ourselves with dignity, he thought, putting down the pen. No need to tell the whole of it for
Elizabeth to read someday. Blue Wind Woman must have
been homesick, lonely. Her family had visited often, looking on Edward's household with pride and curiosity, always expecting a feast and always getting it. But perhaps,
he thought, his wife had been tired of trying to live like a
white woman.

She had left Elizabeth with a good woman nearby who
had a house full of children and had not objected to a
visit from one more. But Elizabeth's visit had lasted for a
week, because Edward Morgan, freighting supplies from
Salt Lake City, had been delayed by snow. He had come
home to find his cabin empty and cold, to find the neighbor woman frantic with concern.

There was no need to tell those details in the journal,
or how unwilling his acquaintances had been to set out to
search for an Indian woman and her baby who were no
doubt settled safely in a tepee miles away.

"They are my wife and child," he had repeated grimly
and had recruited three men to help in the search. He
found the bodies himself and stayed there while the others rode back for shovels to dig a grave.

Tomorrow, he wrote, *my little daughter and I will
leave this place. She will be cared for by Mrs. Clough, a
rancher's wife in the Tumult Valley. I will continue my
freight business, but with headquarters at Elk City.*

He felt more solitary than ever before—excepting the
time when he had lain with his leg broken in the shelter
by that distant mountain creek. And now he could admit
to himself that he had been lonely for a long time. He
wished mightily to confide in someone to ease his grief,
but there was no one.

He wrote a short letter to the bank in Philadelphia,

where he still had a few hundred dollars on deposit, and gave his new address, Elk City.

Four years later, Edward Morgan rearranged his life again, so that he might make a home for Elizabeth. He sold his freight outfit and bought a livery stable that would allow him to stay in town, and during the summer he brought his daughter from the Clough ranch to let her get used to him before school started.

She is willing to try anything, he wrote proudly in the journal, which no longer related anything adventurous about himself. *She even volunteered to make bread, but was satisfied when I said we could buy it from a neighbor, who also does our washing. Elizabeth and I keep house very well. I cook and she wipes the dishes. She attempts to sweep with a broom far taller than herself. She can read a little, even without schooling. My daughter is a more than average bright child.*

She came home jubilant after her first day at school.

"Put your dark apron on," her father admonished, "but never mind peeling the potatoes. You tell me all about school while I get supper."

She sat on a chair, with her feet swinging and her hands clasped. "Well, it was real nice," she reported happily. "I've got a lady for my teacher! Mrs. Bishop, her name is."

"Not Professor Emery? How nice to have a lady! But Missus? Married ladies don't teach school."

"Why not? Oh, I guess they stay home and look after their children. But she said Missus. I sit next to a little girl who has curly hair."

He opened her lunch pail, and said, "Why, you ate both your sandwiches. Good girl."

"Two's too much, but I had one. The other one, there was a boy didn't have any, so Mrs. Bishop said I could give it to him."

"That's fine, my dear." (Oh, proud little Elizabeth, who could be bountiful! She would have two sandwiches every day.)

"Teacher sent a paper for you to write on. I don't know all the answers." She giggled. "She asked what your first name was. I said it was Papa."

Lying in his bunk that night, waiting for sleep, he was amused that his daughter had not known his first name. Still, when had she ever heard it? Men called him Morgan. Blue Wind Woman (she was Jane on the paper he had filled in for the teacher) had called him a pet name in her own language. But now his daughter, or perhaps her teacher, had made him whole again, Edward Morgan, as he had been when he was a boy in the country that Elizabeth, with awe and respect, called Way Back East.

A week later, when Elizabeth skipped in with her book and lunch pail, she said, "Teacher says please she would like to see you."

"Did she say what for? My little girl hasn't been bad in school, has she?"

Elizabeth searched her soul. "Well, I don't think so. If you're bad, she calls you down, like if you talk when you shouldn't. Some of the children are real bad," she added with conscious virtue. "But teacher likes me fine."

Getting slicked up enough to meet the teacher was a problem. He left a clean shirt and his good boots at the barbershop in the morning, and in the afternoon went back there for a bath and a shave. It was a long time since he had been so shined up.

He left his saddle horse at the hitch rack in front of the school and noted Elizabeth's little pinto grazing with a dozen other ponies nearby. When the youngsters surged out with a roar of release, he told Elizabeth to play a while. He tugged at his collar as he limped into the school. The teacher's back was turned and he cleared his throat and said, "Mrs. Bishop?"

When she turned, he heard his own voice saying, "Why, Vicky!"

She stared at him with honest curiosity and then sat down at her desk and said, "I wanted to know whether it was the same Edward Morgan."

He thought of the last seven years. "I guess it isn't," he said. "That Edward Morgan promised to come back. He broke his promise. He was—unavoidably detained. I'm sorry, Vicky. I've always been sorry."

She toyed with a pencil, not looking up. "Vicky Willis promised to wait. But she married a man named Forbes Bishop. He was drowned."

"So Vicky Bishop, forced to earn her own living, came to the frontier to teach school."

"I don't have to earn my living," she said frankly. "It's no coincidence that I came to Elk City. My second cousin works in a bank in Philadelphia. He told me you were here. Getting the information out of him was almost as hard as the journey west. I hope you realize," she added with a trace of a smile, "that this explanation is embarrassing to me."

Unaccustomed laughter rose in his throat. "You've still got the devil in you," he said.

"Devil is a bad word, and we don't say bad words in school," she warned him primly. "I came to find out two facts. You are alive; that's one."

The other was obvious: Why hadn't he come back?

I incurred a debt, and I paid it. He might say that, but he would not, even to save Vicky's pride.

"I married a Crow Indian woman," he said. "Her name was Blue Wind Woman, but I called her Jane. She died four years ago, and my son with her, trying to get back to her own people."

"Yes," Vicky said softly. "Yes, that's what I've heard. Good-by, Edward Morgan. Your daughter is waiting for you. She is a very sweet little girl."

Vicky's back was turned as he answered, "Good-by. Good-by."

That night he opened the Journal of Adventure and wrote, *Today I saw Vicky! She is teaching*— He did not finish. Now he knew for what reader the journal had been intended in the beginning. It was not begun for his descendants, or for the boy who had been Edward Morgan, or for the unknown wanderer who might have found a man's bones in a shallow cave beside a creek.

He did not finish the sentence he had begun, but wrote a new one: *Vicky, this is what became of Edward Morgan.*

He wrapped the book carefully in newspaper and tied it with grocery string. Elizabeth was delighted to take it to school the next morning when he explained, "It's something for your teacher."

Elizabeth was not yet home from school when he reached their cabin that evening. The kettle was boiling before he saw her coming on her pinto pony, and with something close to terror he saw that she was not alone. Vicky walked beside her, laughing. I should go to welcome her, he thought, but he was frightened and trapped. He watched as Elizabeth slid down into Vicky's reaching arms. He could not move until they neared the doorway, walking hand in hand. And then he was able only to say, "Good evening, Mrs. Bishop."

"I asked teacher to supper and we took turns riding," Elizabeth said.

"She is very welcome," Edward Morgan answered, "Vicky, come in."

"I brought back your book," said Vicky Bishop.

They looked at each other across lost years.

"Elizabeth, go gather up some chips for kindling," Edward Morgan ordered. "Hustle!" The child went with lagging feet.

"And what did you find in the book?" he demanded.

Vicky considered. "I found a boy I used to know. And then I found a man, a man of honor."

He could not speak for a moment. At last he said, "Was he there? That man? I hadn't thought of him that way. Vicky?"

She was clutching the door casing with one hand, holding the book with the other. She said, "And I remembered how his grandmother used to say, 'Let us comport ourselves with dignity.' "

Then Vicky was in his arms, weeping softly, with her face pressed against his shoulder.

The Story of Charley

THERE HAD TO BE an obituary for Charity; the preacher would need it for the funeral, and it would go in the weekly paper.

Charity's stepdaughter Leona was a foresighted woman. She had clipped a couple of obituaries from the paper to use as a pattern. There wasn't much to say about Charity. In her early twenties she married Ezra McCutcheon, raised two of his children by his first marriage, gave him four more, homesteaded with him in Nebraska, kept the family together by bitterly hard work after he died.

The only astonishing thing in her life, as far as Leona knew, was that when Charity was close to sixty, a pockmarked, white-haired tramp came to the door, and a few weeks later she married him.

That was Duke, who sat now out by the woodpile, wrapped in silent mourning. He and Charity had known each other in their youth. Leona had been doubtful about that late and somehow embarrassing marriage, but it had been a contented one.

She started to write: "Mrs. Charity Williams passed away July 7, 1912, at her home after a short illness. She was born—" When was she born, and where, and what was her maiden name? That could all be filled in later.

"She married Ezra McCutcheon in"—just what year was that?—"and to this union four children were born, one of whom preceded her in death, as did Mr. McCutcheon, who died in an accident." He was gored by a bull. His youngest daughter shivered, remembering that day.

"Preceded her in death"—that was a stately phrase. Leona could visualize an endless procession passing through a dark gateway, with now and then someone stepping aside to permit another to precede.

The facts she needed were not in her memory. They might be in the small, scarred wooden box that Charity had treasured. And the box was locked.

Leona went, sighing, to the back yard where sat Charity's second husband, with his hands hanging between his knees and the sun warm on his broad, bowed back.

"Would you want to help me with dates and things?" she asked gently. "I don't know what she did with the key to the old box of papers."

"She give it to me," Duke said in a voice of muted thunder. "You can have it, girl." He dug with rheumatic care into his pants pocket.

"I don't know her maiden name or birth date," Leona admitted. "We never celebrated birthdays much, except for the little kids, and Charity wasn't much of a talker about herself."

Duke put the key in her hand. "She was born May 11, 1850, in Council Bluffs. She was a Montgomery. You'll write it real good." As Leona turned away, he added, "One thing I want you to say. Charity was a good woman."

Leona stared. "Of course she was. Everybody knows that."

"When you go through her things," Duke warned softly, "you'll find things there that might make you wonder. So you ask me. Because I know everything that happened to Charity."

Half an hour later, Leona had sorted through the keepsakes in the wooden box. She was disturbed, almost frightened, at what she had found there.

There was a photograph of two young men, and on it was written "From Duke to Charley." The tall young man, wide of mouth and shoulders, could indeed be Duke, before he was scarred with smallpox. Who was Charley, the slighter one, wearing a fringed jacket and a broad-brimmed hat? And why had Charity treasured the picture for so long?

Still, anyone might have a half-forgotten picture. Who would keep another person's letter? But there was a letter to "Dear Charley" from Duke, somewhere in Texas, dated

1867. The writing was barely legible, for the creased paper had worn through.

Duke was, apparently, on a journey to some destination not yet known. He would write again as soon as Wilkins decided where to set up store. He was well and hoped Charley was the same. The letter ended: "I wish I could see my dear wife again and take her in my arms and tell her I love her."

A strange sentiment in a letter from one man to another! Why had Charity kept all these years a letter Duke had written to someone else?

There was a picture of a beautiful young woman looking down at a baby in her arms. Surely no relative of Charity's, for the young woman wore silk, and the baby's dress, yards long, was frothy with embroidery. There had been no such luxury for the children of Charity McCutcheon.

A third photograph struck a faint chord of memory: a dark, gaunt young dandy with deep eyes and a mouth that was bitter though it smiled. Somewhere, Leona thought, she might have seen that man. But written across the bottom was "Mother," and he was not of Charity's brood.

More comforting was a familiar photograph of Charity and Ezra and his four children. Leona saw herself at eight years old, and her younger sister, Bessie, and the two older brothers who had later gone to California and had never come back. That was the wedding picture of her father and his young bride Charity, with his children by his first marriage.

More disturbing than the letter, more than the unidentified photographs of strangers, were the marriage certificates. Three of them. And two had Duke Williams' name. The first was dated 1866—Charity Montgomery must have been sixteen then—the other was dated forty years later, when the widowed Charity McCutcheon married Duke Williams again. But in 1874 she had married Ezra McCutcheon.

And what was in the sealed envelope on which Charity had written, "This is for Duke"?

Leona called, "Duke! Duke, I want to ask you something."

He answered from the kitchen and stood there in the doorway.

"You want me to tell you now? Seems like I have to tell somebody. And she said I could tell you, but not her own children."

We lied to the preacher about our ages, thought it was best that way, because we went all by ourselves to get married. Charity wasn't but sixteen, and I was twenty. We felt guilty running off and still we thought it was the only thing to do. We kept confessing to each other how we didn't amount to anything but was going to improve.

"I ain't got the means to look after you like you deserve," I told her with my heart about breaking of shame. "But there ain't anything I can't do with you beside me."

And it seemed like it was true. It surely seemed that way. I never did tell Charity a knowing lie but once, and that was just before she passed away.

She said, "I'm bone-lazy and good-for-nothing, and Auntie always has to tell me twice, but when we have our own home, I'll be such a good houskeeper!"

We met under an oak tree at midnight and went West. I had the clothes I stood in and a little pack on a bay horse fourteen years old. Charity had a carpet bag and three towels and a linen sheet.

"I wish I'd sewed more," she sighed. "I wish I had more to bring you."

But there was herself, and what more would a man ask?

Mostly, Charity rode the horse, with me beside, holding her hand. But she fretted I must be tired, and once she made me ride a mile or two while she went dancing beside me, laughing because I felt like a fool.

"Me big chief," I says. "Chief ride. Squaw walk a heap."

We went West alone as far's we could, and you could say we was beggars, but the people was kind with what they had, and we worked when they'd let us. But when we got beyond the towns and farms, we couldn't go alone any more.

Then we had to travel with anybody that would have us—wagon trains of freight, or parties of miners and once even some soldiers deserting off the Indian frontier and heading west for gold. We had another horse then, picked it up stray on the prairie.

I had some money, all I could raise from selling the home place, but it didn't add up to much. Kept us going with supplies, though, when we got beyond the farms. I shot game when there was any.

One night by a campfire a big, bearded rough grabbed Charity, and I fought him. Broke his jaw. The others said he had it coming. But I was three days mending enough to travel—that was the worst fight I was ever in, except once later in Mexico—and I worried.

You see, I was only a farm boy, and those were hard men on the frontier. Oh, I had me a revolver, besides the rifle, but I was no gunman. And maybe, I thought, I wouldn't be able to protect my girl the next time. But neither of us said so. There's some things you can't admit.

She fretted about her hair.

"It's too hard to manage," she complained. "Horrid old hair! I wisht you'd cut it short so's it would be easier for me."

Oh, Charity had beautiful hair in those days. Sleek and dark, long enough to sit on, deep enough to drown in. But she kept after me and after me, and one day I cut it all off like a boy's, with tears in my eyes so I hacked it ragged.

After that, she wore a boy's clothes we got from emigrants that had a son that died along the way. We didn't admit it was to save her if I couldn't protect her, or to save my life if there was a worse fight than there'd been already. We let on, the both of us, that it was just to make traveling easier for Charity.

So then she wasn't my wife Charity any more, but my young brother Charley. Sometimes it was hard to remember.

And so we came to Gulch City. It never was on a map, didn't last long enough. It was a gold camp, going great guns, and they said some men got rich there, but I never seen any of them.

Charity and me, we worked for wages, shoveling gravel on a paying placer claim, living in a wickiup. You never seen a wickiup, I guess. We built this'n ourselves, out of poles and brush and rocks against a hill. It was as good as any, but the Injuns lived better. That wickiup was a hell of a thing, but Charity laughed.

"We'll tell our grandchildren about this," she said. "They'll never believe us."

"If they don't believe what you tell 'em," I said, "I'll beat the tar out of 'em."

Such promises I made when I was young! I was a lord in them days, threatening the grandchildren that never got born.

We were just going to stay there till I got the hang of mining, till we got a stake. Then we'd go find our own pay dirt. There was riches to be had in those days. I never happened to catch up with any, though.

I didn't like it, my Charity working with a shovel like she did, but that wickiup was no place for her to spend her days. Anyhow, the other men would have thought there was something funny about a boy Charley's size doing nothing but cook and carry wood and water. And we needed to build our stake.

All we ever wasted money on was powder and ball for the old revolver. We used to practice shooting on Sundays, way out on the sagebrush hills.

In early fall, I had a good opportunity, or so it looked like, but I turned it down.

"Wilkins is going to move his store fixings to Arizona," I told Charity. "Going to set up store there somewheres, trade with the Injuns. Said he'd hire me to drive one wagon, teach me the store business. 'Can my brother go?' I says. 'Only need one man,' he says. So I says, 'No, thanks.'"

But Charity thought I ought to go.

"Then you could send for me," she says. "Or I could leave same time you do, go with some other outfit heading that way."

It wouldn't do, I told her. Not even if she went by stage. Because Wilkins himself wasn't sure where he'd set up his store.

"You couldn't stay here alone, come winter," I says. "And it might take a while before I could send you word. We'd better head for Salt Lake."

"But the store business, your big chance," she says.

That was all we needed, we thought in them days, just one chance for Duke and he'd wrap his bride in satins.

"Don't talk about it no more," I says. "I ain't even thinking of it."

But Charity was. There was a girl with a mind of her own, and every thought in it was for me. She found herself a job in a little shack store in Gulch City that was going to stay open all winter. The old lady that kept it could use a sober, industrious boy to cut wood and do chores in exchange for meals and a place to sleep by the stove.

"No!" I yelled. "I ain't going to have it!"

But she kissed my eyelids, and I began to agree. Ma Harris was sure and all respectable, and she wouldn't stand for no nonsense whether Charity was a boy or a girl.

So I give Charity all our money and gold dust, our stake, so she'd have plenty to carry her through when she come down to join me in the spring.

The night before I left, she cried in my arms because we were going to be separated all winter. That was an awful long, bleak winter. It lasted forty years.

In the morning we took Charity's things to the shed back of the store—not that she had much to take there. And when I went by, driving Wilkins' wagon, she stood waving.

I couldn't kiss her good-by after we left the wickiup. A man don't kiss his brother. But I remember how she looked, waving to me in the street of Gulch City.

"I'll send you word whenever mail's going," I promised. "If you don't hear for a while, don't you fret. Because you'll know I'm thinking of my girl Charity and fixing up so's we can settle down and have a home as good as anybody's."

Before I left, we had our picture made together. It was the last picture that feller took in Gulch City. He was pulling out. Charity's says "From Duke to Charley," and this here's mine, "From Charley to Duke." Mine's dirty, ain't it, and it got broke in my pocket. But I was lucky, I always managed to hang onto that picture.

The rest of it I wouldn't never have known except that Charity told me, and I know she told me true. I want you to remember, in spite of everything that happened, she was a good woman. What happened was my fault, not hers. What she did was only what she had to do, and you'd have done the same, because there was no choice. Not after she decided to stay in Gulch City when Ma Harris left.

Well, I went south with Wilkins, but he was a finicky man, disgusted with how he'd made out in Gulch City, wouldn't settle in a new place until he was sure he'd get rich. Our wagons got lighter and heavier again as he traded along the way, but we never stopped anyplace for long.

Every town the wagons stopped, I mailed a letter to Charity. But of them all, she never got but one. It was a poor thing for a love letter, because it had to be wrote like she was my brother Charley. You never could tell what might become of a letter, and it was safer for her that way. She kept it all these years.

And she was writing letters to me but had no address to mail them. I told her two or three places where mail might have reached me, but those letters I never got. Maybe you don't know what it was like in those days, before the modern times. Mail couldn't go by railroad heading north or south, and there was Injun trouble and some stage drivers didn't give a hang what happened to sacks of mail anyway, throw them in a river to lighten the load, what did they care? In winter, mail didn't travel in or out of Gulch City anyhow, and neither did anything else but the wind.

Wilkins decided he'd trade in Mexico, and I'd throwed in my lot with him, had to stick with him or lose all my time. He didn't pay me wages, just my keep and promises.

It don't matter now what happened in Mexico. I never did know what become of Wilkins. But a bunch of greasers jumped us and I fought and landed in jail. That was the worst fight I was ever in. And there I laid for months in that stinking calabozo, near crazy with worry about my Charity. Then they unlocked the door one day and I walked out.

But I walked out with death on me. Smallpox. I was sick and feverish, starting north, and somewhere I crawled into an old shack or adobe, whatever it was, and laid down. There was scraps of grub there, and when I got well enough I ate it. And I went north as soon as I could stand on my feet again, but even the Injuns was scared of me.

I didn't care whose horses I rode or whose beef I slaughtered, just so I'd keep traveling. What I needed I took, or people give it to me whether they could spare it or not.

So in the spring I came to Gulch City—but another spring had gone before that one since I parted from Charity there. All the way back I asked fellers for news of Gulch City, but all they ever said was it was plumb played out. Nobody there any more, they said, if they knew of it at all.

Still I had to see for myself. If she was gone from there, how would I ever find her?

There was wet gray snow in the gulches and not a living soul around. I went to the wickiup and it was all fallen in from the snow, empty and ruined.

"This is the home I gave my wife," I said. I picked up a scrap of blue cloth and kept it a while because it might have been hers, but then I throwed it away.

No matter what kind of life I'd given her, I knew that wasn't why she left. She had to go if everybody else did, and it was a year and a half since we said good-by.

I went up on the cemetery hill, half crazy, and looked for her name on the crooked slabs of wood they used for markers, if they put any on the graves at all. There never was many graves there, the camp didn't last long enough. If I'd found a board with her name on it, Charity or Charley, I'd have stayed there forever. But there wasn't nothing to keep me.

So I went looking in other gold camps, other towns, but I didn't know if I was looking for my wife Charity or my young brother Charley, and some places they thought I was crazy. They were right, too. After a while I stopped looking.

After that, what happened to me never mattered much. The years slide into each other when you haven't anything special you want to do or be. Sometimes I was outside the law, but a man with a bad-scarred face is easy to identify, so I give that up. I knowed some outlaws in my day and rode with a few. None of them ever got rich or amounted to scratch. But in the law or out of it, what happened to Duke Williams happened to a man that didn't rightly care.

In that first spring after I'd gone with Wilkins, the most of the miners didn't come back to Gulch City, only a few. So Ma Harris, where Charity was working as chore boy, when she see the camp was dying, she decided to pull out too.

"This camp is played out," she says to her boy Charley. "How old are you, I want to know?"

"Seventeen," says Charity.

"Time you was shaving if you was a boy. But I know you ain't," says Ma Harris. "You can come to Oregon with me if you want to. What's your right name?"

"My name is Mrs. Charity Williams," my girl said, "and thank you kindly but I can't leave until I hear from my husband."

"You're good help, boy or girl, and I don't mind having you," said Ma Harris. "And you can't stay here alone."

But she wouldn't go. "I never would get Duke's word of where to meet him. I wrote him letters, but I only got one from him and never mailed most of them I wrote."

Ma Harris said, "Child, accidents happen. If he was able to write you, wouldn't you have heard by now?"

Charity wouldn't listen. She put her hands over her ears and screamed.

She stuck it out till fall, in the shack Ma Harris had moved out of, and then the last storekeeper was leaving too. When it was a full year since I left her there, she still didn't have but that one letter. Every time the stage came in, she asked.

The last time, the storekeeper thumbed through the letters and said, "Nothing here for you, Charley."

Then she broke down, cried like a girl, right there in the store.

A passenger off the stage said, "Mr. Storekeeper, can we have a cup of water for the young lady? Here's a handkerchief, Miss, and a chair."

When she stopped crying, it was like getting well from

a sickness. She wasn't bound any more to Charley nor to Duke. Her husband was dead or she'd have heard from him. But Charity was alive, grieving but alive and young, and she couldn't stay in Gulch City.

Don't forget, she was a good woman. You know that. You was always cared for and safe. You seen hard times maybe, but you never had to face what Charity did.

The passenger off the stage was an Easterner. His name was Howard Benton. His wife would never lack for anything, and Charity should be his wife—and could be, since she was a widow. But he couldn't take her back to his mother with her hair cut short like a boy's. When her hair grew long enough to put up, like a lady, then they would go to Boston.

First they went to St. Louis.

"When are we going to get married?" she asked him. "If you're not ashamed of me, when are you going to marry me?"

"Just as soon as your pretty hair grows a little longer," he said. "Then we'll go home to Boston and you'll see things you never dreamed existed."

"Such things I've seen already," she says, remembering Gulch City.

Before her hair was long enough to please him, she knew she was going to have a baby. When they did go to Boston, there was no more talk of getting married. She knew by then it amused him to take her into his mother's house when she couldn't complain about anything.

The baby was a boy, and Benton loved him.

"I've been cruel," he says, "but it will never happen again. As soon as you can travel, we'll go somewhere that nobody knows me and we'll get married."

"Why, yes," says Charity. "We should have got around to it long ago. Yes, I'll marry you—if your mother comes to the wedding."

When the baby was five months old, Charity ran away. She took all the money she had—Benton was generous with it—and what clothes she could carry, knowing she'd never have such pretty ones again. And she took along that picture of herself holding her baby that she was leaving behind because his pa could give him everything, but she couldn't stay.

She worked here and there, housework and the like of that, and when she was twenty-four, she married your pa. From there on, you know what her life was like.

"My youngest stepbrother was seven when Pa was killed," Leona reflected. "My two older brothers were long gone and never heard from. Sister Bessie was married and moved away. And I was in love and wanted to marry.

"But Charity's children were young—the oldest was only twelve. I never understood how we held out. Charity and I worked like men on the claim. I grieved that I'd die an old maid—twenty-four, I was, and Henry needed a wife. But I had to stay on the claim with Charity, because she needed me.

"Once she talked about giving up and letting the youngest ones go to an orphans' home. But then things got better and she didn't have to, she could spare me, and I got married. I never knew how she did it, but she made out, didn't complain and saw to it the children got some schooling. We were all brought up to work."

Duke nodded. "She could do that because, all of a sudden, there was money coming in. She hated every penny she spent, but what else could she do but take it when it was offered? She needed it for her children, and it came through her oldest boy, the one you never knew she had."

He was two years younger than you, Leona, the baby she left in Boston. She grieved over her guilt in leaving him, but she never regretted it. He was well taken care of, and she wouldn't stay with his father.

The boy was about twenty-two when he traced her. He hired detectives, spent thousands, I shouldn't wonder, finding where his mother was. She met him at a hotel in town, and you went to town with her that day but she didn't tell anybody about meeting her boy that she'd given up forever.

He was a strange young feller, and she said he looked like his pa, dark and gant, with deep eyes. She was shy of him, because of the guilt about deserting him, and he was shy of her but curious. Because his pa had told him what

happened and put a promise on him to keep trying to find
Charity, like his pa had been trying all those years.

She thought her boy had come because he hated her
and wanted to see the face of his wicked mother. But he
didn't hate her, or love her either. He was cool and curious. His father was dead of consumption, and he was
close to dying, but he never told her that. And for Charity, later, that was the hardest thing to know, that he
knowed he wouldn't live long but he didn't say a word to
her about it. She didn't guess it. Her other children was
healthy though so poor.

"Come visit us on the place," says Charity to him. "Let
me feed you up some. You're welcome to what we've got.
Come stay with me and the children for as long as you
can."

But no, he didn't wish to. Was traveling around and
didn't wish to stop. Was glad he'd met her and hoped that
all was well. He'd filled the promise his pa put on him,
and good-by now, Mrs. McCutcheon.

"Or should I call you 'Mother'?" he says with a twisted
smile.

He left her crying, filled with shame.

It wasn't but a few months later that she got a letter
from a Boston lawyer saying her boy was dead of consumption, like his pa. But she would get a sum of money
every year for as long as she lived, from his estate, because his pa had wished it so. The lawyer sent a photograph of him and on it the boy had written "Mother."

They were gone, the both of them so who was there to
tell that she wouldn't take the money? Three hundred
dollars a year, it was. She would have felt proud and
haughty to refuse it, but she needed it too bad.

She could spare you then so's you could marry your
sweetheart, and she could keep her children out of the orphans' home. But there was nobody she could tell her
miseries to, because the son she'd lost was one nobody
knew she ever had.

She raised her young ones and married them off, and
when they didn't need her no more, she moved to town.

And after a few more years—I found her.

I wasn't nobody, just a drifter, a tramp with white hair
and a scarred face and a bent back. I been to lots of

towns, stopped at lots of houses, offered to cut wood for a meal. The last one I ever stopped at was Charity's.

She set me down to a meal in the kitchen, said I could cut wood after I ate. Asked me did I feel all right—she thought I acted like I might be dizzy. Well, I was. My heart was shaking me because I knowed this was my lost Charity.

Oh, not right for the first minute, but while she was filling my plate at the stove—the way she moved, I guess. Here was this white-haired lady in a light-colored dress, putting grub on my plate. But plainer than her I could see Charley in front of the wickiup, dishing my supper out of a pan over the fire. Which of them was real I couldn't be quite sure just then.

She didn't recognize me. How could she, with the scars on my face and the years on me, and rheumatism makes an old man move different from the way he did when he was young. Besides, she'd gave me up for dead. Charity had enough troubles, not to want to look for ghosts.

She let me eat in the kitchen, and afterward I cut a plenty of wood. But I was so upset and full of wonderment that I chopped my foot. She brought me bandages.

I thought, "This is my Charity, that's kind to a tramp, a stranger. I'll go in a few minutes, but it's only right she should know that I went back to Gulch City and tried to find her."

"Are you all right, Mister?" she says. "You don't act right to be going on so soon. You could stay in the shed if you're a mind to."

"I'm all right," I says. Then I took a deep breath and says, "Charley, your hair's grown long in the years that passed between us."

She backed away, whispering, "Duke? Duke? I thought you were dead!"

And I had my lost Charity again. It was more than I ever had coming, more than I'd dreamed of since I stopped being young.

We got married, so as not to shame her children. They shouldn't know she married their pa when she had a husband living and didn't know it.

There's a letter for me in that little wooden box she kept. She told me she wrote it, and I'll take it now.

"I wrote you love letters when we were young," she told me. "You never got any of them. So now you'll have one, finally, to read and keep."

Just before she went, she asked me a question I guess she'd been afraid to ask before.

"Duke," she says, "were you looking for me all those years before you found me?"

"All those years," I says.

That was a lie. I'd stopped looking. Still, that lie was all I had to give her. That was the only time I ever lied to Charity.

Blanket Squaw

THE NEW ROAD to High Valley was opened this past summer, and everybody in Okanasket County turned out to celebrate. Helga Jacobsen, our art teacher, went to the canyon mouth with me in my car to watch the parade. She's so crazy about our part of the state of Washington that she came back before school started.

Behind the band—a good distance behind, so they'd have room to make a grand entrance—came a bunch of young Indians, most of them on their best paint ponies, worth—they claim—a dollar a spot. The boys were all painted up and more than half naked, and they tore out of the woods into the sunshine, leaning low and shrieking in a way that no doubt curdled their own blood. It just sounded like the last day of school to me.

Helga, sitting on the running board, snapped a picture and remarked, "Aren't they having fun!"

"Get off that running board!" I yelped. "The noble red men can't stop!"

I swung the door open and got her into the car just in time. The ponies went past us in a thunder of hoofs and a cloud of dust. The youngsters were trying to pull up, but there wasn't space enough for all those excited horses. Those in front got clear, but the last half dozen piled up right beside my car, with a thumping of boys' bare heels on ponies' bare ribs, and a hullabaloo of yelling, some of which sounded just plain scared. One horse went down.

The rider, a gangling Indian boy wearing swimming trunks, with red and yellow paint streaked over his bare skin, automatically curled up with his arms around his head for protection. Someone caught his pony and another boy helped him to his feet. He shook his head dizzily, but he wore a valiant grin.

"Are you all right?" I called. . . . "Bring him into the car, boys."

"Naw," he said. "The paint might come off on your cushions." But he did condescend to sit on the running board to watch the rest of the show. He had what a medical report would probably call multiple abrasions, and blood was running from a long scraped place on his leg, but he studiously ignored it.

I wondered who he was, because he seemed to know me, but I had never seen quite so much of any Indian boy before, and I didn't recognize him in all his bare skin and war paint. He had a complicated design on his face that made him look positively homicidal.

The next contingent was filing down out of the canyon with more dignity. These were the old braves, gaudy and proud, some of them wearing the great nodding war bonnets they had inherited from their grandfathers, along with a great tradition. Dark-faced and impassive, riding as if they did not know they had horses under them, they filed down singly so as to make a more impressive show. There were not many of these older men; they could not afford to ride in pairs, because that would have made the line too short. Some of them wore their hair in thin gray braids.

The painted youngster on the running board emitted a piercing whistle of greeting, but not one of the older men turned his head.

Helga was taking pictures as fast as she could work her camera, talking happily to herself. All she said to me for ten minutes was "Here, hold this," while she changed a film.

The old men were followed by the younger men, not quite so gaudy as their elders, because when grandpa owns the feathers, grandpa wears the feathers. The rest have to get along with what they can rig up.

"Oh, there come the squaws," remarked Helga. I gave her a jab in the ribs, thinking the youngster on the running board might not like that word used to describe his own relatives.

The women came two by two, but leading them, one woman came alone, a heavy woman, wearing a black kerchief over her head and a gray-and-black-striped shawl. She alone wore dull raiment, but she had dignity and self-possession. She rode a bony gray horse, and she sat in a chairlike saddle that had every visible inch covered with heavy, gaudy patterns of beadwork. She wore at least three petticoats—there were that many showing. I saw her face as she went by—a broad, dark face, unsmiling, distant, wrinkled and serene.

"Who was the one in front?" I asked the boy on the running board.

"Her? My grandmother," he answered.

"A great help you are," I told him. "What's your grandmother's grandson's name?"

His grin went clear to his ears. "Didn't know me, eh? I'm Joe Hawk."

"Oh, my land! I see you in school five days a week—or should, young man—and didn't know you with your war paint on. What's your grandma's name?"

"Mary," he said. Then, dismissing the distaff side of the family, he added boastfully, "My great-grandfather was a medicine man."

Something clicked in my memory. "Her name is Mary. Mary . . . Waters?"

"I got cousins named Waters," he reasoned it out. "So I guess her name might 'a' been that before she married grandpa. The fellers want me, Miss Bunny. G'by now." He galloped off.

"Did you get a picture of the squaw on the gray horse?" I asked Helga, who was aiming at an oncoming cowboy.

She shook her head. "I'm running short of film. She wasn't very special, anyway."

"You wouldn't know," I said. "You never knew Mary Waters."

"Oh, here come the guests of honor!" she exclaimed. "Look!"

They were riding in the old Concord coach that is kept in the firehouse and brought out for big occasions. The band, congregated on the hill behind us, began to blare a welcome to those men, the two state senators, who rode inside the coach and gravely waved their hats to the crowd. They had helped fight for the road from High Valley to the highway, and they deserved honor. But the band was playing for white-bearded Steve Morris, too, the man who had spent more than forty discour. years bringing prosperity to his valley.

Steve Morris rode high above the people, on the driver's seat on the Concord coach. He wore a battered gray hat, pushed back so he could see, not tilted as young men wear their hats. Grizzled old Two Line Tooker, sitting beside him, drove the four horses.

That was the way I saw them, finally—Mary Waters and Steve Morris—a quarter of a mile apart on a brave new road in a bright procession, but a lifetime apart really, with a racial difference between them, and a decision dividing them forever.

I grew up with Mary Waters, the Indian girl, on a ranch that's been deserted now for a good many years. The buildings have fallen in now, and the wild cayuses can find shelter in bitter weather where my folks used to sit beside the heating stove that had been freighted up from Wenatchee by boat, long before the railroad came.

Mary's father worked for my father sometimes, and her mother helped my mother, and Mary kept an eye on me. She was five years older. I was afraid of her father, because people said he was a medicine man. I don't suppose he really was. He was stern and silent, a bulky man with long black braids dangling from under his hat. His trousers always seemed ready to slide off him, and his shirt hung over them.

Mary's mother was a blanket squaw. She wore my mother's old dresses, but when she wore them they looked baggy and unkempt. She usually wore a shawl. What my mother asked her to do around the house, she did, and nothing more. When she finished a task, she simply squatted down on the floor and rested her stooped back against the wall until Ma told her what to do next.

Sometimes the whole family lived in our bunkhouse. Sometimes they lived in a tepee. And sometimes they disappeared between darkness and daylight, no matter if Pa had sheds to be mended and cattle to be driven, no matter if Ma had canning to do and wanted someone around to keep me out from under foot. After a while our Indians would come back and go to work again, and that was all there was to it.

Pa used to grumble about it, but Ma would say, "What

kind of help did you expect in the savage wilderness?"
Ma never relished being a pioneer.

I remember the first time I ever saw Mary Waters. Ma
said to her, "Take good care of the baby," and Mary
took me by the hand. We played down by the creek. Our
game was mostly a business of crouching in the brush and
saying "Listen!" I don't know what Mary was hearing, I
heard nothing but the usual woodsy sounds.

Ma mourned that there was no school for me; and so,
when I was about six, she undertook to teach me herself.
While she was about it, she taught Mary, too, because
otherwise I saw no sense in sitting still. Mary learned so
fast that she had to have a book more advanced than
mine. That kept me humping, because I was jealous, so
we both went faster than the public schools would let
anybody go now. We didn't waste any time coloring
squirrel pictures and making paper chains; we just
learned.

Mary taught me, down by the creek, to braid horsehair
and sew beads and to talk the Chinook jargon—a mixture of French, English and Indian words. I've forgotten
most of it now.

When she was fifteen and I was ten, her older brother
came back from somewhere with another tough young buck.

"Expect we'll be losing our nursemaid soon," Pa said
one night at supper. "I think that young buck that came
with her brother is talking business with the old man.
She's marrying age."

I sat with my mouth open, ready to cry. Ma's eyes wid-
ened and she put down her fork with a clatter. "Do you
mean to tell me these savages marry off their daughters at
fifteen?" she demanded. "Carl, I won't have it!"

"You can't very well stop it," he answered reasonably.
"How would you like to have somebody tell you when
you could marry off Beulah here?"

I got ready to slide under the table. I didn't even like
boys, and here were my own parents planning on having
me marry somebody!

"But you can't have Mary settling down to be just another squaw!" Ma wailed. "You'll have to do something
about it." She began to cut her meat again, as if everything had been settled.

Pa was a patient man. "She's Injun," he said.

"She's bright," said Ma. She glanced up at him. "It would be nice if you'd send her away to school," she remarked. "People do it sometimes. But of course you couldn't afford it."

"I've got some influence," Pa growled.

"You surely haven't got that much," scoffed Ma.

Pa put his fork down hard. "Who says I haven't?"

That was how Mary Waters went back East to school for two years. Ma went on teaching me at home.

I don't know what school Mary went to. She must have known she had not much time to be there, and she must have used that little time well. I remember the day she came back. Ma wanted Pa to go down and get her with the wagon, and I sulked and wept because he wouldn't.

"Let her folks get her," he insisted. "They can ride down and take an extra horse for her. I don't want to have to wait around for the stage and then ride back with an Indian girl in the wagon. It wouldn't look right."

He didn't win that argument, but neither did Ma. He simply didn't go.

Mary and I would ride up in the hills, I planned. I would let her shoot the old rifle Pa had given me over Ma's frenzied protests. We would hide down by the creek and say, "Listen!" And perhaps, being now twelve, I might find out what it was that I was supposed to hear.

I would rush out the door, I planned, and clamber up behind Mary's saddle as soon as she arrived; I'd grasp her around the waist, and we would ride off pell-mell into the coulees and yell to raise the echoes.

But I didn't even hear them come. Suddenly there was movement out in the yard, and I saw a lady swinging down off a horse, with two Indians getting off theirs. The lady turned her back on the Indians and came straight on to the house. She rapped, although the door was open, and stood there smiling.

Her black hair was in two braids around her head, and she wore a long blue dress. (Ma almost cried when she told Pa about it later. "Carl, if you could have seen how wrinkled her pretty dress was! She shouldn't have had to ride up on a pony. You should have taken the wagon. She expected it." But Pa clamped his jaw and answered,

"Injuns ride horses.") I was dumb-struck. I couldn't even say hello.

"Why, Mary!" my mother greeted her. "Do come in. Beulah has made a cake to celebrate."

"Thank you," Mary said. She came in and remained standing.

Ma never asked an Indian to sit down unless there was work to be done that required it, but she looked quickly around and then at Mary in her blue dress. "Have a chair," she said.

"Thank you," Mary answered. She sat down like a lady.

Ma must have realized then what she had done. There was no way she could undo it. When you have made a lady, you must treat her like a lady. Poor Ma, she always tried to make one of me, but the results she got with Mary didn't give her much satisfaction. It was school-teaching that made a lady out of Beulah—if anything ever did.

Mary ate her piece of cake with a fork, from a saucer. I surreptitiously wiped frosting off my fingers onto my petticoat and picked up the fork I had ignored.

They talked about Mary's trip, and her school, and the weather. What they did not talk about, what they dared not talk about, was, "Well, Mary, and what do you plan to do now?"

Next day Mary and I got acquainted again. She wore her old clothes, hand-me-downs, but she had washed them, although she had no way to iron them. She wore them in a temporary kind of way, as if this part of her life were an interlude that would pass.

We walked down by the creek, talking. I stooped in the brush by the water and whispered, "Listen!"

Mary listened, shook her head and smiled brightly. "To what?" she answered. So I still don't know.

Very quietly, without speaking to my parents about it, Mary rode down to Okanasket one day, carrying her blue dress in a bundle on the saddle. In the grove by the river she took off her Indian clothing and put on the blue dress. Then she went into town on foot and applied for a job teaching school. She applied at the store. Then she went from house to house. When it was getting dark, she put on her Indian clothes again and rode home on her pony.

Pa was angry about it, when people told him later. Ma looked as if she wanted to cry.

A week later, Mary came softly to the back door and said to my mother, "I've come to say good-by for a while, Mrs. Bunny. My aunt is cooking for a construction crew out past Okanasket, and I'm going to help her."

It never occurred to Ma to shake hands when they parted, but I saw that Mary had her right hand ready.

Ma told Pa all about Mary's job. He was more interested in the construction crew than in the cookhouse help.

"That's a big thing they're doing up there," he said. "High Valley, Steve Morris calls the territory. Thinks if he can just get water up there, he can make something of it for settlers. Smart fellow, Steve is. Puts his whole heart into anything he undertakes. He's a dreamer though."

"Steve Morris?" my mother inquired.

"Young widower. He wants to open up that valley. I don't know why. There's plenty others. Going to build a dam and an irrigation system—says he can't wait for the Government to do it. Got some settlers up there already. You know the place, Effie—you go through that dark canyon past the Riley ranch."

"Oh, yes. My, I wonder how Esther Riley is. I haven't seen her in months."

For once I was wise enough not to announce pugnaciously that I wanted to go visit the Rileys. For two or three days I asked pensive questions about them. I even suggested that Mrs. Riley had looked to me like a sick lady, which she certainly had not. But Ma got worried enough to decide that a little visit would do us both good.

Having found that pensiveness worked at home, I tried it on Mrs. Riley. She sent one of her boys to tell Mary Waters to come to see me, and Mary came.

She wore her Indian clothes still, in the same temporary way as when she had first put them on after her return. She was gracious to me—not condescending, but gracious as any older girl may be to a younger one. We ran foot races, which I never won, and we rode bareback, with a hackamore instead of a bridle. We had fun.

After Mary went back to wherever she had come from,

I stole up to the back door and heard Mrs. Riley talking to my mother.

"There's been too much talk," she was saying. "Her aunt made her quit working up at the dam. She's staying with relatives now, over the hills somewhere, and they won't let her see Steve."

"Is he a nice man?" my mother inquired.

"Fine man, and nobody would be surprised if he got married again. But he's not the type to be a squaw man. Even if he does turn into one, he's still not the type, if you understand what I mean."

My mother made clicking sounds denoting interest and dismay.

"The girl's own folks wouldn't like it, either," Mrs. Riley said. "They're good people in their own way."

"You never had to put up with them or you might not think so," Ma argued.

"I've put up with others, and I know good Injuns when I see 'em," Mrs. Riley insisted. "Well, that Steve is a dreamer, and he'll dream himself into trouble one way or another, I suppose."

I heard Mr. Riley telling later about the dam, in a masterfully masculine way, as if he didn't expect women to understand.

"It ain't such great shucks as a dam," he explained, "but Steve thinks if he builds it as good as he can, he can convince the Government that the valley needs a real good one. I don't think he's much of a dam builder, but it's none of my business. Hear they're going to let the water on it one of these days soon. That'll be the big day for Steve Morris."

"Could we go up and watch?" Mrs. Riley pleaded, with the hunger of all women in the wilderness who do not have many pleasant disturbances to interrupt the hard routine.

"Sure," Mr. Riley promised expansively. "Unless old Steve keeps it a secret. Next time I see him, I'll ask him when it will be."

Mary came down to visit me two or three times during the week we visited the Rileys. She had changed her attitude toward my mother and Mrs. Riley. She no longer stood with her shoulders straight; she no longer looked them straight in the eye as an equal. She stood a little stooped, looking at the floor. They treated her more gently, and with less bewilderment, because of that. I know now that she did it for that reason, because she had a plan.

Hesitantly she confronted my mother and spoke to my mother's shoes. "Could we—Beulah thought it would be nice—go on a long ride and maybe take a picnic lunch if there was anything to spare? Anyway, maybe just a sandwich for Beulah, and I could bring something for myself?"

Ma patted a finger against her front teeth, considering. "Why, if you'd promise to take good care of Beulah, I think it would be all right, Mary. That is, if Mr. Riley can spare a pony."

"Oh, I can bring another pony," Mary promised.

And so, to my unbounded surprise, we went the next day for a long ride into the woods. The whole thing, including the part about "Beulah thought it would be nice," was a surprise to me. Mary had made that up, and had said nothing about it to me in advance.

Mary did not ask me where I wanted to go. We rode over the hills, out of sight of the house, and then doubled back by a circuitous route and went over more and steeper hills, through the woods for a long way, until we came out in a clearing. At one side the plateau dropped off so that you could see the darkness of treetops below. Down there men were working with horses and lumber and logs. There were shacks there too. Out of one of them came an Indian woman carrying something, which she threw away.

"Get back," Mary whispered. "That's my aunt. We don't want her to see us. We're playing a game."

"What do we pretend now?" I demanded.

"You're a spy," she said. "And I'm the captain of the army. You have to deliver a message for me, and if you're caught, they'll shoot you. You have to find a tall man with brown hair and beard and blue eyes, and say, when nobody's listening, 'Mary's where the trail forks.' Do you understand?"

"Sure. But does the man know about the game?"

"He'll play it," she promised.

I skulked through the brush and lay in wait near where the men were working until I singled out the tall, brown-bearded man where nobody else would hear me. When I whispered, "Mary's where the trail forks," he turned around, startled; then he smiled. When I repeated it, he stopped smiling and answered, "Well. All right."

When he found her, she was standing proudly, with her head up, even in her Indian clothes. I saw the sun on her black hair and his brown head. I saw him take both her hands in his.

Then Mary saw me and pushed his hands away. "Go watch for the enemy," she warned me, and I was glad to go.

I found no enemy attacking party, but there was a nice boy working with the men who were building the dam—a boy perhaps fifteen, lithe and quick and dark, sharply handsome. When he saw me, he made all his actions more exaggerated—his strides were longer, and when he carried an ax over to a man who yelled for it, he swaggered.

That was the first time I ever didn't hate being a girl —when I saw that nice boy and saw that he noticed I was there and put on an act for me. I wonder what ever became of that half-breed boy.

Maybe, I thought, *Steve Morris is building that dam just to show off to Mary.* I know now, of course, that the dam was tremendously more important to him than Mary was, and that he was more important to Mary than anything else in the world; more important even, than her hope of ceasing to be a tepee Indian.

It was only a few minutes that I watched the half-breed boy. Mary had to call me twice before I heard her. We had forgotten to eat our picnic lunch, but we gobbled it just before we reached the ranch.

When we were saying good-by, she did a thing unusual for her—she put her arm around my waist as we walked toward the house. "Could you keep a secret?" she asked.

"Sure. Sure I could. What is it?"

"Steve is going to test the dam tomorrow," she whispered. "And next time I see you, maybe I'll tell you another secret."

That night my mother said we simply had to go home.

I kicked up a fuss that must have broken a record, but Ma was firm.

"I've got work to do," she said flatly. "I can't leave your poor father there alone forever."

"Then let the child stay with us for a few days," Mrs. Riley begged. My, she was a kind, understanding woman. "I haven't any girls of my own. I'd be glad to have a little girl around. One of the boys can ride back with her next week."

I had sense enough to be quiet while they argued it out, and Mrs. Riley won.

The day wore on, and Mary didn't come. I found I didn't like the Rileys' place so well, after all, because I had to be a good girl and not have tantrums. Ma had been pretty outspoken about that.

I was sitting by the window in the parlor, looking at an album full of pictures of people I didn't know, when I glanced out the window and saw brush bending toward me in the canyon. Then I saw water, and I called out proudly, "He's let the water on the dam, Miz Riley! Come look at the water!"

There was a hoarse shout from outside. Mr. Riley thundered in. "Up the hill! Run up the hill! There's water coming down the canyon!"

Mrs. Riley grabbed me by the hand, and we ran without looking back.

Mr. Riley and some other men wrestled with the stock before following us, and then there was no need for them to climb the hill at all, because it was plain that the water would not come even so high as the house.

It could not have been for more than fifteen minutes that the tumbling stream poured down the canyon and spread out where the main highway runs now, bringing with it pieces of lumber and branches and logs. It was not a big flood.

Immediately I wanted to go closer and see it. "Come on!" I called.

Before anyone could tell me not to go, I ran down to the new spreading pond below the house. There was a man lying there, face down in the dirty water with his legs up on the water-flattened grass. I squeaked and turned to run back, and then I saw another man with a brown shirt on. He was lying face up, with his eyes open and a log across his chest. I stumbled back up to the house, screaming.

So I didn't stay at the Rileys' after all. They sent me back that night. One of the Riley boys saddled a pony for me and one for himself, and we started right away. Mrs. Riley's voice was shaking, and so were her hands, as she put my clothes into a bundle to tie on the saddle.

"Go fast, Mike," she pleaded. "Ride fast until you get her home. If her mother should hear of this before Beulah gets home, it would kill her."

We rode all night through the quiet, windless hills. Sometimes I went ahead and sometimes Mike did. It was pretty dark and frightening, though Mike was packing a gun, just in case. After the first excitement died down and I was plain tired and sleepy, I hated that hard night ride, although it was something I had always dreamed of doing, I was nearer grown up after that night, more inclined to concern myself with the real present than with the impossible dream.

They found ten other men after the flood water had gone away. Just one man who had been down in the canyon when the dam broke had not drowned—the man who built the dam, Steve Morris. The boy I had liked had been on high ground with the rest of the crew.

Ma worried about me for a long time; I used to wake up crying and trembling. In the fall she decided to use psychology, though she had probably never heard of it. It was the kind of psychology they use on aviators now, when they make a man go up again right after he has had a crash. I wasn't afraid to go back to the place; I was eager for any change.

"Will Mary be there?" I demanded. "Make her be there."

"I suppose it could be arranged," Ma said. "I'll tell her folks."

Mary was not at the ranch on the day we got there, but Mrs. Riley said she would come. Ma asked a few questions about the valley when she thought I was outside.

"Steve had got several families to settle there," Mrs. Riley said. "But they've got no water to run into their ditches, so they'll starve out. Everything's dried up. The valley was never meant to be settled, I guess."

"Not good land?"

"Oh, yes. It's very fertile, Bob says, but people say it's unlucky."

"That man who built the dam—where did he go?"

"Still there, I guess. My, he took it hard! Every nickel he had he gave to the families of those men who were killed, to help them get a new start. Did I tell you his hair turned gray? Bob was saying yesterday he hadn't seen him for weeks. Said he couldn't talk about anything except what he'd done that was wrong. He has a queer sort of conscience that eats on him. Seems to think this was a terrible punishment that fell on those others for his own sins."

Ma must have been watching to see how I reacted to being back there, but it really didn't bother me. Except for grass that was matted where the water had been, you wouldn't have known there had been a flood. It was important to me, somehow, to see that the water was gone.

Ma and Mrs. Riley pampered me considerably, and when I asked whether Mary and I could go for a long ride Ma said it was all right, and even packed us a lunch.

When Mary and her sullen brother rode down over the hill, I ran to meet them. Mary was thin, and she acted fidgety.

"We can take a lunch and go riding all afternoon!" I crowed.

"Did your mother say so?" she asked sharply.

"You bet she did," I boasted, as if I'd horsewhipped her into it.

Mary turned to her brother without even dismounting and spoke long and forcefully to him in their own language. He argued back, and I heard him growl "No!" in English.

"Yes, you will," she snapped. "Do just as I said."

He argued some more, but when he rode off he acted as if he meant to obey.

"We'll meet him later," she told me. "Don't tell anybody."

She was in such a hurry that I didn't get the saddle cinched up tight enough. That cayuse was wise, and he'd blow himself up like a barrel so the cinch would loosen later. I almost fell off when the saddle turned, after we'd gone over a couple of hills. Mary was sharp and impatient with me while I fixed the cinch and gave the pony a warning punch with my knee.

We rode south and then turned west, down among cedars into darkness that was chilly because fall was coming. I recognized the canyon. This, I realized, was the place where all those men had gone tumbling with the water. I shivered and wished Mary had chosen some other place for us to ride.

"Wait," she commanded suddenly. She called some words I could not understand. There was no answer. Farther on she called again, and a burly man came out of the woods into the trail, leading a horse. I was startled until I saw it was only her brother.

I said hello civilly, and he grunted some question to Mary. After a little argument he got on his horse, and we all rode up the canyon. Nobody talked. We went clear to the end of the canyon, up the steep part that winds to High Valley. I saw the valley for the second time, spreading flat and golden-dry to high hills. It was sere and blasted.

"Wait here," Mary said. We let our horses stand while her brother strolled over a rise and returned, shaking his head. I was wise enough to know that he was unwillingly helping Mary to look for Steve Morris, who should have been in one of the shacks there.

On the way back down the canyon, Mary rode in front, with her shawl over her bowed head. She stopped her horse so abruptly that mine bumped him. She slid out of the saddle and almost fell. She pointed at something on the ground that I could not even see and spoke rapidly to her brother. He dismounted and looked at the ground sharply. Grumbling, he got back on his horse and shouldered through brush down toward the now docile creek that talked to itself over its stones.

He shouted something from below, and Mary plunged her horse recklessly through the brush. Not knowing what else to do, I followed.

I cried out, because there was a man lying on the grassy flat, and I had dreamed of men lying in the water.

This one was not in the water. He was lying on a blanket by the creek, and he was not dead, but he looked near it. His face was so gaunt that it was shiny, and his hair and beard were shot with gray, but he had a look of young-ness about him.

"Steve!" Mary whispered. "Steve! Are you hurt?"

"No," he said and closed his eyes.

She looked about, and my eyes followed hers. The grass was trampled flat; he had been camping there for a long time, but there was no sign of food or of a fire. There was a can that he had used for drinking from the creek, but he had no frying pan. He had only the rusted can and the blanket he lay on, waiting.

Mary stood over him. "Get up, Steve. We'll take you back to the valley."

"I can't go back," he said. "Those men——"

She misunderstood him. "Those men are dead. They can't hurt you."

"They're dead," he said. "My fault."

There was a long silence as she thought with his thoughts until she understood him.

"You won't help by lying here starving to death," she said shortly.

He smiled a little and his teeth showed.

"How long have you been here without eating?" she asked.

"Eleven days," he whispered.

Mary turned her back and covered her face with her shawl. Then she faced him again in desperation.

"You didn't kill those men. The water did it."

"I let the water in."

"No, you didn't. The dam broke."

"I built the dam."

"You can't help them now!" she insisted.

"A life for a life," he said slowly. "I have only one. There were . . . twelve." He looked earnestly up into her face, not moving. "Mary, don't you understand? I wanted something I . . . should not have."

She bowed her head and answered in a muffled voice, "I didn't know . . . white men believed in sacrifices this way."

Then there was forest silence, rippled only by the incoherent speech of the creek talking dangerously to itself under the cedars.

Mary looked at Steve again. "I know a way to make sacrifice," she said softly. "I know a better way than yours."

Steve did not answer, but he watched her face.

"The way of my people," Mary said. "I can make medicine to quiet the spirits of the dead. To pay your debt because you wanted something you should not have."

I was astonished, because I knew that Indian women of Mary's tribe couldn't make medicine. Mary's brother stared at her.

She snapped at her brother, argued with him, flung out her arm in a commanding gesture, repeating some phrase over and over. He grunted, but he went away and then came back, bringing bark and twigs for a fire. She took them from his hands.

"This is big medicine," she said softly. "I can make this medicine. Nobody else can do it. It is a sacrifice."

She stooped and set the twigs and bark for a tiny, peaked fire. She moved her hands over it and murmured. She turned her face to the sky and spoke softly. Then she took a match from her brother's hand and lighted the fire. She knelt by it, swaying and whispering, moving her hands in the thin stream of smoke. I heard the cedars clicking around where I sat, transfixed with fright, on my pony. The smoke went straight up without a quiver. It was not wind that moved the cedars.

Mary took water from the creek into the rusted can and heated it, speaking softly all the while. She opened our picnic lunch and took out a piece of bread. Holding it high in her hands, she spoke to the sky. Then she broke the bread into the hot water in the can.

She spoke to her brother in their own tongue, and he lifted up Steve Morris. Stooping, she kissed Steve Morris on the forehead. Then she held the can to his lips.

"This is magic," she told him. "Take it. . . . No, don't touch my hands. I can't touch you again. Never again. Take it. Drink it."

Too weak to resist, Steve Morris took the bread-and-water mixture into his mouth and swallowed. When he had finished it, Mary's brother laid him down again.

Mary stood with the fire between her and Steve Morris; she stood wrapped in her shawl.

"That is big medicine," she said in the guttural voice of an Indian woman. "But you have to pay back for medicine. I have made an offering for you. I will never speak to you again, and if you ever see me, you will not know. You will have strength now that you did not have before. Steve Morris, go back to the valley!" She bowed her shoulders under the shawl. "Indian woman go back to her people," she said.

If she had seen me, she might have been horrified, as I was, to know that I was there, but she was blind with tears. I rode down the trail behind her after her brother had bundled Steve onto his own pony and had taken him back up the canyon.

I honestly do not believe that she performed any Indian ceremony over that fire. Probably she did not even know any. But she knew what a man needed when he was starving himself to death. He needed to be fed, but he also needed a compulsion put upon him to make him go on fighting. She laid on him such a burden that he did not dare to die. And she took on herself the burden of never seeing him again, so that he would always remember.

They rode in the same bright procession, on the day forty-odd years later when the settlers of High Valley celebrated the road they finally got, years after the Government built them a dam. But Steve Morris could not have known who Mary Waters was, so truly had she done what she had promised. And you would not have known, when he rode wearily in his triumphal procession, that once Steve Morris had been a weak-souled man and a quitter.

It was not Indian magic that Mary Waters made; it was woman magic. But only a great woman could have made that sacrifice.

A few days after school started I stopped Joe Hawk when he was going out of my English class. "Next time you see your grandmother," I said to him, "ask her if she remembers me. I think she used to be a friend of mine."

"Aw, she couldn't be the one," he scoffed. "She wears a blanket. She don't even talk English."

The Hanging Tree

1

JUST BEFORE the road dipped down to the gold camp on Skull Creek, it crossed the brow of a barren hill and went under the out-thrust bough of a great cottonwood tree.

A short length of rope, newly cut, hung from the bough, swinging in the breeze, when Joe Frail walked that road for the first time, leading his laden horse. The camp was only a few months old, but someone had been strung up already, and no doubt for good cause. Gold miners were normally more interested in gold than in hangings. As Joe Frail glanced up at the rope, his muscles went tense, for he remembered that there was a curse on him.

Almost a year later, the boy who called himself Rune came into Skull Creek, driving a freight wagon. The dangling length of rope was weathered and raveled then. Rune stared at it and reflected, If they don't catch you, they can't hang you.

Two weeks after him, the lost lady passed under the tree, riding in a wagon filled with hay. She did not see the bough or the raveled rope, because there was a bandage over her eyes.

Joe Frail looked like any prospector, ageless, anonymous and dusty, in a fading red shirt and shapeless jeans. His matted hair, hanging below his shoulders, would have been light brown if it had been clean. A long mustache framed his mouth, and he wore a beard because he had not shaved for two months.

The main difference between Joe Frail and any other

newcomer to Skull Creek was that inside the pack on his plodding horse was a physician's satchel.

"Now I wonder who got strung up on that tree," remarked his partner. Wonder Russell was Joe Frail's age —thirty—but not of his disposition. Russell was never moody and he required little from the world he lived in. He wondered aloud about a thousand things but did not require answers to his questions.

"I wonder," he said, "how long it will take to dig out a million dollars."

I wonder, Joe Frail thought, if that is the bough from which I'll hang. I wonder who the man is that I'll kill to earn it.

They spent that day examining the gulch, where five hundred men toiled already, hoping the colors that showed in the gravel they panned meant riches. They huddled that night in a brush wickiup, quickly thrown together to keep off the rain.

"I'm going to name my claim after me when I get one," said Wonder Russell. "Call it the Wonder Mine."

"Meaning you wonder if there's any pay dirt in it," Joe Frail answered. "I'll call mine after myself, too. The Frail Hope."

"Hell, that's unlucky," his partner objected.

"I'm usually unlucky," said Joe Frail.

He lay awake late that first night in the gulch, still shaken by the sight of the dangling rope. He remembered the new-made widow, six years ago, who had shrieked a prophecy that he would sometime hang.

Before that, he had been Doctor Joseph Alberts, young and unlucky, sometimes a prospector and sometimes a physician. He struck pay dirt, sold out and went back East to claim a girl called Sue, but she had tired of waiting and had married someone else. She sobbed when she told him, but her weeping was not because she had spoiled her life and his. She cried because she could not possess him now that he was rich.

So he lost some of his youth and all his love and even his faith in love. Before long he lost his riches, too, in a fever of gambling that burned him up because neither winning nor losing mattered.

Clean and new again, and newly named Frail—he

chose that in a bitter moment—he dedicated himself to medicine for a winter. He was earnest and devoted, and when spring came he had a stake that would let him go prospecting again. He went north to Utah to meet a man named Harrigan, who would be his partner.

On the way, he camped alone, he was held up and robbed of his money, his horse and his gun. The robbers, laughing, left him a lame pinto mare that a Digger Indian would have scorned.

Hidden in a slit in his belt for just such an emergency was a twenty-dollar gold piece. They didn't get that.

In Utah he met Harrigan—who was unlucky, too. Harrigan had sold his horse but still had his saddle and forty dollars.

"Will you trust me with your forty dollars?" Joe Frail asked. "I'll find a game and build it bigger."

"I wouldn't trust my own mother with that money," Harrigan objected as he dug into his pocket. "But my mother don't know how to play cards. What makes you think you do?"

"I was taught by an expert," Joe Frail said briefly.

In addition to two professions, doctor and miner, he had two great skills: he was an expert card player and a top hand with a pistol. But he played cards only when he did not care whether he won or lost. This time winning was necessary, and he knew what was going to happen— he would win, and then he would be shattered.

He found a game and watched the players—two cowboys, nothing to worry about; a town man, married, having a mildly devilish time; and an older man, probably an emigrant going back East with a good stake. The emigrant was stern and tense and had more chips before him than anyone else at the table.

When Doc sat in, he let the gray-haired man keep winning for a while. When the emigrant started to lose, he could not pull out. He was caught in some entangling web of emotions that Doc Frail had never felt.

Doc lost a little, won a little, lost a little, began to win. Only he knew how the sweat ran down inside his dusty shirt.

The emigrant was a heavy loser when he pulled out of the game.

"Go to find my wife," was his lame excuse. But he went only as far as the bar and was still there, staring into the mirror, when Doc cashed in his chips and went out with two hundred dollars in his pockets.

He got out to the side of the saloon before the shakes began.

"And what the hell ails you?" Harrigan inquired. "You won."

"What ails me," said Doc with his teeth chattering, "is that my father taught me to gamble and my mother taught me it was wicked. The rest of it is none of your business."

"You sound real unfriendly," Harrigan complained. "I was admiring your skill. It must be mighty handy. The way you play cards, I can't see why you waste your time doctoring."

"Neither can I," said Doc.

He steadied himself against the building. "We'll go someplace and divide the money. You might as well have yours in your pocket."

Harrigan warned, "The old fellow, the one you won from, is on the prod."

Doc said shortly, "The man's a fool."

Harrigan sounded irritated. "You think everybody's a fool."

"I'm convinced of it."

"If you weren't one, you'd clear out of here," the cowboy advised. "Standing here, you're courting trouble."

Doc took that as a challenge. "Trouble comes courting me, and I'm no shy lover."

He felt as sore as raw meet. Another shudder shook him. He detested Harrigan, the old man, himself, everybody.

The door swung open and the lamplight showed the gray-haired emigrant. The still night made his words clear: "He cheated me, had them cards marked, I tell you!"

Salt stung unbearably on raw meat. Doc Frail stepped forward.

"Are you talking about me?"

The man squinted. "Certainly I'm talking about you. Cheating, thieving tin horn—"

Young Doc Frail gasped and shot him.

Harrigan groaned, "My God, come on!" and ducked back into darkness.

But Doc ran forward, not back, and knelt beside the fallen man as the men inside the saloon came cautiously out.

Then there was a woman's keening cry, coming closer: "Ben! Ben! Let me by—he's shot my husband!"

He never saw her, he only heard her wailing voice: "You don't none of you care if a man's been killed, do you! You'll let him go scot free and nobody cares. But he'll hang for this, the one who did it! You'll burn in hell for this, the lot of you—"

Doc Frail and Harrigan left that place together—the pinto carried both saddles and the men walked. They parted company as soon as they could get decent horses, and Doc never saw Harrigan again.

A year or so later, heading for a gold camp, Doc met the man he called Wonder, and Wonder Russell, it seemed to him, was the only true friend he had ever had.

But seeing him for the first time, Joe Frail challenged him with a look that warned most men away, a slow, contemptuous look from hat to boots that seemed to ask, "Do you amount to anything?"

That was not really what it asked, though. The silent question Joe Frail had for every man he met was "Are you the man? The man for whom I'll hang?"

Wonder Russell's answer at their first meeting was as silent as the question. He smiled a greeting, and it was as if he said, "You're a man I could side with."

They were partners from then on, drifting through good luck and bad, and so finally they came to Skull Creek.

They built more than one wickiup in the weeks they spent prospecting there, moving out from the richest part of the strike, because that was already claimed.

By September they were close to broke.

"A man can go to work for wages," Wonder Russell suggested. "Same kind of labor as we're doing now, only we'd get paid for it. I wonder what it's like to eat."

"You'll never be a millionaire working someone else's mine," Doc warned.

"I wonder how a man could get a stake without working," his partner mused.

"I know how," Joe Frail admitted. "How much have we got between us?"

It added up to less than fifty dollars. By morning of the following day, Joe Frail had increased it to almost four hundred and was shuddering so that his teeth chattered.

"What talent!" Wonder Russell said in awe. He asked no questions.

Four days after they started over again with a new supply of provisions, they struck pay dirt. They staked two claims, and one was as good as the other.

"Hang on or sell out?" Joe Frail asked.

"I wonder what it's like to be dirty rich," Wonder mused. "On the other hand, I wonder what it's like to be married?"

Joe Frail stared. "Is this something you have in mind for the immediate future, or are you just dreaming in a general kind of way?"

Wonder Russell smiled contentedly. "Her name is Julie and she works at the Big Nugget."

And she already has a man who won't take kindly to losing her, Joe Frail recollected. Wonder Russell knew that as well as he did.

She was a slim young dancer, beautiful though haggard, this Julie at the Big Nugget. She had tawny hair in a great knot at the back of her neck, and a new red scar on one shoulder; it looked like a knife wound and showed when she wore a low-necked dress.

"Let's sell, and I'll dance at your wedding," Joe Frail promised.

They sold the Wonder and the Frail Hope on a Monday and split fifteen thousand dollars between them. They could have got more by waiting, but Wonder said, "Julie don't want to wait. We're going out on the next stage, Wednesday."

"There are horses for sale. Ride out, Wonder." Doc could not forget the pale, cadaverous man called Dusty Smith who would not take kindly to losing Julie. "Get good horses and start before daylight."

"Anybody's think it was you going to get married,

you're in such a sweat about it," Wonder answered, grinning. "I guess I'll go tell her now."

A man should plan ahead more, Joe Frail told himself. I planned only to seek for gold, not what to do if I found it, and not what to do if my partner decided to team up with someone else.

He was suddenly tired of being one of the anonymous, bearded, sweating toilers along the creek. He was tired of being dirty. A physician could be clean and wear good clothes. He could have a roof over his head. Gold could buy anything—and he had it.

He had in mind a certain new cabin. He banged on the door until the owner shouted angrily and came with a gun in his hand.

"I'd like to buy this building," Joe Frail told him. "Right now."

A quarter of an hour later, he owned it by virtue of a note that could be cashed at the bank in the morning, and the recent owner was muttering to himself out in the street, with his possessions on the ground around him, wondering where to spend the rest of the night.

Joe Frail set his lantern on the bench that constituted all the cabin's furniture. He walked over to the wall and kicked it gently.

"A whim," he said aloud. "A very solid whim to keep the rain off."

Suddenly he felt younger than he had in many years, light-hearted, completely carefree, and all the wonderful world was his for the taking. He spent several minutes leaping into the air and trying to crack his heels together three times before he came down again. Then he threw back his head and laughed.

Lantern in hand, he set out to look for Wonder. When he met anyone, as he walked toward the Big Nugget, he lifted the lantern, peered into the man's face, and asked hopefully, "Are you an honest man?"

Evans, the banker, who happened to be out late, answered huffily, "Why, certainly!"

Wonder Russell was not in the saloon, but tawny-haired Julie was at the bar between two miners. She left them and came toward him smiling.

"I hear you sold out," she said. "Buy me a drink for luck?"

"I'll buy you champagne if they've got it," Joe Frail promised.

When their drinks were before them, she said, "Here's more luck of the same kind, Joe." Still smiling gaily, she whispered, "Go meet him at the livery stable." Then she laughed and slapped at him as if he had said something especially clever, and he observed that across the room Dusty Smith was playing cards and carefully not looking their way.

"I've got some more places to visit before morning," Joe Frail announced. "Got to find my partner and tell him we just bought a house."

He blew out the lantern just outside the door. It was better to stumble in the darkness than to have Dusty, if he was at all suspicious, be able to follow him conveniently.

Wonder was waiting at the livery stable corral.

"Got two horses in here, paid for and saddled," Wonder reported. "My war sack's on one of 'em, and Julie's stuff is on the other."

"I'll side you. What do you want done?"

"Take the horses out front of the Big Nugget. They're yours and mine, see? If anybody notices, we bought 'em because we made our pile and we've been drinking. Hell, nobody'll notice anyway."

"You're kind of fidgety," Joe Frail commented. "Then what?"

"Get the horses there and duck out of sight. That's all. I go in, buy Julie a drink, want her to come out front and look at the moon."

"There isn't any moon," Joe warned him.

"Is a drunk man going to be bothered by that?" Wonder answered. "I'll set 'em up for the boys and then go show Julie the moon while they're milling around. That's all."

"Good luck," Joe Frail said, and their hands gripped. "Good luck all the way for you and Julie."

"Thanks, partner," Wonder Russell said.

And where are you going, friend? Joe Frail wondered.

Your future is none of my business, any more than your past.

He staggered as he led the horses down the gulch, in case anyone was watching. A fine performance, he told himself; too bad it is so completely wasted. Because who's going to care, except Dusty Smith, if Julie runs off and gets married?

He looped the lines over the hitch rail so that a single pull would dislodge them. Then he stepped aside and stood in the shadows, watching the door.

Wonder Russell came out, singing happily: "Oh, don't you remember sweet Betsy from Pike, who crossed the big desert with her lover Ike?"

Another good performance wasted, Joe Frail thought. The lucky miner with his claim sold, his pockets full of money, his belly full of whiskey—that was Wonder's role, and nobody would have guessed that he was cold sober.

Wonder capped his performance by falling on the steps and advising them to get out of the way and let a good man pass. Joe grinned and wished he could applaud.

Two men came out and, recognizing Russell, loudly implored him to let some golden luck rub off on them. He replied solemnly, "Dollar a rub, boys. Every little bit helps." They went away laughing as he stumbled through the lighted doorway.

Joe Frail loosened his guns in their holsters and was ready in the shadows. The best man helps the happy couple get away, he remembered, but this time not in a shower of rice with tin cans tied to the buggy and bunting on the team!

Wonder Russell was in the doorway with Julie beside him, laughing.

"Moon ain't that way," Russell objected. "It's over this way." He stepped toward the side of the platform where the saddled horses were.

Inside the lighted room a white-shirted gaunt man whirled with a gun in his hand, and Dusty Smith was a sure target in the light for three or four seconds while Joe Frail stood frozen with his guns untouched. Then the noise inside the saloon was blasted away by a gunshot, and Wonder Russell staggered and fell.

The target was still clear while Dusty Smith whirled

and ran for the back door. A pistol was in Joe Frail's right hand, but the pistol and the hand might as well have been blocks of wood. He could not pull the trigger—until the miners roared their shock and anger and Dusty Smith had got away clean.

Joe Frail stood frozen, hearing Julie scream, seeing the men surge out the front door, knowing that some of them followed Dusty Smith out the back.

There were some shots out there, and then he was no longer frozen. His finger could pull the trigger for a useless shot into the dust. He ran to the platform where Julie was kneeling. He shouldered the men aside, shouting, "Let me by. I'm a doctor."

But Wonder Russell was dead.

"By God, Joe, I wish you'd have come a second sooner," moaned one of the men. "You could have got him from the street if you'd been a second sooner. It was Dusty Smith."

Someone came around the corner of the building and panted the news that Dusty had got clean away on a horse he must have had ready out back.

Joe Frail sat on his heels for a long time while Julie held Wonder's head in her arms and cried. One of the little group of miners still waiting asked, "You want some help, Joe? Where you want to take him?"

He looked down at Julie's bowed head.

My friend—but her lover, he remembered. She has a better right.

"Julie," he said. He stooped and helped her stand up.

"It doesn't matter," she said dully. "To my place, I guess."

Joe Frail commissioned the building of a coffin and bought burying clothes at the store—new suit and shirt that Wonder had not been rich long enough to buy for himself. Then, carrying a pick and shovel, he climbed the hill.

While he was digging, another friend of Wonder's came, then two more, carrying tools of the same kind.

"I'd rather you didn't," Joe Frail told them. "This is something I want to do myself."

The men nodded and turned away.

When he stopped to rest, standing in the half-dug grave, he saw another man coming up. This one, on horseback, said without dismounting, "They got Dusty hiding about ten miles out. Left him for the wolves."

Joe Frail nodded. "Who shot him?"

"Stranger to me. Said his name was Frenchy Plante."

Joe went back to his digging. A stranger had done what he should have done, a stranger who could have no reason except that he liked killing.

Joe Frail put down his shovel and looked at his right hand. There was nothing wrong with it now. But when it should have pulled the trigger, there had been no power in it.

Because I shot a man in Utah, he thought, I can't shoot any more when it matters.

Julie climbed the hill before the grave was quite finished. She looked at the raw earth, shivering a little in the wind, and said, "He's ready."

Joe stood looking at her, but she kept her eyes down.

"Julie, you'll want to go away. You'll have money to go on—all the money for his claim. I'll ride with you as far as Elk Crossing, so you'll have someone to talk to if you want to talk. I'll go with you farther than that if you want."

"Maybe. Thanks. But I kind of think I'll stay in Skull Creek."

She turned away and walked down the hill.

Sometime that night, Julie cut her throat and died quietly and alone.

2

Elizabeth Armistead, the lost lady, came to Skull Creek the following summer.

About four o'clock one afternoon, a masked man rode out of the brush and held up a stage coach some forty miles south of the diggings. Just before this, the six persons aboard the stage were silently wrapped in their separate thoughts, except the stage line's itinerant blacksmith, who was uneasily asleep.

A tramp printer named Heffernan was dreaming of riches to be got by digging gold out of the ground. A whiskey salesman beside him was thinking vaguely of suicide, as he often did during a miserable journey. The driver, alone on his high seat, squinted through glaring light and swiped his sleeve across his face, where sand scratched the creases of his skin. He envied the passengers, protected from the sand-sharp wind, and was glad he was quitting the company. He was going back to Pennsylvania, get himself a little farm. Billy McGinnis was fifty-eight years old on that last day of his life.

The sick passenger, named Armistead, was five years older and was planning to begin a career of schoolteaching in Skull Creek. He had not intended to go there. He had thought he had a good thing in Elk Crossing, a more stable community with more children who needed a school. But another wandering scholar had got there ahead of him, and so he and his daughter Elizabeth traveled on toward the end of the world.

The world ended even before Skull Creek for Mr. Armistead.

His daughter Elizabeth, aged nineteen, sat beside him with her hands clasped and her eyes closed but her back straight. She was frightened, had been afraid for months, ever since people began to say that Papa was dishonest. This could not be, must not be, because Papa was all she had to look after and to look after her.

Papa was disgraced and she was going with him into exile. She took some comfort from her own stubborn, indignant loyalty. Papa had no choice, except of places to go. But Elizabeth had had a choice—she could have married Mr. Ellerby and lived as she had always lived, in comfort.

If Papa had told her to do so, or even suggested it, she would have married Mr. Ellerby. But he said it was for her to decide and she chose to go away with Papa. Now that she had an idea how harsh life could be for both of them, she was sick with guilt and felt that she had been selfish and willful. Mr. Ellerby had been willing to provide Papa with a small income, as long as he stayed away, and she had deprived him of it.

These two had no real idea about what the gold camp at Skull Creek would be like. The towns they had stopped in had been crude and rough, but they were at least towns, not camps. Some of the people in them intended to stay there, and so made an effort toward improvement.

Mr. Armistead was reasonably certain that there were enough children in Skull Creek for a small private school, and he took it for granted that their parents would be willing to pay for their education. He assumed, too, that he could teach them. He had never taught or done any other kind of work, but he had a gentleman's education.

He was bone-tired as well as sick and hot and dusty, but when he turned to Elizabeth and she opened her eyes, he smiled brightly. She smiled back, pretending that this endless, unendurable journey to an indescribable destination was a gay adventure.

He was a gentle, patient, hopeful man with good intentions and bad judgment. Until his financial affairs went wrong, he had known no buffeting. Catastrophe struck him before he acquired the protective calluses of the spirit that accustomed misfortune can produce.

All the capital they had left was in currency in a small silk bag that Elizabeth had sewed under her long, full traveling dress.

Elizabeth was wondering, just before the holdup, whether her father could stand it to travel the rest of the days and all night on the final lap of the journey. But the stage station would be dirty and the food would be horrible—travel experience had taught her to be pessimistic—and probably it would be better if they went on at once to Skull Creek where everything, surely, would be much, much pleasanter. Papa would see to that. She could not afford to doubt it.

Billy McGinnis, the driver, was already in imagination in Pennsylvania when a masked rider rode out of scanty timber at his right and shouted, "Stop there!"

Billy had been a hero more than once in his career, but he had no leanings that way any more. He cursed dutifully but hauled on the lines and stopped his four horses.

"Drop that shotgun," the holdup man told Billy. He obeyed, dropping the weapon carefully, making no startling movement.

"Everybody out!" yelled the masked man. "With your hands up."

The printer, as he half fell out of the coach (trying to keep his hands up but having to hang on with one of them), noted details about the bandit: tall from the waist up but sort of short-legged, dusty brown hat, dusty blue shirt, red bandanna over his face.

The whiskey salesman stumbled out hastily—he had been through this a couple of times before and knew better than to argue—and wondered why a man would hold up a stage going into a gold camp. The sensible thing was to hold up one going out.

The blacksmith, suddenly wide awake, was the third to descend. He accepted the situation philosophically, having no money with him anyway, and not even a watch.

But Mr. Armistead tried to defend his daughter and all of them. He warned her, "Don't get out of the coach."

As he stepped down, he tried to fire a small pistol he had brought along for emergencies like this.

The bandit shot him.

Billy McGinnis, jerking on the lines to hold the frightened horses, startled the masked man into firing a second shot. As Billy pitched off the seat, the team lit out running, with Elizabeth Armistead screaming in the coach.

She was not in it any more when the three surviving men found it, overturned, with the frantic horses tangled in the lines, almost an hour later.

"Where the hell did the lady go to?" the blacksmith demanded. The other two agreed that they would have found her before then if she had jumped or fallen out during the runaway.

They did the best they could. They shouted and searched for another hour, but they found no sign of the lost lady. At the place where the coach had turned over, there was no more brush or scrubby timber by the road, only the empty space of the Dry Flats, dotted with greasewood.

One of the horses had a broken leg, so the whiskey salesman shot it. They unhitched the other three, mounted and searched diligently, squinting out across the flats, calling for the lost lady. But they saw nothing and heard no answering cry.

"The sensible thing," the printer recommended, "is to get on to the station and bring out more help."

"Take the canteen along?" suggested the whiskey salesman.

"If she gets back here, she'll need water," the blacksmith reminded him. "And she'll be scared. One of us better stay here and keep yelling."

They drew straws for that duty, each of them seeing himself as a hero if he won, the lady's rescuer and comforter. The blacksmith drew the short straw and stayed near the coach all night, with the canteen, but the lady did not come back.

He waited alone in the darkness, shouting until he grew hoarse and then voiceless. Back at the place of the holdup, Billy McGinnis and Mr. Armistead lay dead beside the road.

Doc Frail was shaving in his cabin, and the boy called Rune was sullenly preparing breakfast, when the news came about the lost lady.

Doc Frail was something of a dandy. In Skull Creek, cleanliness had no connection with godliness and neither did anything else. Water was mainly used for washing gold out of gravel, but Doc shaved every morning or had the barber do it.

Since he had Rune to slave for him, Doc had his boots blacked every morning and started out each day with most of the dried mud brushed off his coat and breeches. He was a little vain of his light brown curly hair, which he wore hanging below his shoulders. Nobody criticized this, because he had the reputation of having killed four men.

The reputation was unearned. He had killed only one, the man in Utah. He had failed to kill another, and so his best friend had died. These facts were nobody's business.

Doc Frail was quietly arrogant, and he was the loneliest man in the gold camp. He belonged to the aristocracy of Skull Creek, to the indispensable men like lawyers, the banker, the man who ran the assay office, and saloon owners. But these men walked in conscious rectitude and carried pistols decently concealed. Doc Frail wore two guns in visible holsters.

The other arrogant ones, who came and went, were the men of ill will, who dry-gulched miners on their way out with gold. They could afford to shoulder lesser men aside.

Doc Frail shouldered nobody except with a look. Where he walked, other men moved aside, greeting him respectfully: "Morning, Doc. . . . How are you, Doc? . . . Hear about the trouble down the gulch, Doc?"

He brandished no pistol (though he did considerable target practice, and it was impressively public) and said nothing very objectionable. But he challenged with a look.

His slow gaze on a stranger, from hat to boots, asked silently, "Do you amount to anything? Can you prove it?"

That was how they read it, and why they moved aside.

What he meant was, "Are you the man I'm waiting for, the man for whom I'll hang?" But nobody knew that except himself.

By Skull Creek standards, he lived like a king. His cabin was the most comfortable one in camp. It had a wood floor and a half partition to divide his living quarters from his consulting room.

The boy Rune, bent over the cookstove, said suddenly, "Somebody's hollering down the street."

"That's a fact," Doc answered, squinting in his shaving mirror.

Rune wanted, of course, to be told to investigate, but Doc wouldn't give him the satisfaction and Rune wouldn't give Doc the satisfaction of doing anything without command. The boy's slavery was Doc's good joke, and he hated it.

There was a pounding on the door and a man's voice shouting, "Doc Frail!"

Without looking away from his mirror, Doc said, "Well, open it," and Rune moved to obey.

A dusty man shouldered him out of the way and announced, "Stage was held up yestiddy, two men killed and a lady lost track of."

Doc wiped his razor and permitted his eyebrows to go up. "She's not here. One of us would have noticed."

The messenger growled. "The boys thought we better warn you. If they find her, you'll be needed."

"I'll keep it in mind," Doc said mildly.

"They're getting up a couple posses. I don't suppose you'd care to go?"

"Not unless there's a guarantee I'd find the lady. What's the other posse for?"

"To get the road agent. One of the passengers thinks he'd recognize him by the build. The driver, Billy Mc-

Ginnis, was shot, and an old man, the father of the lost lady. Well, I'll be going."

The messenger turned away, but Doc could not quite let him go with questions still unasked.

"And how," he inquired, "would anybody be so careless as to lose a lady?"

"Team ran off with her in the coach," the man answered triumphantly. "When they caught up with it, she wasn't in it any more. She's lost somewheres on the Dry Flats."

The boy Rune spoke unwillingly, unable to remain silent and sullen: "Kin I go?"

"Sure," Doc said with seeming fondness. "Just saddle your horse."

The boy closed down into angry silence again. He had no horse; he had a healing wound in his shoulder and a debt to Doc for dressing it. Before he could have anything he wanted, he had to pay off in service his debt to Doc Frail—and the service would end only when Doc said so.

Doc Frail set out after breakfast to make his rounds— a couple of gunshot wounds, one man badly burned from falling into his own fire while drunk, a baby with colic, a miner groaning with rheumatism, and a dance-hall girl with a broken leg resulting from a fall off a table.

The posses were setting out then with considerable confusion and some angry arguments over the last of the horses available at the livery stable.

"You can't have that bay!" the livery stable man was shouting. "That's a private mount and I dassent rent it!"

"You certainly dassent," Doc agreed. "The bay is mine," he explained to three scowling men. The explanation silenced them.

Doc had an amusing thought. Rune would sell his soul to go out with the searchers.

"Get the mare ready," Doc said, and turned back to his cabin.

"I've decided to rent you my horse," he told the sullen boy. "For your services for—let's see—one month in addition to whatever time I decide you have to work for me anyway."

It was a cruel offer, adding a month to a time that

might be endless. But Rune, sixteen years old, was a gambler. He blinked and answered, "All right."

"Watch yourself," Doc warned, feeling guilty. "I don't want you crippled." The wound was two weeks old.

"I'll take good care of your property," the boy promised. "And the horse too," he added, to make his meaning clear.

Doc Frail stood back, smiling a little, to see which crowd Rune would ride with. There was no organized law enforcement in the gravel gulches of Skull Creek, only occasional violent surges of emotion, with mob anger that usually dissolved before long.

If I were that kid, thought Doc, which posse would I choose, the road agent or the lady? He watched the boy ride to the milling group that was headed for the Dry Flats and was a little surprised. Doc himself would have chosen the road agent, he thought.

So would Rune, except that he planned to become a road agent himself if he ever got free of his bondage.

Rune dreamed, as he rode in the dust of other men's horses, of a bright, triumphant future. He dreamed of a time when he would swagger on any street in any town and other men would step aside. There would be whispers: "Look out for that fellow. That's Rune."

Doc Frail's passage in a group earned that kind of honor. Rune, hating him, longed to be like him.

Spitting dust, the boy dreamed of more immediate glory. He saw himself finding the lost lady out there on the Dry Flats in some place where less keen-eyed searchers had already looked. He saw himself comforting her, assuring her that she was safe now.

He was not alone in his dreaming. There were plenty of dreams in that bearded, ragged company of gold-seekers (ragged even if they were already rich, bedraggled with the dried mud of the creek along which sprawled the diggings). They were men who lived for tomorrow and the comforts they could find somewhere else when, at last, they pulled out of Skull Creek. They were rough and frantic seekers after fortune, stupendously hard workers, out now on an unaccustomed holiday.

Each man thought he was moved by compassion, by pity for the lost and lovely and mysterious lady whose name most of them did not yet know. If they went instead because of curiosity and because they needed change from the unending search and labor in the gravel gulches, no matter. Whatever logic moved them, they rode out to search, fifty motley, bearded men, each of whom might find the living prize.

Only half a dozen riders had gone over the sagebrush hills to look for the road agent who had killed two men. The miners of Skull Creek gambled for fortune but, except when drunk, seldom for their lives. About the worst that could happen in looking for the lost lady was that a man might get pretty thirsty. But go looking for an armed bandit—well, a fellow could get shot. Only the hardy adventurers went in that posse.

When the sun went down, nobody had found anybody, and four men were still missing when the rest of the lady's seekers gathered at the stage line's Station Three. The state company superintendent permitted a fire to be set to a pile of stovewood (freighted in at great expense, like the horse feed and water and everything else there) to make a beacon light. The missing men came in swearing just before midnight. Except for a few provident ones, most of the searchers shivered in their broken sleep, under inadequate and stinking saddle blankets.

They were in the saddle, angry and worried, before dawn of the day Elizabeth Armistead was found.

The sun was past noon when black-bearded Frenchy Plante stopped to tighten his cinch and stamp his booted feet. He pulled off a blue kerchief that protected his nose and mouth from the wind-borne grit, shook the kerchief and tied it on again. He squinted into the glare and, behind a clump of greasewood, glimpsed movement.

A rattler, maybe. Might as well smash it. Frenchy liked killing snakes. He had killed two men, too, before coming to Skull Creek, and one since—a man whose name he found out later was Dusty Smith.

He plodded toward the greasewood, leading his horse, and the movement was there—not a rattler but the wind-whipped edge of a blue skirt.

"Hey!" he shouted, and ran toward her.

She lay face down, with her long, curling hair, once glossy brown, dull and tangled in the sand. She lay flat and drained and lifeless, like a dead animal. Elizabeth Armistead was not moving. Only her skirt fluttered in the hot wind.

"Lady!" he said urgently. "Missus, here's water."

She did not hear. He yanked the canteen from his saddle and pulled out the stopper, knelt beside her and said again, "Lady, I got water."

When he touched her shoulder, she moved convulsively. Her shoulders jerked and her feet tried to run. She made a choking sound of fear.

But when he held the canteen to her swollen, broken lips, she had life enough to clutch at it, to knock it accidentally aside so that some of the water spilled on the thankless earth. Frenchy grabbed the canteen and set it again to her lips, staring at her face with distaste.

Dried blood smeared it, because sand cut into the membranes of the nose like an abrasive. Her face was bloated with the burn of two days of sun, and her anguished lips were shapeless.

Frenchy thought, I'd rather be dead. Aloud he said, "No more water now for a minute. Pretty soon you can have more, Missus."

The lost lady reached blindly for the canteen, for she was blind from the glaring sun, and had been even before she lost her bonnet.

"You gotta wait a minute," Frenchy warned. "Don't be scared, Missus. I'm going to fire this here gun for a signal, call the other boys in. We'll get you to the stage station in no time."

He fired twice into the air, then paused. Two shots meant "found dead." Then he fired the third that changed the pattern and told the other searchers, listening with their mouths open slightly, that the lady had been found living.

The first man to get there was tall, fair-haired Rune, aching with sunburn and the pain of his wound, which had pulled open. When Frenchy found the lady, Rune had been just beyond a little rise of barren ground, stubbornly dreaming as he rode.

I should have been the one, he thought with dull anger. I should have been the one, but it's always somebody else.

He looked at the lady, drained and half dead, dull with dust. He saw the frail and anxious hands groping for the canteen, clutching it as Frenchy guided it to her mouth. He saw the burned, blind face. He said, "Oh, God!"

Frenchy managed a friendly chuckle.

"You're going to be all right, Missus. Get you to a doctor right away. That's a promise, Missus. Frenchy Plante's promise."

He put his name on her, he staked his claim, Rune thought. Who cares? She's going to die anyway.

"I'll go for Doc," Rune said, turning his horse toward the stage station.

But he couldn't go for Doc, after all. He took the news to Station Three; he had that much triumph. Then there was vast confusion. The stage line superintendent ordered a bed made up for the lady, and it was done—that is, the stocktender took the blankets off his bunk and gave them a good shaking and put them back on again. Riders began to come in, shouting, "How is she? Who found her?"

By the time Frenchy Plante arrived, with the lady limp in his arms, and an escort of four other searchers who had gone in the direction of his signal shots, it was discovered that nobody at all had started for Skull Creek to get the doctor.

Rune sat on the ground in the scant shade of the station with his head bowed on his knees, as near exhausted as he had ever been in his life. His shoulder wound hurt like fury, and so did his stomach whenever he remembered how the lost lady looked.

Frenchy Plante was the hero again. He borrowed a fresher horse and rode on to Skull Creek.

He found Doc Frail at home but occupied with a patient, a consumptive dancer from the Big Nugget. With her was another woman, who looked up scowling, as Doc did, when Frenchy came striding in.

"Found the lady, Doc," Frenchy announced. "Want you to come right away."

"I have a patient here," Doc said in controlled tones, "as you will see if you're observant. This lady also needs me."

The consumptive girl, who had seldom been called a

lady, was utterly still, lying on Doc's own cot. Her friend was holding her hands, patting them gently.

"Come out a minute," Frenchy urged, "so I can tell you."

Doc closed the door behind him and faced Frenchy in the street.

Frenchy motioned toward the door. "What's Luella doing in your place?"

"Dying," Doc answered. "She didn't want to do it where she works."

"How soon can you come? The lost lady's real bad. Got her to the stage station, but she's mighty sick."

"If she's as sick as this one," Doc said, "it wouldn't do her any good for me to start out there anyway."

"Damned if you ain't a hard-hearted scoundrel," commented Frenchy, half shocked and half admiring. "You ain't doing Luella no good, are you?"

"No. Nobody ever has. But I'm not going to leave her now."

Frenchy shrugged. "How long'll it be?"

"Couple hours, maybe. Do you expect me to strangle her to hurry it along?"

Frenchy's eyes narrowed. "I don't expect nothing. Get out there when you feel like it. I done my duty anyhow."

Was that a reminder, Doc wondered as he watched Frenchy ride on to the Big Nugget, that once you did a duty that should have been mine? That you killed Dusty Smith—a man you didn't even know—after I failed?

Doc Frail went back into his cabin.

A few hours later, Luella released him by dying.

It was dawn when he flung himself off a rented horse at the station and stumbled over a couple of the men sleeping there on the ground.

The lost lady, her face glistening with grease that the stocktender had provided, was quiet on a bunk, with a flickering lamp above her on a shelf. Cramped and miserable on his knees by the bunk was Rune, whose wrist she clutched with one hand. Her other arm cradled Frenchy's canteen.

There was a spot of blood on Rune's shoulder, soaked through Doc's neat dressing, and he was almost too numb to move, but he looked up with hostile triumph.

"She let me be here," he said.

"Now you can go back to Skull Creek," Doc told him, stating a command, not permission. "I'll stay here until she can be moved."

Dispossessed, as he had often been before, but triumphant as he had longed to be, Rune moved away, to tell the sleepy, stirring men that Doc had come. He was amused, when he started back to the gold camp a little later, by the fact that he still rode Doc's mare and Doc would be furious when he discovered it.

The searchers who delayed at Station Three because of curiosity were relieved at the way Doc Frail took charge there. The lost lady seemed to be glad of his presence, too. He treated her burns and assured her in a purring, professional tone, "You'll get your sight back, madam. The blindness is only temporary, I can promise you that."

To the clustering men, he roared like a lion: "Clean this place up—she's got to stay here a few days. Get something decent for her to eat, not this stage-line diet. That's enough to kill an ox. Clean it up, I say—with water. Don't raise a lot of dust."

The superintendent, feeling that he had done more than his duty by letting the stocktender feed the search posse, demurred about wasting water.

"Every drop has to be hauled clear from Skull Creek," he reminded Doc, who snapped back, "Then hitch up and start hauling!"

The stocktender was caught between Doc's anger and the superintendent's power to fire him. He said in a wheedling voice, "Gonna make her some good soup, Doc. I shot a jackrabbit and had him in the pot before he quit kicking."

"Get out of here," snarled Doc. He bent again to the burned, anguished lady.

"You will be able to see again," he promised her. "And your burns will heal."

But your father is dead and buried, and Skull Creek is no place for you, my dear.

3

Frenchy Plante was still around when Rune got back to Skull Creek. Frenchy swaggered, as he had a right to do, being the man who had found the lost lady. But he spent only half a day or so telling the details over. Then he went back to the diggings, far up the gulch, to toil again in the muck and gravel. He had colors there, he was making wages with a small sluice, he had high hopes of getting rich. It had happened before.

The curious of Skull Creek left their own labors to stand by and get the story. When Frenchy was out of the way, Rune became the belligerent center of attention. He had just finished applying a bunchy bandage to his painful shoulder when he jumped guiltily at a pounding on Doc's door. He finished putting his shirt on before he went to take the bar down.

"Doc ain't back yet?" the bearded caller asked.

Rune shook his head.

"Expecting him?" the man insisted.

"He don't tell me his plans."

The man looked anxious. "Look here, I got a boil on my neck needs lancing. Don't suppose you could do it?"

"Anybody could do it. Wrong, maybe. Doc could do it right—I guess."

The man sidled in. "Hell, you do it. Ain't he got some doctor knives around, maybe?"

Rune felt flattered to have someone show confidence in him.

"I'll find something," he offered. He did not know the name of the thing he found, but it was thin and sharp and surgical. He wiped it thoroughly on a piece of clean bandage and, after looking over the boil on the man's neck, opened it up with a quick cut.

The patient said, "Wow!" under his breath and shuddered. "Feels like you done a good job," he commented. "Now tie it up with something, eh?"

He stretched out his booted legs while he sat back in Doc's best chair and waited for Rune to find bandaging material that pleased him.

"You was right on the spot when they found her, I hear," he hinted.

"I was second man to get there," Rune answered, pretending that to be second was nothing at all, but knowing that it was something, knowing that the man's boil could have waited, or that anyone could have opened it.

"Heard she's a foreigner, don't talk no English," the man hinted.

"She didn't say nothing to me," Rune answered. "Couldn't talk any language. She's an awful sick lady."

The man touched his bandage and winced. "Well, I guess that fixes it. Your fee the same as Doc Frail's, I suppose?"

As coolly as if he were not a slave, Rune nodded, and the man hauled a poke from his pocket, looking around for the gold scales.

For a little while after he had gone, Rune still hated him, even with the man's payment of gold dust stowed away in his pocket. So easy to get a doctor—or somebody with a knife, anyway—when you had the dust to pay for it! So easy to enter servitude if you were penniless and had to have a shoulder wound dressed and thought you were going to die!

Before the morning was half done, another visitor came. This time it was a woman, and she was alone. The ladies of Skull Creek were few and circumspect, armored with virtue. Rune guessed that this one, wife of Flaunce the storekeeper, would not have visited Doc Frail's office without a companion if she had expected to find Doc there.

But she asked in her prissy way, "Is the doctor in?" and clucked when Rune shook his head.

"Well, I can see him another day," she decided. "It was about some more of that cough medicine he gave me for my little ones."

And what for do they need cough medicine in warm weather? Rune would have liked to ask her. He said only, "He ain't here."

"He's out at the stage station, I suppose, with the poor lady who was rescued. Have you heard how she's getting along?"

"She's alive but blind and pretty sick," he said. "She'll get her sight back afterwhile."

"I don't suppose anyone knows why she was coming here?" the woman probed.

"Was with her pa, that's all I know. He's dead and she can't talk yet," Rune reported, knowing that what

Flaunce's wife really wanted to know was, Is she a lady or one of those others? Was he really her father?

"Dear me," she asked, "is that blood on your shirt?" Another one, then, who did not know his shame.

"I shot a rabbit, ma'am," he lied. That satisfied her, even though a man would not normally carry a freshly killed rabbit over his shoulder.

The woman decided the cough medicine could wait and minced up the deep-rutted street of the gulch, carefully looking neither to right nor left.

At the store, buying supplies for Doc's account, Rune inquired, "Any news of the other posse? Them that was after the road agent?"

"It's bigger'n it was, now they found the lost lady. Some of the men figure there's got to be a lesson taught."

"If they catch him, that is," Rune suggested, and the storekeeper nodded, sighing, "If they catch him."

In Doc's absence, Rune carried out a project he had in mind, now that there was no fear of interruption by Doc himself. He searched with scrupulous care for the place where Doc hid his gold.

There should be some in the cabin somewhere. Doc had much more than a physician's income, for he had grub-staked many miners, and a few of them had struck it rich. Doc could afford to be careless with his little leather pokes of nuggets and dust, but apparently he wasn't careless. Rune explored under every loose board and in every cranny between the logs, but he didn't find anything. He did not plan to take the gold yet anyway. It could wait until he was free to leave.

And why don't I pull out now? he wondered. Two men that morning had asked if he wanted to work for wages, and he had turned them down.

It was not honor that kept him there—he couldn't afford the luxury of honor. It was not his wound; he knew now he wasn't going to die of that. The reason he was going to stay, he thought, was just because Doc expected him to run out. He would not give his master that much satisfaction.

He was Rune, self-named, the world's enemy. The world owed him a debt that he had never had much luck in collecting.

He thought he was going to collect when he came to Skull Creek in triumph driving a freight team and carrying his whole fortune—eighty dollars in gold—inside a canvas belt next to his skin. He drew his pay, had a two-dollar meal, and set out for the barber shop.

There was music coming from the Big Nugget. He went in to see the source. Not for any other purpose; Rune spent no money that he didn't have to part with. He did not mean to gamble, but while he watched, a miner looked up and said, scowling, "This is a man's game."

He began to lose, and he could not lose, he must not lose, because if you did not have money you might as well be dead.

When he left the saloon, he was numb and desperate and dead.

Toward morning he tried to rob a sluice. He was not yet hungry, but he would be hungry sometime. He had been hungry before and he was afraid of it. He lurked in shadows, saw the sluice had no armed guard. He was scrabbling against the lower riffles, feeling for nuggets, when a shot came without warning. He fell, pulled himself up and ran, stumbling.

Twenty-four hours later he came out of hiding. He was hungry then, and his shoulder was still bleeding. By that time, he knew where the doctor lived, and he waited, huddling outside the door, while the sun came up.

Doc, in his underwear, opened the door at last to get his lungs full of fresh air and, seeing the tall boy crouching on the step, said, "Well!" Noticing the blood-stiffened shirt he stepped back, sighing, "Well, come in. I didn't hear you knock."

Rune stood up carefully, trying not to move the injured shoulder, holding it with his right hand.

"I didn't knock," he said, hating this man of whom he must ask charity. "I can't pay you. But I got hurt."

"Can't pay me, eh?" Doc Frail was amused. "Guess you haven't heard that the only patients who didn't pay me are buried up on the hill."

Rune believed his grim joke.

"You've been hiding out with this for quite a spell," Doc guessed, as he teased the shirt away from the wound, and the boy shuddered. "You wouldn't hide out without a reason, would you?"

He was gentle from habit, but Rune did not recognize gentleness. He was being baited and he was helpless. He gave a brazen answer:

"I got shot trying to rob a sluice."

Doc, working rapidly, commented with amusement, "So now I'm harboring a criminal! And doing it for nothing, too. How did you figure on paying me, young fellow?"

The patient was too belligerent, needed to be taken down a peg.

"If I could pay you, I wouldn't have tackled the sluice, would I?" the boy demanded. "I wouldn't have waited so long to see you, would I?"

"You ask too damn many questions," Doc grunted. "Hold still. . . . Your wound will heal all right. But of course you'll starve first."

Sullen Rune made no answer.

Doc Frail surveyed him. "I can use a servant. A gentleman should have one. To black his boots and cook his meals—you can cook, I hope?—and swamp out the cabin."

Rune could not recognize kindness, could not believe it, could not accept it. But that the doctor should extract service for every cent of a debt not stated—that he could understand.

"For how long?" he bargained, growling.

Doc Frail could recognize what he thought was ingratitude.

"For just as long as I say," he snapped. "It may be a long time. It may be forever. If you bled to death, you'd be dead forever."

That was how they made the bargain. Rune got a home he needed but did not want to accept. Doc got a slave who alternately amused and annoyed him. He resolved not to let the kid go until he learned to act like a human being—or until Doc himself became too exasperated to endure him any more. Rune would not ask for freedom, and Doc did not know when he would offer it.

There was one thing that Rune wanted from him: skill with a gun. Doc's reputation as a marksman trailed from him like a tattered banner. Men walked wide of him and gave him courtesy.

But I won't lower myself by asking him to teach me, Rune kept promising himself. There were depths to which even a slave did not sink.

A letter came from Doc Frail the day after Rune returned to Skull Creek. It was brought by a horseback rider who came in from Station Three ahead of the stage.

Rune had never before in his life received a letter, but he took it as casually as if he had had a thousand. He turned it over and said, "Well, thanks," and turned away, unwilling to let the messenger know he was excited and puzzled.

"Ain't you going to read it?" the man demanded. "Doc said it was mighty important."

"I suppose you read it already?" Rune suggested.

The man sighed. "I can't read writing. Not that writing, anyhow. Print, now, I can make out with print, but not writing. Never had much schooling."

"He writes a bad hand," Rune agreed, mightily relieved. "Maybe the store man, he could make it out."

So there was no need to admit that he could not read, either. Even Flaunce, the storekeeper, had a little trouble, tracing with his finger, squinting over his glasses.

Doc had no suspicion that his servant could not read. He had never thought about the matter. If he had known, he might not have begun the letter, "White Sambo."

Hearing that, his slave reddened with shame and anger, but the store man merely commented, "Nickname, eh? 'White Sambo: Miss Elizabeth Armistead will arrive in Skull Creek in three or four days. She is still weak and blind. She must have shelter and care. I will provide the care, and the shelter will have to be in the cabin of the admirable and respectable Ma Fisher across the street from my own mansion.

" 'Convey my regards to Mrs. Fisher and make all the necessary arrangements. Nothing will be required of Mrs. Fisher except a temporary home for Miss Armistead, who will of course pay for it.' "

The storekeeper and the messenger stared at Rune.

"I'm glad it ain't me that has to ask Ma Fisher a thing

like that," the messenger remarked. "I'd as soon ask favors of a grizzly bear."

Flaunce was kinder. "I'll go with you, son. She wants a sack of flour anyhow, over to the restaurant. I'll kind of back you up—or pick up the pieces."

Ma Fisher served meals furiously in a tent restaurant to transients and miners who were tired of their own cooking in front of the wickiups along the gulch. She seldom had any hired help—too stingy and too hard to get along with, it was said. Her one luxury was her cabin, opposite Doc's, weather-tight and endurable even in cold weather. Most of the population, willing to live miserably today in the hope of a golden tomorrow, housed itself in shacks or lean-to's or caves dug into the earth, eked out with poles and rocks and sods.

Ma Fisher fumed a little when she was informed that the lost lady would be her guest, but she was flattered, and besides she was curious.

"I won't have time to wait on her, I want that understood," she warned. "And I won't stand for no foolishness, either."

"She's too sick for foolishness, I'd say," the storekeeper said soothingly. "Hasn't got her sight back yet. She mighty near died out there, you know."

"Well," Ma Fisher agreed without enthusiasm. "Well."

The first words Elizabeth Armistead spoke in the stage station were, faintly, "Where is Papa?"

"Your father is dead," Doc Frail answered gently. "He was shot during the holdup."

Why didn't she know that? She had seen it happen.

She answered with a sigh: "No." It was not an exclamation of shock or grief. It was a soft correction. She refused to believe, that was all.

"They buried him there by the road, along with the driver," Doc Frail said.

She said again, with more determination, "No!" And after a pause she pleaded, "Where is Papa?"

"He is dead," Doc repeated. "I am sorry to tell you this, Miss Armistead."

He might as well not have told her. She did not accept it.

She waited patiently in darkness for someone to give a reasonable explanation for her father's absence. She did not speak again for several hours because of her weakness and because of her swollen, broken lips.

Doc wished he could give her the comfort of a sponge bath, but he did not dare offend her by offering to do so himself, and she was not strong enough to move her arms. She lay limp, sometimes sleeping.

When he judged that the girl could better bear the trip to Skull Creek in a wagon than she could stand the stage station any longer, he explained that she would stay at Mrs. Fisher's—a very respectable woman, she would be perfectly safe there—until she could make plans for going back East.

"Thank you," the lost lady answered. "And Papa is in Skull Creek waiting?"

Doc frowned. The patient was beginning to worry him. "Your father is dead, you know. He was shot in the holdup."

She did not answer that.

"I will try again to comb your hair," Doc offered. "To-morrow you can wash, if you want to try it. There will be a blanket over the window, and one over the door, and I will be outside to make sure no one tries to come in."

Her trunk was there, brought from the wrecked coach. He searched out clean clothes that she could put on, and carefully he combed her long, dark, curling hair. He braided it, not very neatly, and wound the two thick braids up over her head.

4

The wagon was slow, but Doc Frail preferred it for his patient; she could ride easier than in the coach. He ordered the wagon bed well padded with hay, and she leaned back against hay covered with blankets. He had a canvas shade rigged to protect her from the sun. The stage-line superintendent himself was the driver—mightily relieved to be getting this woman to Skull Creek where she would be no more concern of his.

Doc Frail had not looked ahead far enough to expect

the escort that accompanied them the last mile of the journey. He sat with the lost lady in the wagon bed, glaring at the curiously silent miners who came walking or riding or who stood waiting by the road.

None of them spoke, and there was no jostling. They only stared, seeing the lady in a blue dress, with a white cloth over her eyes. From time to time, the men nearest the wagon fell back to let the others have their turn.

Once, Doc got a glimpse of the boy Rune, lanky and awkward, walking and staring with the rest. Doc scowled, and the boy looked away.

For a while, the doctor closed his eyes and knew how it must be for the girl who could hear but could not see. The creak of the wagon, the sound of the horses' hoofs —too many horses; she must know they were accompanied. The soft sound of many men's feet walking. Even the restless sound of their breathing.

The lady did not ask questions. She could not hide. Her hands were clasped tightly together in her lap.

"We have an escort," Doc murmured. "An escort of honor. They are glad to see that you are safe and well."

She murmured a response.

At the top of the hill, where the road dipped down to the camp, they lost their escort. The riders and the walkers stepped aside and did not follow. Doc Frail glanced up as the wagon passed under the great, out-thrust bough of the gnarled tree and felt a chill tingle the skin along his spine.

Well, the fellow deserved the hanging he would get. Doc regretted, however, that the mob that would be coming in from the north would have to pass Ma Fisher's cabin to reach the hanging tree. He hoped they would pass in decent silence. But he knew they would not.

Rune waited near the tree with the other men, torn between wanting to help the lost lady into the cabin and wanting to see the road agent hang. Whichever thing he did, he would regret not having done the other. He looked up at the great bough, shivered, and decided to stay on the hill.

He could see Doc and the stage superintendent help Miss Armistead down from the wagon. As they took her into Ma Fisher's cabin, he could see something else: dust in the distance.

A man behind him said, "They're bringing him in."

Rune had two good looks at the road agent before he died and one brief, sickening glance afterward. The angry miners were divided among themselves about hanging the fellow. The men who had pursued him, caught him, and whipped him until his back was bloody were satisfied and tired. Four of them even tried to defend him, standing with rifles cocked, shouting, "Back! Get back! He's had enough."

He could not stand; men pulled him off his horse and held him up as his body drooped and his knees sagged.

But part of the crowd roared, "Hang him! Hang him!" and shoved on. The mob was in three parts—those for hanging, those against it, and those who had not made up their minds.

Rune glimpsed him again through the milling miners beneath the tree. The posse men had been pushed away from him, and men who had not pursued him were bringing in a rope.

The black-bearded giant, Frenchy Plante, tied the noose and yanked the road agent to his feet. Frenchy's roar came over the rumbling of the mob: "It's his fault the lost lady pridnear died! Don't forget that, boys!"

That was all they needed. Order came out of chaos. Fifty men seized the rope and at Frenchy's signal "Pull!" jerked the drooping, bloody-backed road agent off the ground. Rune saw him then for the third time, dangling.

A man beside him said knowingly, "That's the most humane way, really—pull him up all standing."

"How do you know?" Rune sneered. "You ever get killed that way?"

With the other men, he walked slowly down the hill. He waited in Doc's cabin until Doc came in.

"You had to watch," Doc said. "You had to see a man die."

"I saw it," Rune growled.

"And the lost lady might as well have. She might as well have been looking, because Ma Fisher kindly told her what the noise was about. And was offended, mind you, when I tried to shut her up!"

Doc unbuckled his gun belt and tossed it on his cot.

"You're going to wait on Miss Armistead," he announced. "I told her you would do her errands, anything that will make her a little easier. Do you hear me, boy? She keeps asking for her father. She keeps saying. 'Where is Papa?' "

Rune stared. "Didn't you tell her he's dead?"

"Certainly I told her! She doesn't believe it. She doesn't remember the holdup or the team running away. All she can remember is that something happened so the coach stopped, and then she was lost, running somewhere, and after a long time a man gave her a drink of water and took the canteen away again."

"Did she say where she's going when she gets her sight back?" Rune asked.

Doc let out a gusty breath. "She has no place to go. She says she can't go back because she has to wait for Papa. He was going to start a school here, and she was going to keep house for him. She has no place to go, but she can't stay alone in Skull Creek. It's unthinkable."

Ma Fisher came flying over to get Doc.

"The girl's crying and it'll be bad for her eyes," she said.

Doc asked coolly, "And why is she crying?"

"I'm sure I don't know," Ma answered, obviously injured. "I wasn't even talking to her. She started to sob, and when I asked her what was the matter, she said, 'Papa must be dead, or he would have been waiting here to meet me.' "

"Progress," Doc growled. "We're making progress." He went out and left Ma Fisher to follow if she cared to do so.

Doc was up before daylight next morning.

"When Ma Fisher leaves that cabin," Doc told Rune, when he woke him, "you're going to be waiting outside the door. If the lady wants you inside for conversation, you will go in and be as decently sociable as possible. If she wants to be alone, you will stay outside. Is that all perfectly clear?"

It was as clear as it was hateful. Rune would have taken delight in being the lady's protector if he had had any choice. (And Doc would, too, except that he wanted to protect her reputation. It wouldn't look good for him to be in the cabin with her except on brief professional visits.)

"Nursemaid," Rune muttered sourly.

Ma Fisher scowled when she found him waiting outside her door, but Miss Armistead said she would be glad of his company.

The lost lady was timid, helpless, but gently friendly, sitting in the darkened cabin, groping now and then for the canteen that had been Frenchy's.

Rune asked, "You want a cup to drink out of?" and she smiled faintly.

"I guess it's silly," she answered, "but water tastes better from this canteen."

Rune kept silent, not knowing how to answer.

"Doctor Frail told me your first name," the lost lady said, "but not your last."

"Rune is all," he answered. He had made it up, wanting to be a man of mystery.

"But everybody has two names," she chided gently. "You must have another."

She was indeed ignorant of frontier custom or she would not make an issue of a man's name. Realizing that, he felt infinitely superior and therefore could be courteous.

"I made it up, ma'am," he told her. "There's lots of men here go by names they wasn't born with. It ain't a good idea to ask questions about folks' names." Then, concerned lest he might have offended her, he struggled on to make conversation:

"There's a song about it. 'What was your name in the States? Was it Johnson or Olson or Bates?' Goes that way, sort of."

The lady said, "Oh, my goodness. Doctor Frail didn't make up his name, I'm sure of that. Because a man wouldn't take a name like that, would he?"

"A man like Doc might," Rune decided. The idea interested him. "Doc is a sarcastic fellow."

"Never to me," Miss Armistead contradicted softly. "He is the soul of kindness! Why, he even realized that I might wish for someone to talk to. And you are kind, too, Rune, because you came."

To get her off that subject, Rune asked, "Was there any errands you'd want done or anything?"

"Doctor Frail said he would send my meals in, but I am already so much obligated to him that I'd rather not. Could you cook for me, Rune, until I can see to do it myself?"

"Sure," he agreed. "But I cook for Doc anyhow. Just as easy to bring it across the street."

"No, I'd rather pay for my own provisions." She was firm about that, with the pathetic stubbornness of a woman who for the first time must make decisions and stick to them even if they are wrong.

"I have money," she insisted. "I can't tell what denomination the bills are, of course. But you can tell me."

Poor, silly lady, to trust a stranger so! But Rune honestly identified the bills she held out.

"Take the five dollars," she requested. "and buy me whatever you think would be nice to eat. That much money should last for several days, shouldn't it?"

Rune swallowed a protest and murmured, "Kind of depends on what you want. I'll see what they got at Flaunce's." He backed toward the door.

"I must be very businesslike," Miss Armistead said with determination. "I have no place to go, you know, so I must earn a living. I shall start a school here in Skull Creek."

Arguing about that was for Doc, not for his slave. Rune did not try.

"Doc's going in his cabin now," he reported, and fled across the street for instructions.

The storekeeper's inquisitive wife got in just ahead of him, and he found Doc explaining, "The lady is still too weak for the strain of entertaining callers, Mrs. Flaunce. The boy here is acting as amateur nurse, because she needs someone with her—she can't see, you know. But it would not be wise for anyone to visit her yet."

"I see," Mrs. Flaunce said with cold dignity. "Yes, I understand perfectly." She went out with her head high, not glancing at the cabin across the street.

Doc thus cut the lost lady off from all decent female companionship. The obvious conclusion to be drawn—which Mrs. Flaunce passed on to the other respectable women of the camp—was that the doctor was keeping the mysterious Miss Armistead. Ma Fisher's stern respectability was not enough to protect her, because Ma herself was strange. She chose to earn her living in a community where no sensible woman would stay if she wasn't married to a man who required it.

When Mrs. Flaunce was gone, Rune held out the greenback.

"She wants me to buy provisions with that. Enough for several days, she says."

Doc's eyebrows went up. "She does, eh? With five dollars? Why, that'd buy her three cans of fruit, wouldn't it? And how much is Flaunce getting for sugar, say?"

"Dollar a pound."

Doc scowled thoughtfully. "This is a delicate situation. We don't know how well fixed she is, but she doesn't know anything about the cost of grub in Skull Creek. And I don't want her to find out. Understand?"

Rune nodded. For once, he was in agreement with his master.

Doc reached into his coat pocket and brought out a leather poke of dust.

"Put that on deposit to her account at the store," he ordered.

"Lady coming in on the stage wouldn't have gold in a poke, would she?" Rune warned.

Doc said with approval, "Sometimes you sound real smart. Take it to the bank, get currency for it, and take the currency to Flaunce's. And just pray that Ma Fisher doesn't take a notion to talk about the price of grub. Let the lady keep her stake to use getting out of here as soon as she's able."

A week passed before he realized that Elizabeth Armistead could not leave Skull Creek.

5

Elizabeth could find her way around the cabin, groping, stepping carefully so as not to fall over anything. She circled sometimes for exercise and to pass the long, dark time and because she did not feel strong enough to think about important matters.

The center of her safe, circumscribed world was the sagging double bed where she rested and the table beside it, on which was the water bucket. She still clung to Frenchy Plante's canteen and kept it beside her pillow but only when she was alone so that no one would guess her foolish fear about thirst. But every few minutes she fumbled for the dipper in the bucket. She was dependent on strangers for everything, of course, but most important of them was Rune, who filled the water bucket at the creek that he said was not far outside the back door.

She had explored the cabin until she knew it well, but its smallness and scanty furnishings still shocked her. Papa's house back East had had nine rooms, and until his money began to melt away, there had been a maid as well as a cook.

She moved cautiously from the table a few steps to the front door—rough planks with a strong wooden bar to lock it from the inside; around the wall to a bench that Rune had placed so she would not hurt herself on the tiny stove; then to the back door.

But the need for decision gnawed at her mind and made her head ache.

"You must go back East just as soon as you can travel," Doctor Frail had said—how many times?

But how could she travel again when she remembered the Dry Flats that had to be crossed? How could she go without Papa, who was dead, they kept telling her?

The cabin was uncomfortably warm, but she could not sit outside the back door, where there was grass, unless Rune was there. And she must not open the door unless she knew for sure who was outside.

She could not go back East yet, no matter what they said. To stay in Skull Creek was, of course, an imposition on these kind people, but everything would work out all right after a while—except for Papa, who they said was dead.

She remembered what Papa had said when his investments were dwindling.

"We do what we must," he had told her with his gentle

smile when he made the hard decision to go West. And
so his daughter would do what she must.

I must find a place for the school, she reminded herself. Perhaps Mrs. Fisher will let me use this cabin. I
must offer her pay, of course, very tactfully so she will
not be offended.

It was a relief to keep her mind busy in the frightening
darkness, safe in the cabin with an unknown, raucous settlement of noisy men just outside the door. There were
women, too; she could hear their laughter and screaming
sometimes from the saloon down the street. But ladies did
not think about those women except to pity them.

They were very strange, these people who were looking
after her—Doc, who sounded strained and cross; Rune,
whose voice was sullen and doubtful: Mrs. Fisher, who
talked very little and came to the cabin only to groan into
bed. Elizabeth was a little afraid of all of them, but she
reminded herself that they were really very kind.

There was cautious knocking on the door, and she
called out, "Yes?" and turned. Suddenly she was lost in
the room, not sure of the position of the door. Surely the
knocking was at the back? And why should any of
them come that way, where the little grassy plot went
only down to the creek?

She stumbled against a bench, groping. The knocking
sounded again as she reached the door. But she was cautious. "Who is it?" she called, with her hand on the bar.

A man's voice said, "Lady! Lady, just let me in."

Elizabeth stopped breathing. The voice was not Doc
Frail's nor Rune's. But it was cordial, enticing: "Lady,
you ever seen a poke of nuggets? I got a poke of gold
right here. Lady, let me in."

She trembled and sank down on the floor in her darkness, cowering. The voice coaxed, "Lady? Lady?"

She did not dare to answer. She did not dare to cry.
After a long time the pounding and the coaxing stopped.

She could not escape any more by planning for the
school. She was remembering the long horror of thirst,
and the noise the mob had made, going past to hang a
man on a tree at the top of the hill. She hid her burned
face in her trembling hands, crouching by the barred

door, until a familiar and welcome voice called from another direction, "It's me. Rune."

She groped to the front door, reached for the bar. But was the voice familiar and therefore welcome? Or was this another importunate, lying stranger? With her hand on the unseen wooden bar, she froze, listening, until he called again. His voice sounded concerned: "Miss Armistead, are you all right in there?"

This was Rune. She could open the door. He was not offering a poke of nuggets, he was only worried about her welfare.

"I was frightened," she said as she opened the door.

"You're safer that way in Skull Creek," he said. "Anything you want done right now?"

"You are so kind," she said gently. "No, there is nothing. I have plenty of drinking water in the bucket. Oh—if you go to the store, perhaps there would be some potatoes and eggs?"

After a pause he said, "I'll ask 'em." (A month ago there had been a shipment of eggs; Doc had mentioned it. There had not been a potato in camp since Rune came there.)

"Doc says to tell you you'll have your unveiling this evening, get your eyes open. I got to go find him now, give him a message from the Crocodile."

"The—what?"

"Ma Fisher, I mean." She could hear amusement in his voice.

"Why, it's not nice to speak of her so. She is very kind to me, letting me share her home!"

There was another pause. He said, "Glad to hear it," and "I'll go find Doc now. He went to get a haircut."

Doc's haircut was important. He went often to the barbershop for a bath, because he could afford to be clean, but never before in Skull Creek had he let scissors touch his hair, hanging in glossy waves below his shoulders.

A miner might let his hair and whiskers grow, bushy and matted, but Doc Frail was different. His long hair was no accident, and it was clean. He wore it long as a challenge, a quiet swagger, as if to tell the camp, "You may make remarks about this if you want trouble." Nobody did in his presence.

Except the barber, who laughed and said, "I been wantin' to put scissors to that, Doc. You gettin' all fixed up for the lost lady to take a good look?"

Doc had dignity even in a barber's chair. "Shut up and tend to business," he advised. There was no more conversation even when the barber handed him a mirror.

Rune had too much sense to mention the reformation. The tall boy glanced at him, smiled tightly, and reported, "Ma Fisher wants to see you. She's tired of having the lost lady underfoot."

Doc snorted. "Ma has no weariness or distaste that a poke of dust won't soothe." He turned away, but Rune was not through talking.

"Can I come when you take the bandage off her eyes?"

"No. Yes. What do I care?" Doc strode away, trying to put his spirits into a suitably humble mood to talk business with Ma Fisher.

The girl was a disturbing influence for him, for Rune, for the whole buzzing camp. She must get out in a few days, but she must not be made any more miserable than she already was.

He did not wait for Ma Fisher to attack, from her side of the dirty wooden counter in her tent restaurant. He spoke first: "You would no doubt like to be paid for Miss Armistead's lodging. I will pay you. I don't want you to get the idea that I'm keeping her. My reason for wishing to pay is that I want her to keep thinking the world is kind and that you have welcomed her."

Ma Fisher shrugged. "You can afford it. It's an inconvenience to me to have her underfoot."

Doc put a poke on the counter. "You can heft that if you want to. That's dust you'll get for not letting her know she's unwelcome. You'll get it when she leaves, in a week or so."

Ma lifted the leather sack with an expert touch. "All right."

Doc swept it back again. "One compliment before I leave you, Mrs. Fisher: you're no hypocrite."

"Two-faced, you mean? One face like this is all a woman can stand." She cackled at her own wit. "Just the same, I'd like to know why you're willing to pay good clean dust to keep the girl from finding out the world is cruel."

"I wish I knew myself," he answered.

I'll take off the dressings now, he decided, and let her get a glimpse of daylight, let her see what she's eating for a change.

He crossed the street and knocked, calling, "Doc Frail here." Rune opened the door.

Elizabeth turned her face toward him. "Doctor? Now will you let me see again? I thought if you could take the dressings off now, you and Rune might be my guests for supper."

You and Rune. The leading citizen and the unsuccessful thief.

"I'll be honored," Doc replied. "And I suppose Rune realizes that it is an honor for him."

He removed the last dressings from her eyes and daubed the closed lids with liquid.

"Blink," he ordered. "Again. Now try opening them."

She saw him as a blurred face, close up, without distinguishing characteristics. The one who protected in the darkness, the one who had promised to bring light. The only dependable creature in the world. There was light again, she had regained her sight. She must trust him, and she could. He had not failed her in anything.

But he was a stranger in a world of terror and strangers. He was too young. A doctor should be old, with a gray chin beard.

"Hurts a little?" he said. "You can look around now."

He stepped aside and she was lost without him. She saw someone else, tall in the dimness; that was Rune, and he was important in her life. She tried to smile at him but could not tell whether he smiled back.

Doc said, "Don't look in a mirror yet. When your face is all healed, you will be a pretty girl again. Don't worry about it."

Unsmiling, she answered, "I have other things to concern me."

Elizabeth tried to make conversation as they ate the supper Rune had cooked. But now that she could see them dimly, they were strangers and she was lost and afraid.

"It's like being let out of jail, to see again," she offered. "At least I suppose it is. When may I go outside to see what the town is like?"

"There is no town, only a rough camp," Doc told her. "It's not worth looking at, but you may see it tomorrow. After sunset, when the light won't hurt your eyes."

The following day, after supper, when she heard knocking on the front door, she ran to answer. Dr. Frail had changed his mind about waiting until later, she assumed. He must have come back sooner than he had expected from a professional call several miles away.

She swung the door wide—and looked up through a blur into the black-bearded, grinning face of a stranger. Then she could not shut it again. A lady could not do a thing so rude as that.

The man swept off his ragged hat and bowed awkwardly. "Frenchy Plante, ma'am. You ain't never seen me, but we sure enough met before. Out on the Dry Flats."

"Oh," she said faintly. He looked unkempt and she could smell whiskey. But he had saved her life. "Please come in," she said, because there was no choice. She hoped he did not notice that she left the door open. With this man in the cabin, she wanted no privacy.

He remembered to keep his hat in his hand but he sat down without waiting to be invited.

"Figure on doing a little prospecting, ma'am," he said jovially. "So I just dropped in to say good-by and see how you're making out."

Frenchy was well pleased with himself. He was wearing a clean red shirt, washed though not pressed, and he had combed his hair, wanting to make a good impression on the lost lady.

"I have so much to thank you for," Elizabeth said earnestly. "I am so very grateful."

He waved one hand. "It's nothing, lady. Somebody would of found you." Realizing that this detracted from his glory, he added, "But of course it might have been too late. You sure look different from the first time I seen you!"

Her hands went up to her face. "Doctor Frail says there won't be any scars. I wish I could offer you some refreshment, Mr. Plante. If you would care to wait until I build up the fire to make tea?"

Doc Frail remarked from the doorway, "Frenchy would miss his afternoon tea, I'm sure."

There were a few men in the camp who were not afraid of Doc Frail—the upright men, the leading citizens, and Frenchy Plante.

Frenchy had the effrontery to suggest, "Come on in, Doc," but the wisdom to add, "Guess I can't stay, ma'am. Going prospecting, like I told you."

Doc Frail stood aside so as not to bar his progress in leaving. "I thought your claim was paying fairly well."

Frenchy made an expansive gesture. "Sold it this morning. I want something richer."

Elizabeth said, "I hope you'll find a million dollars, Mr. Plante."

"With a pretty lady like you on my side, I can't fail, can I?" replied the giant, departing.

Elizabeth put on her bonnet. With her foot on the threshold, she murmured, "Everyone is so kind." She took Doc's arm as he offered it.

"To the left," he said. "The tougher part of the camp is to the right. You must never go that way. But this is the way you will go to the hotel, where the stage stops. Next week you will be able to leave Skull Creek."

She did not seem to hear him. She trembled. She was staring with aching eyes at the rutted road that led past Flaunce's store and the livery stable, the road that took a sudden sweep upward toward a cottonwood tree with one great out-thrust bough.

"You are perfectly safe," Doc reminded her. "We will not go far this time. Only past the store."

"No!" she moaned. "Oh, no!" and tried to turn back.

"Now what?" Doc demanded. "There is nothing here to hurt you."

But up there where she had to go sometime was the hanging tree, and beyond was the desert. Back all that distance, back all alone—a safe, quiet place was what she must have now, at once.

Not here in the glaring sun with the men staring and the world so wide that no matter which way she turned she was lost, she was thirsty, burning, dying.

But there must be some way out, somewhere safe, the cool darkness of a cabin, if she could only run in the right direction and not give up too soon—

But someone tried to keep her there in the unendurable sun glare with the thirst and endless dizzying space—someone held her arms and said her name urgently from far away as she struggled.

She jerked away with all her strength because she knew the needs of her own anguished body and desperate spirit—she had to be free, she had to be able to hide.

And where was Papa, while this strange and angry man carried her back to the cabin that was a refuge from which she would not venture forth again?

And who was this angry boy who shouted, "Doc, if you've hurt her, I'll kill you!"

When she was through with her frantic crying and was quiet and ashamed, she was afraid of Doc Frail, who gripped her wrists as she lay on Ma Fisher's bed.

"What was it, Elizabeth?" he demanded. "Nothing is going to hurt you. What did you think you saw out there?"

"The Dry Flats," she whispered, knowing he would not believe it. "The glaring sun on the Dry Flats. And I was lost again and thirsty."

"It's thirty miles to the Dry Flats," he told her brusquely. "And the sun went down an hour ago. It's getting dark here in the gulch."

She shuddered.

"I'll give you something to make you sleep," he offered.

"I want Papa," she replied, beginning to cry again.

Back in his own cabin, Doc walked back and forth, back and forth across the rough floor boards, with Rune glaring at him from a corner.

Doc Frail was trying to remember a word and a mystery. Someone in France had reported something like this years ago. What was the word, and what could you do for the suffering patient?

He had three books in his private medical library, but they treated of physical ailments, not wounds of the mind. He could write to Philadelphia for advice, but—he

calculated the weeks required for a letter to go East and a
reply to come back to Skull Creek.

"Even if they know," he said angrily, "we'll be snowed
in here before the answer comes. And maybe nobody
knows, except in France, and he's probably dead now,
whoever he was."

Rune spoke cuttingly. "You had to be in such a hurry
to make her start back home!"

Doc said, "Shut your mouth."

What was the word for the mystery? Elizabeth remembered nothing about the runaway of the coach horses,
nothing about the holdup that preceded it, only the horror that followed.

"Hysteria?" he said. "Is that the word? Hysteria? But
if it is, what can you do for the patient?"

The lost lady would have to try again. She would have
to cross the imaginary desert as well as the real one.

6

I will not try to go out for a few days, Elizabeth told
herself, comforted by the thought that nobody would expect her to try again after what had happened on her first
attempt.

The desert was not outside the cabin, of course. It was
only a dreadful illusion. She realized that, because she
could look out and see that the street was in a ravine.
Nothing like the Dry Flats.

Next time, she assured herself, it will be all right. I will
not look up toward the tree where they—no, I will simply
not think about the tree at all, nor about the Dry Flats.
Other people go out by stage and nothing happens to
them. But I can't go right away.

Doctor Frail did not understand at all. He came over
the next morning, implacable and stern.

"I have a patient to see down at the diggings," he said,
"but he can wait half an hour. First you will walk with
me as far as Flaunce's store."

"Oh, I couldn't," she answered with gentle firmness.
"In a few days, but not now. I'm not strong enough."

He put his hat on the table and sat on one of the two benches.

"You will go now, Elizabeth. You have got to do it now. I am going to sit here until you are ready to start."

She stared at him in hurt surprise. Of course he was a doctor, and he could be expected to be always right. He was a determined man, and strength came from him. It was good, really, not to make a decision but to have him make it, even though carrying it out would be painful. Like the time Papa made her go to a dentist to have a tooth pulled.

"Very well," she replied with dignity. She put her bonnet on, not caring that there was no mirror.

"You are only going for a walk to the store," he told her, offering his arm at the door. "You will want to tell your friends back home what a store in a gold camp is like. You will have a great many things to tell your friends."

She managed a laugh as she walked with her eyes down, feeling the men staring.

"They would not believe the things I could tell them," she agreed.

The sun was not yet high over the gulch and the morning was not warm but she was burning and thirsty and could not see anything for the glare and could not breathe because she had been running, but he would not let her fall. He was speaking rapidly and urgently, telling her she must go on. He was not Papa because Papa was never angry; Papa would never have let her be afraid and alone in the glare and thirsty and going to die here, now, if he would only let her give up and fall. . . .

She was lying down—where? On the bed in the cabin? And turning her head away from something, the sharp odor of something the doctor held under her nose to revive her.

The men had seen her fall, then, the staring men of Skull Creek, and she had fainted, and they must think she was insane and maybe she was.

She was screaming and Doc Frail was slapping her cheek, saying, "Elizabeth! Stop that!"

Then she was crying with relief, because surely now nobody would make her go out again until she was ready.

The doctor was angry, a cruel man, a hateful stranger. Angry at a helpless girl who needed only to be let alone until she was stronger!

She said with tearful dignity, "Please go away."

He was sarcastic, too. He answered, "I do have other patients," and she heard the door close.

But she could not lie there and cry as she wanted to do, because she had to bar the door to keep out fear.

At noontime she was calmer and built a fire in the little stove and brewed some tea to eat with a cold biscuit of the kind Rune called bannock. Nobody came, and in the afternoon she slept for a while, exhausted, but restless because there was a great deal of racket from down the gulch.

Rune leaned against a building with his thumbs in his belt, watching two drunk miners trying to harness a mule that didn't want to be harnessed. Rune was amused, glad to have something to think about besides Doc Frail's cruelty to the lost lady.

"Leave her strictly alone till I tell you otherwise," Doc had commanded.

Rune was willing, for the time being. She had cold grub in the cabin and the water bucket was full. He didn't want to embarrass her by going there anyway. He had seen her stumble and struggle and fall. He had watched, from Doc's shack, as Doc carried her back to the cabin, had waited to be called and had been ignored.

The plunging mule kicked one of the miners over backward into the dust, while a scattering of grinning men gathered and cheered.

The other drunk man had a long stick, and as he struck out with it, the mule went bucking, tangled in the harness. A man standing beside Rune commented with awe and delight, "Right toward Ma Fisher's restaurant! Now I'd admire to see that mule tangle with her!"

He shouted, and Rune roared with him. A roar went up from all the onlookers as the far side of Ma Fisher's tent went down and Ma came running out on the near side, screaming. The mule emerged a few seconds behind her, but the drunk miner was still under the collapsed, smoke-stained canvas.

There was a frenzied yell of "Fire!" even before Rune

saw the smoke curl up and ran to the nearest saloon to grab a bucket.

They kept the flames from spreading to any buildings although the lean-to behind the tent was badly charred and most of the canvas burned.

Ma Fisher was not in sight by the time they got the fire out. Rune slouched away, grinning.

Ma Fisher made only one stop on the way from her ruined restaurant to the cabin. She beat with her fist on the locked door of the bank until Mr. Evans opened it a few inches and peered cautiously out.

"I want to withdraw all I've got on deposit," she demanded. "I'm going to my daughter's in Idaho."

He unfastened the chain on the inside and swung the door open.

"Leaving us, Mrs. Fisher?"

"Sink of iniquity," she growled. "Of course I'm leaving. They've burned my tent and ruined my stove, and now they can starve for all I care. I want to take out every dollar.

"But you needn't think I want to carry it with me on the stage," she warned. "I just want to make the arrangements now. Transfer it or whatever you do, so's I can draw on it in Idaho."

"Will you need some for travel expenses?" the banker asked, opening his ledger.

"I've got enough dust on hand for that. Just let me sign the papers and get started."

Rune, lounging in Doc's doorway, saw Ma Fisher jerk at her own door handle and then beat angrily with her fists, yelling, "Girl, you let me in! It's Ma Fisher."

She slammed the door behind her, and Rune grinned. He worried a little though, wondering how her anger would affect the gentle Miss Armistead. But he had his orders not to go over there. His own opinion was that the lost lady was being mighty stubborn, and maybe Doc Frail was right in prescribing the let-alone treatment till she got sensible.

Elizabeth listened with horror to Ma Fisher's description of the wrecking of her restaurant. Ma paced back and forth across the floor and she spat out the news.

"How dreadful!" Elizabeth sympathized. "What can I do to help you?"

Ma Fisher stopped pacing and stared at her. It was a long time since anyone had offered sympathy. Having had little of it from anyone else, she had none to give.

"I don't need nothing done for me," she growled. "I'm one to look after myself. Oh, laws, the cabin. I've got to sell this cabin."

"But then you'll have no place to live!" Elizabeth cried out.

"I'm going to Idaho. But I got to get my investment out of the cabin. You'll have to leave, Miss. I'm going tomorrow on the stage."

She was pacing again, not looking to see how Elizabeth was affected by the news, not caring, either.

"Man offered me five hundred dollars in clean dust for it not long ago, but I turned it down. Had to have a place to live, didn't I? Now who was that? Well, it won't be hard to find a buyer. . . . You've got your things all over the place. You better start packing. Could come on the same stage with me if you're a mind to."

Out into the open, away from refuge? Out across the Dry Flats—and before that, under the hanging tree? When she could not even go as far as Flaunce's store!

There was no one to help her, no one who cared what became of her. The doctor was angry, the boy Rune had deserted her, and this hag, this witch, thought only of her own interests. Papa had said, "We do what we must."

"I will give you five hundred dollars for the cabin," Elizabeth said coolly.

Doc Frail did not learn of the transaction until noon the next day. He had been called to a gulch ten miles away to care for a man who was beyond help, dying of a self-inflicted gunshot wound. Crippled with rheumatism, the man had pulled the trigger of his rifle with his foot.

Doc rode up to his own door and yelled, "Rune! Take care of my horse."

Rune came around from the back with the wood-chopping axe in his hand.

"Hell's broke loose," he reported. "Old lady Fisher left on the stage this morning, and the girl must be still in the cabin, because she didn't go when Ma did."

Doc sighed.

"Fellow that came by said she's bought Ma's cabin," Rune said, watching to see how Doc Frail would take that news.

Doc disappointed him by answering, "I don't care what she did," and went into his own building.

But while Rune was taking the mare to the livery stable, Doc decided he did care. He cared enough to cross the road in long strides and pound on the door, shouting, "Elizabeth, let me in this instant."

She had been waiting for hours for him to come, to tell her she had done the right thing, the only thing possible.

But he said, "If what I hear is true, you're a fool. What are you going to do in Skull Creek?"

She stepped back before the gale of his anger. She drew herself up very straight.

"Why, I am going to start a school for the children," she replied. "I have been making plans for it all morning."

"You can't. You can't stay here," Doc insisted.

"But I must, until I am stronger."

Doc glared. "You'd better get stronger in a hurry then. You've got to get out of this camp. You can start by walking up to the store. And I'll go with you. Right now."

Elizabeth was angry too. "I thank you for your courtesy," she said. "I must look out for myself now, of course." Looking straight into his eyes, she added, "I will pay your fee now if you will tell me what I owe."

Doc flinched as if she had struck him.

"There is no charge, madam. Call on me at any time."

He bowed and strode out.

He told Rune, "The order to leave her alone still stands," and told him nothing else.

Rune endured it for twenty-four hours. The door across the street did not open. There was no smoke from the chimney.

She's got just about nothing in the way of grub over there now, Rune fretted to himself. Ain't even building a fire to make a cup of tea.

But when Rune crossed the street, he did not go for pity. He had convinced himself that his only reason for

visiting Elizabeth was that Doc had forbidden him to go
there.

He knocked on the slab door but no answer came. He
pounded harder, calling, "Miss Armistead!" There was no
sound from within, but there was a waiting silence that
made his skin crawl.

"It's Rune!" he shouted. "Let me in!"

A miner, passing by, grinned and remarked, "Good
luck, boy. Introduce me sometime."

Rune said, "Shut your foul mouth," over his shoulder
just as the door opened a crack.

Elizabeth said coolly, "What is it?" Then, with a
quick-drawn breath like a sob, "Rune, come in, come in."

As she stepped away from the entrance, her skirt
swung and he saw her right hand with a little derringer in
it.

"The gun—where'd you get it?" he demanded.

"It was Papa's. They brought it to me with his things
after—" Remembering that she must look after herself,
not depending on anyone else, she stopped confiding.
"Won't you sit down?" she invited formally.

"I just come to—to see how everything is. Like if you
needed something."

She shook her head, but her eyes flooded with tears.
"Need something? Oh, no. I don't need a thing. Nobody
can do anything for me!"

Then she was sobbing, sitting on a bench with her face
hidden in her hands, and the little gun forgotten on the
floor.

"Listen, you won't starve," he promised. "I'll bring
your grub. But have you got money to live on?" He
abased himself, admitting, "I ain't got anything. Doc
don't pay me. If I had, I'd help you out."

"Oh, no. I will look after myself." She wiped her eyes
and became very self-possessed. "Except that for a while
I should appreciate it if you will go to the store for me.
Until I am strong enough to walk so far myself."

But Doc had said she was strong enough, and Doc
Frail was no liar. Rune scowled at Elizabeth. He did not
want to be bound to her by pity. It was bad enough to be
bound to Doc by debt.

This tie, at least, he could cut loose before it became a serious burden.

"You got to get out of Skull Creek," he said harshly. "Unless you've got a lot of money."

"I have sufficient," she said.

Now she was playing the great lady, he thought. She was being elegant and scornful.

"Maybe where you come from, folks don't talk about such things," he burst out with bitterness. "It ain't nice, you think. Don't think I'm asking how much you got. But you don't know nothing about prices here. You ain't been paying full price for what you got, not by a long ways. You want to know?"

She was staring at him wide-eyed and shocked.

"Sugar's ninety cents a pound at Flaunce's," he told her. "It went down. Dried codfish—you're tired of it, I guess, and so's everybody—it's sixty cents. Dried apples —forty cents a pound last time they had any. Maybe you'd like a pound of tea? Two and a half, that costs you. Potatoes and eggs, there ain't been any in a long time. Fresh meat you can't get till another bunch of steers come in. Now how long will your money last you if you stay in Skull Creek?"

She had less than five hundred dollars left after buying the cabin. Stage fare—that was terribly high. She had never had to handle money, and only in the last year had she even had to be concerned about it, since Papa's affairs had gone so badly.

But she said coolly, "I have a substantial amount of money, thank you. And I am going to start a school. Now tell me, please, who paid for my supplies if I didn't?"

Rune gulped. "I can't tell you that."

"So it was Doctor Frail," Elizabeth said wearily. "I will pay him. Tell him that."

"He'd kill me," Rune said. "Remember, I never said it was him."

Between two dangers, the lesser one seemed to be telling Doc himself. He did so at the first opportunity.

Doc did not explode. He only sighed and remarked, "Now she hasn't even got her pride. How much money has she got to live on?"

"She didn't tell me. Won't tell you, either, I'll bet."

"And she thinks she can make a fortune teaching school!" Doc was thoughtful. "Maybe she can earn part of her living that way. How many children are there in camp, anyway?" He scrabbled for a sheet of paper and began writing the names of families, muttering to himself.

"Go to the livery stable," he said without looking up, "and get a string of bells. They've got some. Then figure out a way to hitch them over her door with a rope that she can pull from inside her cabin."

"What for?" Rune demanded.

"So she can signal for help next time somebody tries to break in," Doc explained with unusual patience.

And what will I do to protect her when the time comes? Doc Frail wondered. Look forbidding and let them see two guns holstered and ready? That will not always be enough.

The noted physician of Skull Creek can outshoot anyone within several hundred miles, but will he fire when the target is a man? Never again. Then his hand and his eye lose their cunning, and that is why Wonder Russell sleeps up on the hill. If I could not pull the trigger to save the life of my friend, how can I do it for Elizabeth? I must have a deputy.

Rune was on his way out when Doc asked, "Can you hit a target any better than you dodge bullets?"

Rune hesitated, torn between wanting to boast and wanting to be taught by a master. If he admitted he was no marksman, he was not a complete man. But a slave didn't have to be.

He answered humbly, "I never had much chance to try. Target practice costs money."

"Stop at the store and get a supply of ammunition," Doc ordered. "I'm going to give you the world's best chance to shoot me."

Rune shrugged and went out, admitting no excitement. He was going to have his chance to become the kind of man from whose path other men would quietly step aside.

Doc watched him go, thinking, Are you the one for whom I'll hang? Put a gun in your hand, and skill with it, and there's no telling. But your lessons start tomorrow.

"I wish the school didn't matter so much to her," Doc muttered. "I wish she wasn't so set on it."

He had made some calls early that morning and was back in his cabin, scowling across the street at Elizabeth's, with its door standing open to welcome the children of Skull Creek.

Her floor was scrubbed; the rough plank table was draped with an embroidered cloth, and her father's books were on it. She visualized the children: shy, adorable, anxious to learn. And their mothers: grateful for a school, full of admonitions about the little ones' welfare, but trusting the teacher.

Doc turned to Rune, saw the rifle across his knees.

"You planning to shoot the children when they come?" he demanded.

"Planning to shoot any miner that goes barging in there with her door open," Rune answered. "Because I don't think there's going to be any children coming to school."

Doc sighed. "I don't either. After all the notes she wrote their mothers, all the plans she made."

At eleven o'clock, they saw Elizabeth shut her door. No one had crossed the threshold.

Doc growled, "Bring my mare. I've got a patient up the gulch. Then go see about getting her dinner."

Rune muttered, "I'd rather be shot."

Elizabeth had the derringer in her hand, hidden in a fold of her skirt, when she unbarred the door. She did not look at him but simply stepped aside.

"I don't care for anything to eat," she said faintly.

"If you don't eat nothing, I don't either."

She sipped a cup of tea, but she set it down suddenly and began to cry.

"Why didn't anybody come?" she wailed.

"Because they're fools," he told her sturdily.

But he knew why. He had guessed from the way the women acted when he delivered the notes. Elizabeth Armistead, the lost lady, was not respectable. She had come under strange circumstances, and the protection of Doc Frail was like a dark shadow upon her.

"I thought I would teach the children," she said hopelessly. "I thought it would be pleasant."

Rune drew a deep breath and offered her all he had—his ignorance and his pride.

"You can teach me," he said. "I ain't never learned to read."

The look of shock on her face did not hurt quite so much as he had supposed it would.

7

Early cold came to Skull Creek, and early snow. Halfway through one gloomy, endless morning, someone knocked at Elizabeth's door, but she had learned caution. She called, "Who is it?"

A voice she did not know said something about books. When she unbarred the door, the derringer was in her hand, but she kept it decently hidden in the folds of her skirt.

He was a big man with a beard. He swept off a fur cap and was apologetic.

"I didn't mean to frighten you, ma'am. Please don't be afraid. I came to see if you would rent out some of your books."

Elizabeth blinked two or three times, considering the matter. "But one doesn't rent books!" she objected. "I have never heard of renting books. . . . It's cold, won't you come in so I can close the door?"

The man hesitated. "If you're sure you will let me come in, ma'am. I swear I'll do you no harm. It's only for books that I came. Some of the boys are about to go crazy for lack of reading matter. We drew straws, and I got the short one. To come and ask you."

It's my house, Elizabeth told herself. And surely no rascal would care for books.

This man happened not to be a rascal, though he acted so fidgety about being in there that Elizabeth wondered who he thought might be chasing him.

"They call me Tall John, ma'am," he said in introduction, cap in hand. "Any book would do, just about. We've worn out the newspapers from the States and we're tired of reading the labels on canned goods. And the winter's only just begun."

He paid five dollars apiece for the privilege of keeping three books for a month. (His listeners, when he read aloud in a hut of poles and earth, were a horse thief, a half-breed Arapaho Indian and the younger son of an English nobleman.)

Doc scolded Elizabeth for letting a stranger in, although he admitted that Tall John was a decent fellow.

"He was a perfect gentleman," she insisted. What bothered her was that she had accepted money for lending books.

Rune complained bitterly because his book supply was cut by three.

"Listen, boy," Doc said, "you can read like a house afire, but can you write? Your schooling isn't even well begun. Do you know arithmetic? If you sold me eight head of horses at seventy dollars a head, how much would I owe you?"

"I wouldn't trust nobody to owe me for 'em," Rune told him earnestly. "You'd pay cash on the barrel head, clean dust, or you wouldn't drive off no horses of mine."

But thereafter his daily lessons in Elizabeth's cabin included writing, spelling and arithmetic. When the only books she had left were readers through which he had already ploughed his impetuous way, he was reduced to sneaking a look at the three medical books in Doc's cabin —Doc's entire medical library.

When Rune boasted of how much he was learning in his classes at the lost lady's cabin, Doc listened and was pleased.

"Each week, you will take her a suitable amount of dust for tuition," Doc announced. "I will have to decide how much it's going to be."

"Dust? Where'm I going to get dust?" Rune was frantic; the only delight he had was being barred from him, as everything else was, by his poverty.

"From me, of course. I can properly pay for the education of my servant, surely?"

"The lady teaches me for nothing," Rune said in defense of his privilege. "She don't expect to get paid for it."

"She needs an income, and this will help a little." Doc felt lordly. He was doing a favor for both his charges,

Rune and the pathetic girl across the street. "If you don't care to accept a favor from me," he told Rune, "you'd better get used to the idea." With a flash of insight, he explained, "It is necessary sometimes to let other people do something decent for you."

That is, he considered, it is necessary for everybody but me. And I have a sudden very excellent idea about the uses of gold.

He had an interest in several paying placer claims, which he visited often because the eye of the master fatteneth the cattle, and the eye of an experienced gold miner can make a shrewd guess about how many ounces there should be on the sluice riffles at the weekly cleanup. His various partners seldom tried to cheat him any more.

With the ground and the streams frozen, placer mining had come to a dead stop, but Dr. Frail's professional income had dwindled only a little, and there was so much dust to his credit with the bank that he had no financial problems anyway.

He strode up the street to visit Evans, the banker.

"Your dealings with your customers are strictly confidential, are they not?" he inquired.

"As confidential as yours," Evans replied stiffly.

"I want to make a withdrawal. The dust is to be put into leather pokes that can't be identified as the property of anyone around here. Old pokes, well worn."

"Very well," said Evans, as if it happened every day.

"Weigh it out in even pounds," Doc instructed, and Evans' eyebrows went up. "I want—oh, six of them. I'll be back for them this afternoon."

He sat with Elizabeth just before supper, drinking tea, listening to the sounds Rune made chopping firewood outside the back door. Rune had the bags of gold and orders to conceal them in the woodpile to be found accidentally.

"And remember, I know very well how much is in there," Doc had warned him. "I know how much she's supposed to find when she does find it."

Rune had glared at him in cold anger, replying, "Did you think I would steal from *her?*"

Tall John's shack burned when he built the fire too hot

on a bitter cold day. The three men who shared it with him were away. He ran out, tried to smother the flames with snow, then ran back to save what he could, and the roof fell in on him.

When help came, he was shouting under the burning wreckage. His rescuers delivered him to Doc's office with a broken leg and serious burns on his shoulders and chest.

Doc grumbled, "You boys think I'm running a hospital?" and started to work on the patient.

"He's got no place to go; our wickiup burned," the horse thief apologized. "The rest of us, we can hole up some place, but John can't hardly."

"He needs a roof over his head and conscientious nursing," Doc warned.

"I could sort of watch him," Rune suggested, wondering if they would sneer at the idea.

"Guess you'll have to," Doc agreed. "All right, he can have my bunk."

Then there was less company to help Elizabeth pass the time. Rune bought her supplies and carried in firewood, but he was always in a hurry. There were no more interesting evenings with Doc and Rune as her guests for supper, because Doc never stayed with her more than a few minutes.

Winter clamped down with teeth that did not let go. Elizabeth began to understand why Tall John had found it necessary to borrow books—she was reading her father's books over and over to pass the time. She began to understand, too, why a man of pride must pay for such borrowing.

She sewed and mended her own clothes until there was no more sewing to do. Doc commissioned her to make him a shirt and one for Rune. She finished them and was empty-handed again.

Then she peeled every sliver of bark from the logs that made her prison.

Rune came dutifully twice a day to bring supplies, and do her chores, but he no longer had lessons.

"Tall John's teaching me," he explained.

"And what are you studying?" she asked with some coolness.

"Latin. So I can figure out the big words in Doc's books."

"Now I wonder whether Papa brought his Latin grammar," she cried, running to look at the books she could not read.

"You ain't got one," Rune said. "I looked. We get along without. Sometimes we talk it."

"I didn't think anybody talked Latin," Elizabeth said doubtfully.

"Tall John can. He studied it in Rome. Told me where Rome is, too."

Elizabeth sighed. Her pupil had gone far beyond her.

She faced the bleak fact that nobody needed her at all any more. And Doc said there would be at least another month of winter.

"I don't want to impose on you, now that you're so busy," she told Rune with hurt dignity. "Hereafter I will bring in my own firewood and snow to melt for water. It will give me something to do."

"Don't hurt yourself," he cautioned. He didn't seem to see anything remarkable in her resolve to do hard physical labor. Elizabeth had never known any woman who carried water or cut wood. She felt like an adventurer when she undertook it.

Rune told Doc what she was planning, and Doc smiled.

"Good. Then you won't have to find what's in her woodpile. She can find it herself."

He visited her that evening, as he did once a day, briefly. She was a little sulky, he noticed, and he realized that she deserved an apology from him.

"I'm sorry not to spend more time in your company," he said abruptly. "There is no place I'd rather spend it. But for your own protection, to keep you from being talked about—do you understand why I'd rather not be here when Rune can't be here too?"

Elizabeth sniffed. "Have I any good name left to protect?"

The answer was No, but he would not say it.

"Rune says you're going to do your own chores," he remarked.

"Beginning tomorrow," she said proudly, expecting either a scolding or a compliment.

Doc disappointed her by saying heartily, "Good idea. You need some exercise."

Then he wondered why she was so unfriendly during the remainder of his visit.

Her venture into wood cutting lasted three days. Then, with a blister on one hand and a small axe cut in one shoe—harmless but frightening—she began to carry in wood that Rune had already chopped and piled earlier in the winter.

She was puzzled when she found a leather bag, very heavy for its size, and tightly tied. Unable to open the snow-wet drawstring with her mittened hands, she carried the bag into the house and teased the strings open with the point of a knife.

She glimpsed what was inside, ran to the shelf for a plate, and did not breathe again until the lovely yellow treasure was heaped upon it.

"Oh!" she said. "Oh, the pretty!" She ran her chilled fingers through the nuggets and the flakes that were like fish scales. "Maybe it belongs to Ma Fisher," she said angrily to the emptiness of the cabin. "But I bought the place and it's mine now. And maybe there's more out there!"

She found them all, the six heavy little bags, and completely demolished the neat woodpile.

Then she ran to the rope of the warning bells and pulled it for the first time, pulled it again and again, laughing and crying, and was still pulling it when Rune came shouting.

She hugged him, although he had a cocked pistol in his hand. She did not even notice that.

"Look!" she screamed. "Look what I found in the woodpile!"

Doc came to admire, later in the day, and stayed for supper, but Elizabeth was too excited to eat—or to cook, for that matter. The table was crowded, because all the golden treasure was on display in plates or cups. She kept touching it lovingly, gasping with delight.

"Now you know," Doc guessed, "why men search for that. And why they kill for it."

"I know," she crooned. "Yes, I understand."

He leaned across the table. "Elizabeth, with all that for a stake, you needn't be afraid to go out next spring, go home."

She caressed a pile of yellow gold. "I suppose so," she answered, and he knew she was not convinced.

The woodpile was a symbol after that. She restored the scattered sticks to make a neat heap, but did not burn any of them. She went back to chopping wood each day for the fire.

She was hacking at a stubborn, knotty log one afternoon, her skirts soggy with snow, when a man's voice not far behind her startled her into dropping the axe.

He was on the far side of the frozen creek, an anonymous big man bundled up in a huge and shapeless coat of fur.

"It's me, Frenchy," he shouted jovially. "Looks like you're working too hard for a young lady!"

Elizabeth picked up the axe. When the man who once saved your life speaks to you, you must answer, she decided. Especially when you had nobody to talk to any more.

"I like to be in the fresh air," she called.

He waded through the snow. "Let me do that work for you, little lady."

Elizabeth clung to the axe, and he did not come too close.

"Sure having a cold spell," he commented. "Been a bad winter."

This is my own house, Elizabeth told herself. This man saved my life on the Dry Flats.

"Won't you come in and thaw out by the stove?" she suggested. "Perhaps you'd like a cup of tea."

Frenchy was obviously pleased. "Well, now, a day like this, a man can sure use something hot to drink."

Elizabeth felt guilty, ushering him into her cabin by the back way, as if trying to hide her doings from her guardians across the street. But he had come the back way, and not until later did it occur to her that his choice of routes had been because he wanted to avoid being seen.

He sat across the table from her, affable and sociable, waiting for the tea to steep. When his clothing got warmed, he smelled, but a lady could not tell a guest that he should go home and take a bath.

Frenchy had in mind to tell a fine big lie and perhaps to get himself a stake. The lost lady, he guessed, had brought lots of money with her. For her Rune bought the very best supplies available. She was strange, of course, about staying in her cabin all the time, and he had seen her almost fall down in a kind of struggling fit when she went outside. But she was very pretty, and she was nice to him. Doc Frail was her protector, but Frenchy had a strong suspicion that Doc Frail was frail indeed.

Frenchy went into his lie.

"Just can't hardly wait for a warm spell. I got the prettiest little claim you ever seen—colors galore. I'm going to be the rich Mr. Plante, sure enough. That is," he sighed, "if I can just keep eating till the ground thaws."

He blew politely into his tea to cool it.

"Yes, sir," mused Frenchy, "all I need is a grubstake. And whoever stakes me is going to be mighty lucky. That's how Doc Frail made his pile, you know. Grubstaking prospectors."

He did not ask her for anything. He did not suggest that she stake him. She thought of it all by herself.

"Tell me more, Mr. Plante," she said. "Maybe I will stake you."

He argued a little—couldn't possibly accept a stake from a lady. She argued—he must, because she owed him her life, and she would like to get rich. How much did he need?

Anything, anything—but with prices so high—and he'd have to hire labor, and that came high, too—

She calculated wildly. Six pokes of gold, a pound in each one. She had no basis for computing how much a prospector needed.

"I will give you half of what I have," she offered. "And you will give me half the gold you find. I think we should have some sort of written contract, too."

Frenchy was dazzled. He had nothing to lose. He did not expect to have any gold to divide. His luck had been bad for months, and he intended to leave Skull Creek as soon as the weather permitted travel.

He dictated the contract as Elizabeth wrote in her prettiest penmanship, and both of them signed.

"The contract's yours to keep," he told her. It was a valid grubstake contract—if the holder could enforce it.

"I'll name the mine after you," he promised, vastly cheerful. "A few weeks from now—next summer anyway —you'll have to get gold scales to keep track of your take. When you see me again, you can call me Solid Gold Frenchy!"

At the Big Nugget, Frenchy took care to stand at the end of the bar nearest the table where Doc Frail was killing time in a card game.

The bartender was polite to Frenchy because business was poor, but his tone was firm as he warned, "Now, Frenchy, you know you ain't got no more credit here."

Frenchy was jovial and loud in his answer: "Did I say a word about credit this time? Just one drink, and I'll pay for it." He pulled out a poke.

Doc Frail was paying no attention to Frenchy and not much to the game. He took care to be seen in public most evenings, in the vain hope of weakening the camp's conviction that the lost lady was his property. He succeeded only in confusing the men, who felt he was treating her badly by leaving her in solitude.

Frenchy held up his glass and said with a grin, "Here's to the gold that's there for the finding, and here's to my grubstake partner."

Doc could not help glancing up. Frenchy had worn out three or four stakes already. Doc himself had refused him and did not know of a single man in camp who was willing to give him another start.

He looked up to see Frenchy grinning directly at him.

A challenge? Doc wondered. What's he been up to?

A suspicion of what Frenchy had been up to was like a burning coal in his mind.

Are you the man? he thought. Are you, Frenchy Plante, the man for whom I'll hang?

He stayed on for about an hour, until Frenchy had gone. He found Elizabeth in a cheerful mood, mending one of his shirts.

"The tea's been standing and it's strong," she apologized, getting a cup ready for him.

Drinking it, he waited for her to say that Frenchy had been there, but she only asked about Tall John's health.

Finally Doc remarked, "Frenchy Plante has suddenly come into comparative riches. He's got a grubstake from somewhere."

Elizabeth said mildly, "Is that so?"

"He said so when he bought a drink just now," Doc added, and Elizabeth was indignant.

"Is that what he's doing with it—drinking it up? I declare, I don't approve. I grubstaked him, if that's what you're trying to find out. But that was so he wouldn't starve and could go on mining when the weather moderates."

Doc said sadly, "Oh, Elizabeth!"

"It was mine," she maintained. "I simply invested some of it. Because I have plenty—and I want more."

Frenchy went on a prolonged, riotous and dangerous drinking spree. He was so violent that Madame Dewey, who kept the rooms above the Big Nugget, had him thrown out of there—at some expense, because two men were injured in removing him.

When he was almost broke, he really did go prospecting.

Doc and Rune treated Elizabeth with distant courtesy, mentioning casually the less scandalous highlights of Frenchy Plante's orgy. They did not scold, but their courtesy was painful. She had no friends any more, no alternately laughing and sarcastic friend name Joe Frail, no rude but faithful friend named Rune. They were only her physician and the boy who did her errands. She lived in a log-lined, lamp-lit cave, and sometimes wished she were dead.

There was a window by her front door; Rune had nailed stout wooden bars across it on the inside. For privacy, an old blanket was hung over the bars. She could peek through a small hole in the blanket for a narrow glimpse of the street, but nothing ever happened that was worth looking at. To let in daylight by taking the blanket off the window was to invite stares of men who happened to pass by—and sometimes the curious, yearning, snow-bound miners were too drunk to remember that Doc Frail was her protector, or if they remembered, too drunk to care.

One of them, who tried to get in one evening in mid-April, was cunning when he made his plans. He was sober enough to reconnoiter first.

He knew where Doc Frail was—playing cards at the Big Nugget, bored but not yet yawning. Rune was in Doc's cabin with a lamp on the table, bent over a book. Tall John was limping down the gulch with a lantern to visit friends. And Frenchy Plante, who had some right to the lady because he had found her, was somewhere out in the hills.

The intruder felt perfectly safe about the warning bells. If the lady pulled the rope, there would be no noise, because he had cut the rope.

Elizabeth was asleep on her bed, fully clothed—she slept a great deal, having nothing else to do—when knuckles rapped at the back door and a voice not quite like Doc's called, "Miss Armistead! Elizabeth!"

She sat up, frozen with fright. Then the pounding was louder, with the slow beats of an axe handle. She did not answer, and with senseless anger the man began to chop at the back door.

She ran and seized the bell rope. It slumped loose in her hands. She heard the dry wood crack and splinter. She did not even try to escape by the front door. She reached for the derringer that had been her father's, pointed it blindly and screamed as she pulled the trigger.

Then she was defenseless, but there was no more chopping, no sound at all, until she heard Rune's approaching shout. She was suddenly calm and guiltily triumphant. Making very sure that Rune was indeed Rune, she unbarred the front door and let him in.

"I fired the little gun!" she boasted.

"You didn't hurt anybody," Rune pointed out. The bullet had lodged in the splintered back door. "We'll just wait right here till Doc comes."

But Doc solved no problems when he came. He sat quietly and listened to Elizabeth's story.

"I don't know," Doc said hopelessly. "I don't know how to protect you." He motioned toward the shattered, splintered door. "Rune, fix that. I'll repair the bell rope."

Rune nailed the back door solid again and was noisy outside at the woodpile for a few minutes. When he came back, he said briefly, "Nobody will try that entrance again tonight. I'm going to bring blankets and sleep on the woodpile."

In Doc Frail's cabin he bundled blankets together. He straightened up and blurted out a question: "How much time do I still owe you?"

"Time? That old nonsense. You don't owe me anything. I just wanted to cut you down to size."

"Maybe somebody will cut you down to size sometime," Rune said. "I suppose you were never licked in your life. The great Joe Frail, always on top of the heap. It's time you got off it."

Doc said, "Hey! What's this sudden insurrection?"

"All you do is boss Elizabeth around. Why don't you get down on your knees instead? Didn't it ever dawn on you that if you married her, you could take her out of here to some decent place?" Rune was working himself up to anger. "Sure, she'd say she couldn't go, but you could make her go—tie her up and take her out in a wagon if there's no other way. How do you know the only right way to get her out of Skull Creek is to make her decide it for herself? Do you know everything?"

Doc answered, "No, I don't know everything," with new humility. He was silent for a while. "Don't think the idea is new to me. I've considered it. But I don't think she'd have me."

Rune picked up his blankets. "That's what I mean," he said. "You won't gamble unless you're sure you'll win." He slammed the door behind him.

8

When Doc set out to court Elizabeth Armistead, he put his whole heart into it, since this was what he had been wanting to do for a long time anyway. He was deferential and suitably humble. He was gentle. He was kind. And Elizabeth, who had never had a suitor before (except old Mr. Ellerby, who had talked across her head to her father), understood at once what Doc's intentions were.

He crossed the street more often and stayed longer. He came at mealtime, uninvited, and said he enjoyed her cooking. He even cut and carried in firewood. He brought his socks to be mended. They sat in pleasant domesticity at the table, while Elizabeth sewed and sometimes glanced across at him.

In his own cabin, Rune studied with the patient, Tall John.

And fifteen miles away, Frenchy Plante panned gravel. The ground had thawed, and rain made his labors miserable, but Frenchy had a hunch. Ninety-nine times out of a hundred, his hunches didn't pan out, but he trusted them anyway.

On a slope by a stream there was a ragged old tree. Beside it he had a pit from which he had dug gravel that showed occasional colors. He groaned out of his blankets one gray dawn, in his ragged tent, to find that the tree was no longer visible. Its roots washed by rain, it had fallen headfirst into his pit.

Frenchy swore.

"A sign, that's what it is," he growled. "A sign there wasn't nothing there to dig for. Damn tree filled up my pit. Going to leave here, never go back to Skull Creek."

But he had left a bucket by the tree, and he went for the bucket. The tree's head was lower than its roots, and the roots were full of mud, slick with rain. Mud that shone, even in the gray light.

He tore at the mud with his hands. He shelled out chunks like peanuts, but peanuts never shone so richly yellow. He forgot breakfast, forgot to build a fire, scrabbled in the oozing mud among the roots.

He held in his hand a chunk the size of a small crabapple, but no crabapple was ever so heavy.

He stood in the pouring rain with a little golden apple in his muddy hands. He threw his head back so the rain came into his matted beard, and he howled like a wolf at the dripping sky.

He staked his claim and worked it from dawn to dusk for a week, until he was too exhausted by labor and starvation to wash gravel any more. He might have died there in the midst of his riches, because he was too weak to go back to Skull Creek for grub, but he shot an unwary deer and butchered it and fed. The discovery that even he could lose his strength—and thereby his life and his treasure—frightened him. He caught his horse, packed up, and plodded toward Skull Creek, grinning.

He slogged down the gulch at dusk, eager to break the news to Elizabeth Armistead, but he had another important plan. He shouted in front of a wickiup built into the side of the gulch: "Bill you there? It's Frenchy."

The wickiup had been his until he sold it for two bottles of whiskey. Bill Scanlan looked out and said without enthusiasm, "Broke already? Well, we got beans."

A man known as Lame George, lying on a dirty blanket, grunted a greeting.

"Crowded here," he murmured. "But we can make room."

"Anything happening?" Frenchy asked, wolfing cold fried pork and boiled beans.

"Stages ain't running yet. This camp's played out. What'd you find?"

"Some good, some bad. Mostly bad." That was honest, not that honesty mattered much, and not that prospectors expected it even among friends. "I was thinking about that time the boys drove the mules through the old lady's tent. I bet there ain't been a funny joke like that for a long time."

Lame George said sadly, "There ain't, for a fact. Nothing much to do, nothing to laugh about. We been digging but couldn't raise a color."

"I got a good idea for a funny joke," Frenchy hinted. "On Doc Frail."

Lame George snorted. "Nobody jokes him."

"I'd make it worth a man's while," Frenchy said with great casualness, and Lame George sat up to demand, "What'll you do it with? You find something?"

"What you got, Frenchy?" Scanlan asked tensely.

"The joke," Frenchy reminded them. "What about the joke on Doc?"

"Hell, yes!" Lame George exploded. "Let us in on something good and we'll take our chances on Doc." He glanced at Scanlan, who nodded agreement.

"All I want," Frenchy explained, spreading his hands to show his innocent intentions, "is to make a social call on the lady, Miss Armistead, without getting my head blowed off. Is Tall John still living at Doc's?"

"He got better and moved to a shack. Rune still lives with Doc. But what," Lame George demanded with justifiable suspicion, "do you want with the lady?"

"Wouldn't hurt her for the world. Won't lay a hand on her. Just want to talk to her." Frenchy added with a grin, "Just want to show her something I found and brought back in my pocket."

They swarmed at him, grabbed his arms, their eyes eager. "You made a strike, Frenchy? Sure you did—and she grubstaked you!"

Elizabeth sat at the table, mending by lamplight. Doc was across from her, reading aloud to their mutual contentment. He sat in comfort, in his shirt sleeves, his coat and gun belt hanging on a nail by the front door. The fire in the cookstove crackled, and the teakettle purred.

Doc chose his reading carefully. In an hour and a half, he worked through portions of the works of Mr. Tennyson and Mr. Browning and, apparently by accident, looked into the love sonnets of William Shakespeare—exactly what he had been aiming at from the beginning.

"Why," Elizabeth asked, "are you suddenly so restless? Are you tired of reading to me?"

Doc discovered that he was no longer sitting. He was walking the floor, and the time had come to speak.

"My name," he said abruptly, "is not really Frail."

She was not shocked. "Why did you choose that one, then?"

"Because I was cynical. Because I thought it suited me. Elizabeth, I have to talk about myself. I have to tell you some things."

She said, "Yes, Joe."

"I killed a man once."

She looked relieved. "I heard it was four men!"

He frowned. "Does it seem to you that one does not matter? It matters to me."

She said gently, "I'm sorry, Joe. It matters to me, too. But one is better than four."

And even four killings, he realized, she would have forgiven me!

He bent across the table.

"Elizabeth, I enjoy your company. I would like to have it the rest of my life. I want to protect you and work for you and love you and—make you happy, if I can."

"I shouldn't have let you say that," she answered quietly. Her eyes were closed, and there were tears on her cheeks. "I am going to marry a man named Ellerby. And I expect I'll make his life miserable."

He said teasingly, "Does a girl shed tears when she mentions the name of a man she really plans to marry? I've made you cry many a time, but—"

He was beside her, and she clung as his arms went around her. He kissed her until she fought for breath.

"Not Ellerby, whoever he is, my darling. But me. Because I love you. When the roads are passable—soon, soon—I'll take you away and you'll not need to set foot on the ground or look at—anything."

"No, Joe, not you. Mr. Ellerby will come for me when I write him, and he will hate every mile of it. And I will marry him because he doesn't deserve any better."

"That's nonsense," Doc Frail said. "You will marry me."

Across the street, a man with a bad cold knocked at Doc's door. He kept a handkerchief to his face as he coughed out his message to Rune:

"Can Doc come, or you? Tall John's cut his leg with an axe, bleeding bad."

"I'll come," gasped Rune, and grabbed for Doc's bag. He knew pretty well what to do for an axe cut; he had been working with Doc all winter. "Tell Doc—he's right across the street."

"Go to Tall John's place," the coughing man managed to advise. As far as Rune knew, he went across the street to call Doc. Rune did not look back; he was running to save his patient.

When he was out of sight, another man who had been standing in the shadows pounded on Elizabeth's door, calling frantically, "Doc, come quick! That kid Rune's been stabbed at the Big Nugget!"

He was out of sight when Doc Frail barged out, hesitated a moment, decided he could send someone for his bag, and ran toward the saloon.

He tripped and, as he fell, something hit him on the back of the head.

He did not lie in the mud very long. Two men solicitously carried him back in the opposite direction and laid him in the slush at the far side of Flaunce's store. They left him there and went stumbling down the street, obviously drunk.

Frenchy Plante did not use force in entering Elizabeth's cabin. He knocked and called out, "Miss Armistead, it's Frenchy." In a lower tone, he added, "I got good news for you!"

She opened the door and demanded, "Is Rune hurt badly? Oh, what happened?"

"The boy got hurt?" Frenchy was sympathetic.

"Someone called Dr. Frail to look after him—didn't you see him go?"

Frenchy said good-humoredly, "Miss, I'm too plumb damn excited. Listen, can I come in and show you what I brought?"

She hesitated, too concerned to care whether he came in or not.

"Remember," he whispered, "what I said once about Solid Gold Frenchy?"

She remembered and gasped. "Come in," she said.

Doc reeled along the street, cold, soaking wet, and with his head splitting. He would have stopped long enough to let his head stop spinning, but he was driven by cold fear that was like sickness.

What about Elizabeth alone in her cabin? Where was Rune and how badly was he hurt? Doc was bruised and aching, tricked and defeated. Who had conquered him was not very important. Skull Creek would know soon enough that someone had knocked the starch out of Doc Frail without a shot being fired.

Rune, wherever he was, would have to wait for help if he needed it.

At Elizabeth's door Doc listened and heard her voice between tears and laughter: "I don't believe it! I don't think it's really true!"

The door was not barred. He opened it and stood watching with narrowed eyes. Elizabeth was rolling something crookedly across the table, something yellow that looked like a small, misshapen apple. When it fell and boomed on the floor boards, he knew what it was.

He asked in a controlled voice, "Has the kid been here?"

Elizabeth glanced up and gasped. She ran to him, crying, "Joe, you're hurt—what happened? Come sit down. Oh, Joe!"

Frenchy Plante was all concern and sympathy. "My God, Doc, what hit you?"

Doc Frail brushed Elizabeth gently aside and repeated, "Has the kid been here?"

"Ain't seen him," Frenchy said earnestly. "Miss Armistead was saying you'd been called out, he was hurt, so we thought you was with him."

Doc turned away without answering. He ran, stumbling, toward the Big Nugget. He stood in the doorway of the saloon, mud-stained, bloody and arrogant. He asked in a voice that did not need to be loud, "Is the kid in here?"

Nobody answered that, but someone asked, "Well, now, what happened to you?" in a tone of grandfatherly indulgence.

They were watching him, straight-faced, without concern, without much interest, the way they would look at any other man in camp. But not the way they should have looked at Doc Frail. There was nothing unusual in their attitudes, except that they were not surprised. And they should have been. They expected this, he understood.

"I was informed," Doc said, "that Rune had been knifed in a fight here."

The bartender answered, "Hell, there ain't been a fight here. And Rune ain't been in since he came for you two-three days ago."

Doc was at bay, as harmless as an unarmed baby. He turned to the door—and heard laughter, instantly choked.

Outside, he leaned against the wall, sagging, waiting for his head to stop spinning, waiting for his stomach to settle down.

There was danger in the laughter he had heard. And there was nothing he could do. Frail, Frail, Frail.

He realized that he was standing on the spot where Wonder Russell stood when Dusty Smith shot him, long ago.

He began to run, lurching, toward Elizabeth's cabin.

She was waiting in the doorway. She called anxiously, "Joe! Joe!"

Frenchy said, "I kept telling her you'd be all right, but I figured it was best to stay here with her in case anything else happened."

Doc did not answer but sat down, staring at him, and waited for Elizabeth to bring a pan of water and towels.

"Is Rune all right?" she demanded.

"I presume so. It was only a joke, I guess."

Golden peas and beans were on the table with the little golden apple. When Doc would not let Elizabeth help him clean the blood off his face, she turned toward the table slowly as if she could not help it.

"He named the mine for me," she whispered. "He calls it the Lucky Lady." Her face puckered, but she did not cry. She laughed instead, choking.

Rune came in at that moment, puzzled and furious, with Doc's bag.

"They said Tall John was hurt," he blurted out, and stopped at sight of Doc Frail.

"The way I heard it," Doc said across the towel, "you were knifed at the saloon. And somebody hit me over the head."

Rune seemed not to hear him. Rune was staring at the nuggets, moving toward them, pulled by the same force that had pulled Elizabeth.

Frenchy chortled, "Meet the Lucky Lady, kid. I got a strike, and half of it is hers. I'll be leaving now. No, the nuggets are yours, Miss, and there'll be more. Sure hope you get over that crack on the head all right, Doc."

Doc's farewell to Elizabeth was a brief warning: "Bar the door. From now on, there'll be trouble."

He did not explain. He left her to think about it.

She did not go to bed at all that night. She sat at the table, fondling the misshapen golden apple and the golden peas and beans, rolling them, counting them. She held them in her cupped hands, smiling, staring, but not dreaming yet. Their value was unknown to her; there would be plenty of time to get them weighed. They were only a token, anyway. There would be more, lots more.

She hunted out, in its hiding place, a letter she had written to Mr. Ellerby, read it through once, and burned it in the stove.

The golden lumps would build a wall of safety between her and Mr. Ellerby, between her and everything she didn't want.

She sat all night, or stood sometimes by the front window, smiling, hearing the sounds she recognized although she had never heard the like before: the endless racket of a gold rush. Horses' hoofs and the slogging feet of men, forever passing, voices earnest or anxious or angry, the creak of wagons. She listened eagerly with the golden apple cupped in her hand.

Even when someone pounded on her door, she was not afraid. The walls are made of gold, she thought. Nobody can break them down. A man called anxiously, "Lucky Lady, wish me luck! That's all I want, lady, all in the world I want."

Elizabeth answered, "I wish you luck, whoever you are," and laughed.

But when, toward morning, she heard an angry racket outside the back door, she was frightened for Rune. She ran to listen.

"I've got a gun on you," he was raging. "Git going, now!" And men's voices mumbled angrily away.

She spoke to him through the closed back door.

"Rune, go and get Doc. I have been making plans."

The three of them sat at the table before dawn. Coffee was in three cups, but only Rune drank his.

Doc listened to Elizabeth and thought, This is some other woman, not the lost lady, the helpless prisoner. This is the Lucky Lady, an imprisoned queen. This is royalty. This is power. She has suddenly learned to command.

"I would like to hire you, Rune, to be my guard," she began.

Rune glanced at Doc, who nodded. Rune did not answer. Elizabeth did not expect him to answer.

"I would like you to buy me a gold scale as soon as

possible," she continued. "And please find out from Mr. Flaunce what would be the cost of freighting in a small piano from the States."

Doc said wearily, "Elizabeth, that's defeat. If you order a piano and wait for it to get here, that means you're not even thinking of leaving Skull Creek."

"When I thought of it, thinking did me no good," she answered, and dismissed the argument.

"Rune, please ask Mr. Flaunce to bring over whatever bolts of dress material he has—satin, in a light gray. I shall have a new dress."

Rune put down his coffee cup. "You could build a lean-to on the back here. I'd ought to stay pretty close, and I don't hanker to sleep on that woodpile often."

She nodded approval. "And another thing: grubstaking Frenchy brought me luck. Other miners will think of the same thing, and I will grubstake them, to keep my luck."

Rune growled, "Nonsense. Hand out a stake to every one that asks for it, and you'll be broke in no time. Set a limit—say every seventh man that asks. But don't let anybody know it's the seventh that gets it."

Elizabeth frowned, then nodded. "Seven is a lucky number."

Doc picked up his cup of cool coffee.

A handful of gold has changed us all, he thought. Elizabeth is the queen—the golden Queen Elizabeth. Rune is seventeen years old, but he is a man of sound judgment —and he is the second best shot in the territory. And I, I am a shadow.

Doc said gently, "Elizabeth, there may not be very much more gold for Frenchy to divide with you. You are planning too much grandeur."

"There will be a great deal more," she contradicted, serenely. "I am going to be very rich. I am the Lucky Lady."

9

At the end of a single week, the fragility of the Skull Creek gold camp was plain. The town was collapsing, moving to the new strike at Plante Gulch.

The streets swarmed and boomed with strangers—but they were only passing through. Flaunce's store was open day and night to serve prospectors replenishing grub supplies and going on to the new riches. Flaunce was desperately trying to hire men to freight some of his stock on to the new diggings to set up another store before someone beat him to it.

Doc Frail lounged in his own doorway waiting for Rune to come from Elizabeth's cabin, and watched the stream of men passing by—bearded, ragged, determined men on foot or on horseback, leading donkeys or mules, driving bull teams with laden wagons, slogging along with packs on their shoulders. Almost all of them were strangers.

Let's see if I'm what I used to be, Doc thought, before Frenchy tricked me and got me hit over the head.

He stepped forward into the path of a pack-laden man, who was walking fast and looking earnestly ahead. When they collided, Doc glared at him with his old arrogance, and the man said angrily, "Damn you, stay out of the way," shoved with his elbow, and went on.

No, I am not what I used to be, Doc admitted silently. The old power, which had worked even on strangers, was gone, the challenge in the stare that asked, Do you amount to anything?

Rune came weaving through the crowd, and Doc saw in him power that was new. Rune looked taller. He wore new, clean clothing and good boots, although the gun in his holster was one Doc had given him months before. Rune was no longer sullen. He wore a worried frown, but he was sure of himself.

Doc pointed with his thumb to a vacant lot, and Rune nodded. It was time for his daily target practice, purposely public. In the vacant space where nobody would get hurt, Doc tossed an empty can, and Rune punctured it with three shots before it fell. The steady stream of passing men became a whirlpool, then stopped, and the crowd grew.

Someone shouted, "Hey, kid," and tossed another can. Doc's pistol and Rune's thundered a duet, and the crowd was pleased.

When Rune's gun was empty, Doc kept firing, still with

his right hand but with his second gun, tossed with a flashing movement from his left hand as the first weapon dropped to the ground. No more duet, but solo now, by the old master. He heard admiration among the men around them, and that was all to the good. It was necessary that strangers should know the Lucky Lady was well protected. The border shift, the trick of tossing a loaded gun into the hand that released an empty one, was impressive, but Rune had not yet perfected it enough for public demonstration.

That was all there was to the show. The crowd moved on.

"Go take yourself a walk or something," Doc suggested. "I'll watch Elizabeth's place for a while."

"There's a crazy man in town," Rune said. "Did you see him?"

"There are hundreds of crazy men in town. Do you mean that fanatical preacher with red whiskers? I've been on the edge of his congregation three or four times but never stopped to listen. I wouldn't be surprised if the camp lynched him just to shut him up."

"He scares me," Rune admitted, frowning. "They don't like him, but he gets everybody mad and growling. He don't preach the love of God. It's all hell fire and damnation."

Doc asked, suddenly suspicious, "Has he been to Elizabeth's?"

"He was. I wouldn't let him in. But when I said he was a preacher, she made me give him some dust. She'd like to talk to him, figuring she'd get some comfort. He's not the kind of preacher that ever comforted anybody. Go listen to him when you have time."

"I have more time than I used to," Doc Frail admitted. Two new doctors had come through Skull Creek, both heading for the booming new settlement at Plante Gulch.

Doc had an opportunity to listen to the preacher the next afternoon. The piano player at a dance hall far down the street threw his back out of kilter while trying to move the piano. Doc went down to his shack, gave him some pain killer and with a straight face prescribed bed rest and hot bricks.

The man squalled, "Who'll heat the bricks? And I

can't stay in bed—we've moving this shebang to Plante Gulch soon as they finish laying a floor."

"They need a piano player when they get there," Doc reminded him. "I'll tell the boss to see to it you get the hot bricks. You are an important fellow, professor."

"Say, guess I am," the man agreed. "Unless they get a better piano player."

Doc left the proprietor tearing his hair because of the threatened delay, then went out to the street. It was crowded with men whose movement had been slowed by curiosity, for across the street on a packing box the red-haired man was preaching.

His eyes were wild, and so were his gestures, and his sermon was a disconnected series of uncompleted threats. He yelled and choked.

"Oh, ye of little faith! Behold I say unto you! Behold a pale horse: and his name that sat on him was Death, and Hell followed with him! Verily, brethren, do not forget hell—the eternal torment, the fire that never dieth. And I heard a great voice out of the temple saying to the seven angels, go your ways, and pour out the vials of the wrath of God upon the earth.

"Lo, there is a dragon that gives power unto the beast, and you worship the dragon and the beast, saying, 'Who is like unto the beast?' And the dragon is gold and the beast is gold, and lo, ye are eternally damned that seek the dragon or the beast."

The preacher was quoting snatches of Revelation, Doc realized, with changes of his own that were not exactly improvements. But gold may be a dragon and a beast, indeed.

A man in the crowd shouted, "Aw, shut up and go dig yourself some beast!" and there was a roar of approving laughter.

"Remember Sodom and Gomorrah!" screamed the red-haired man. "For their wickedness they were burned—yea, for their sin and evil! Lo, this camp is wicked like unto those two!"

Doc Frail was caught in an impatient eddy in the moving crowd, and someone growled, "Give that horse a lick or we'll never get out of Sodom and on to Gomorrah by dark!"

The preacher's ranting stirred a kind of futile anger in Joe Frail. What makes him think he's so much better than his congregation? Doc wondered. There's a kind of hatred in him.

"A sinful nation," shouted the preacher. "A people laden with iniquity, the seed of evildoers, children that are corrupters. Hear the word of the Lord, ye rulers of Sodom; give ear unto the law of our God, ye people of Gomorrah!"

The Book of the Prophet Isaiah, reflected Joe Frail, who was the son of a minister's daughter. Immediately the red-haired man returned to Revelation:

"There is given unto me a mouth speaking great things, and power is given unto me to continue forty and two months!"

A man behind Joe Frail shouted, "We ain't going to listen that long."

"If any man have an ear, let him hear! He that leadeth into captivity shall go into captivity; he that killeth with the sword must be killed with the sword."

Joe Frail shivered in spite of himself, thinking, And he that killeth with a pistol?

In that moment a man's voice said behind him, *"That is the man,"* and Doc went tense as if frozen, staring at the red-haired madman.

"That's the man I told you about," the voice went on, moving past him. "Crazy as a loon. His name is Grubb."

How could it be? Doc wondered. How could that be the man for whom I'll hang?

After a few days, the madman went on to Plante Gulch.

By August, Elizabeth Armistead was rich and getting richer. The interior log walls of her cabin were draped with yards of white muslin, her furniture was the finest that could be bought in Skull Creek, her piano had been ordered from the East, and she dressed in satin. But only a few men ever saw her, only every seventh man who came to beg a grubstake from the Lucky Lady, and Frenchy Plante when he came to bring her half the cleanup from the mine.

This is Saturday, Doc Frail remembered. Cleanup day

at the sluices. Frenchy will be in with the gold. And I will spend the evening with Elizabeth, waiting for him to come. The Lucky Lady hides behind a golden wall.

He found Elizabeth indignantly arguing with Rune.

"Frenchy sent a man to say they have a big cleanup this time," she told Doc. "And they want a man with a reputation to help guard it on the way in. But Rune refuses to go!"

"I don't get paid to guard gold," Rune said. "I hired out to guard you."

"Half of it's mine," she argued.

"And half of it's Frenchy's. He'll look after it. The bank's going to open up whenever he comes. But I'm going to be right here."

Doc said without a smile, "Young lady, you seem to have a sensible fellow on your payroll," and was pleased to see Rune blush.

By George, he thought, that's probably the first decent thing I ever said to him!

"I'll be here, too," Doc promised. "Just making a social call."

He was too restless to sit down and wait. He stood in the doorway, looking out, thinking aloud: "The month is August, Elizabeth. The day is lovely, even in this barren cleft between barren hills. And you are young, and I am not decrepit. But you're a prisoner." He turned toward her and asked gently, "Come for a walk with me, Elizabeth?"

"No!" she whispered instantly. "Oh, no!"

He shrugged and turned away. "There was a time when you couldn't go because you didn't have any place to go or enough money. Now you can afford to go anywhere, but you've got a pile of nuggets to hide behind."

"Joe, that's not it at all! I can't go now for the same reason I couldn't go before."

"Have you tried, Elizabeth?"

She would not answer.

He saw that Rune was watching him with slitted eyes and cold anger in the set of his mouth.

"Maybe your partner will bring you some new and unusual nuggets," Doc remarked. "I wonder where he gets them from."

"From his mine, of course," Elizabeth answered. Her special nuggets were not in sight, but Doc knew they were in the covered sugar bowl on the table.

"Madam, I beg to differ. The Lucky Lady is a placer operation. Water is used to wash gold out of dirt and gravel. Most of your nuggets came from there, all right. But—spread them out and I'll show you.'"

Unwillingly, she tipped the sugar bowl. It was packed with gold; she had to pry it out with a spoon. And this was not her treasure, but her hobby, the private collection she kept just because it was so beautiful.

Doc touched a golden snarl of rigid strands. "That's wire gold, hardened when it cooled. It squeezed through crevices in rock. Rock, Elizabeth. That's hard-rock gold, not placer, and it never came from diggings within a couple of hundred miles from here. Neither did those sharpened nuggets with bits of quartz still on them. That gold never came from the mine Frenchy named for you."

Elizabeth stared, fascinated and frightened. "It was in with some other lumps he brought. Where did he get it?"

"He sent for it, to give you. Some men go courting with flowers. Frenchy gives his chosen one imported gold nuggets."

"Don't talk that way! I don't like it."

"I didn't suppose you would, but it was time to tell you."

Frenchy was cleverly succeeding in two purposes: to please Elizabeth and to taunt Joe Frail.

And we are harmless doves, both of us, Doc thought.

"I wish you'd keep those grubstake contracts at the bank," Doc remarked. Four of them were paying off, and some of the others might. "Why keep them in that red box right here in your cabin?"

"Because I like to look at them sometimes," she said stubbornly. "They're perfectly safe. I have Rune to guard me."

Doc smiled with one corner of his mouth, and she hastened to add, "And I have you, too."

"As long as I live, Elizabeth," he said gently.

Rune tried to clear the air by changing the subject. "I hear the preacher, Grubb, is back."

"Then I would like to talk to him," said Elizabeth. "If he comes to the door, please let him in."

"No!" Doc said quite loudly. "Rune, do not let him in. He's a lunatic."

Elizabeth said coolly, "Rune will let him in. Because I want to talk to him. And because I say so!"

Doc said, "Why, Elizabeth!" and looked at her in astonishment. She sat stiff-backed with her chin high, pale with anger, imperious—the queen behind the golden wall, the Lucky Lady, who had forgotten how vulnerable she was. Doc Frail, newly vulnerable and afraid since the great joke Frenchy played on him, could not stare her down.

"Rune," he began, but she interrupted, "Rune will let him in because I say so."

Rune looked down at them both. "I will not let him in, and not because Doc says to keep him out. I won't let him in—because he shouldn't get in. And that's how it is."

Doc smiled. "The world has changed, Elizabeth. That's how it is. Rune holds all the winning cards—and nobody needs to tell him how to play them."

Rune guessed dimly in that moment that, no matter how long he lived or what he accomplished to win honor among men, he would never be paid any finer compliment.

"Guess I'll go see what's doing around town," he said, embarrassed.

"Both of you can go!" Elizabeth cried in fury.

To her surprise, Doc answered mildly, "All right," and she was left alone. The nuggets from the sugar bowl were scattered on the table. She touched them, fondled them, sorted them into heaps according to size and shape. She began to forget anger and imprisonment. She began to forget that she was young and far from home.

Doc Frail was only a hundred yards away from the cabin when a messenger on a mule hailed him: "Hey, Doc! My partner Frank's hurt up at our mine. There's three men trying to get him out, or hold up the timbering anyway."

He flung himself off the mule and Doc, who had his

satchel, leaped into the saddle. He knew where the mine was.

"Send some more men up there," he urged, and started for it.

Rune, strolling, saw him go and turned at once back to the Lucky Lady's cabin. He did not go in. He hunkered down by the front door and began to whittle.

Down beyond the Big Nugget, the red-haired man was preaching a new sermon, lashing himself to fury—and attracting a more favorably inclined audience than usual. His topic was the Lucky Lady. There was no more fascinating topic in Skull Creek, for she was young and desirable and mysterious, and she represented untold riches, even to men who had never seen her, who knew her only as a legend.

"Lo, there is sin in this camp, great sin!" Grubb was intoning. "The sin that locketh the door on deliverance, that keepeth a young woman prisoner against her will. There is a wicked man who shutteth her up in a cabin, that she escape not, and putteth a guard before her door that righteousness may not enter!"

His listeners were strangers. They believed him, because why not?

One nudged another and murmured, "Say, did you know that?" The other shook his head, frowning.

"She cannot be delivered from evil," intoned Grubb, "because evil encompasseth her round about. She has no comfort within those walls because the servant of the Lord is forbidden to enter."

Someone asked, "Did you try?"

Grubb had tried just once, weeks earlier. But he remembered it as today, and anger was renewed in him. He began to yell.

"Verily, the servant of the Lord tried to enter, to pray with her for deliverance, to win her from evil. But the guard at the door turned him away and bribed him with nuggets. Lo, the guard was as evil as the master, and both of them are damned!"

His audience saw what he saw, the arrogant doctor who would not let the Lucky Lady go, and the young man who idled at her doorway to keep rescuers away. His audience stirred and murmured, and someone said, "By

damn, that's a bad thing!" His audience increased, and
Grubb, for once delivering a message to which men listened without reviling him, went on screaming words that
he convinced himself were true.

One man on the edge of the crowd walked away—the
horse thief who was a friend of Tall John, and of Doc
who had cured him, and of Rune who had nursed him.
The horse thief passed the barbershop and observed that
Frenchy Plante was inside, getting his hair cut. Frenchy's
mule was hitched in front, and the gold from the weekly
cleanup was no doubt in the pack on the mule. But Frenchy was watching from the barber chair with a rifle across
his knees, so the horse thief did not linger.

Walking fast, but not running, he paused in front of
the Lucky Lady's cabin and spoke quietly to Rune:

"The red-haired fellow is raising hell, working the men
up. Saying the girl could get away if it wasn't Doc pays
you to keep her locked up. Don't act excited, kid. We're
just talking about the weather. I think there's going to be
hell to pay, and I'll go tell Tall John. Where's Doc?"

"Went on a call, on Tim Morrison's mule—to Tim's
mine, I guess. Thanks."

Unhurried, Rune entered the Lucky Lady's cabin and
sat down.

The horse thief, who did not happen to possess a horse
just then, went to the livery stable and rented one. At a
trot, he rode to the place where Tall John was washing
gravel. Tall John dropped his pick and said, "Go look for
Doc." He himself started back toward Elizabeth's cabin
at a brisk limp.

Tall John observed that a fairly large crowd had gathered down beyond the Big Nugget, and occasionally a
shout came from it.

If they ever get into her cabin, he told himself, they'll
have to kill the boy first—and if that happens, she won't
care to live either. He and I, between us, will have to
keep Frenchy out. Heaven forbid that he should be her
rescuer!

Tall John knocked on Elizabeth's door and after he
identified himself, Rune let him in. He sat down to chat
as if he had come only for a friendly visit.

The horse thief met Doc Frail walking. The man trapped in the cave-in had died. He was still trapped.

"There's trouble," the horse thief said bluntly, and told him what the trouble was.

"I'll take that horse, please," Doc replied. He rode at a trot; he did not dare attract attention by going faster. And he did not know what he was going to do when he got to the cabin—if he got there.

It is too late to try to take her out of Skull Creek now, he realized. I wonder how much ammunition Rune has. I haven't much—and what can I do it with anyway, except to shoot through the roof and make a noise?

He heard Frenchy shout "Hey Doc!" from down the street, but he did not turn.

The crowd beyond the Big Nugget was beginning to stir and to scatter on the edges. Rune, watching from a peephole in the blanket on the window, let Doc in before he had a chance to knock.

The three inside the cabin were still as statues. Elizabeth said, "They've just told me. Joe, I'll go out when they come in and I'll tell Grubb it isn't so."

"You'll stay right here," Doc answered. "I hope you will not think I am being melodramatic, but I have to do something that I have been putting off for too long. Tall John, can I make a legal will by telling it to you? There's not time to write it. I want to watch that window."

Elizabeth gasped.

Tall John said, "Tell me. I will not forget."

"My name is Joseph Alberts. I am better known as Joseph Frail. I am of sound mind but in imminent danger of death. I bequeath two thousand dollars in clean gulch gold to—Rune, what's your name?"

Rune answered quietly, "Leonard Henderson."

"To Leonard Henderson, better known as Rune, to enable him to get a medical education if he wants it. Everything else I leave to Elizabeth Armistead, called the Lucky Lady."

"Oh, so lucky!" she choked.

He did not say that he wanted Rune to take her away from Skull Creek. It was not necessary.

"That mob is getting noisier," Doc commented. "Tall John, you'd better go out by the back door."

"I will not forget," Tall John promised. He left the cabin, not stopping even to shake hands.

Just outside the window, Frenchy shouted, "Lucky Lady! I got gold for you! Open the door for Frenchy, Lucky Lady."

No one inside the cabin moved. No one outside could see in.

Frenchy hiccuped and said, "Aw, hell, she ain't home." He rode on, then shouted, "But she's always home, ain't she?"

Doc spoke rapidly. "If I go out this door, both of you stay inside—and bar it. Do you understand?"

"I get it," Rune replied. Elizabeth was crying quietly.

Frenchy's voice came back. "Doc, you in there? Hey, Doc Frail! Come on out. You ain't scared, are you?"

Joe Frail went tense and relaxed with an effort of will.

"You wouldn't shoot me, would you, Doc?" Frenchy teased. "You wouldn't shoot nobody, would you, Doc?" He laughed uproariously, and Doc Frail did not move a muscle.

He heard the muttering mob now, the deep, disturbed murmur that he had heard from the hill on the day the road agent swung from a bough of the great tree.

He heard a shrill scream from Grubb, who saw Frenchy coaxing at the window and had seen Frenchy enter the cabin before.

Grubb's topic did not change, but his theme did, as he led his congregation. His ranting voice reached them:

"Wicked woman! Wicked and damned! Will all your gold save you from hell fire? Wanton and damned—"

Doc forgot he was a coward. He forgot a man lying dead in Utah. He forgot Wonder Russell, sleeping in a grave on the hill. He slammed the bar upward from the door and stepped into the street.

His voice was thunder: "Grubb, get down on your knees!"

Grubb was blind to danger. He did not even recognize Doc Frail as an obstacle. Clawing the air, he came on, screaming, "Babylon and the wicked woman—"

Doc Frail gasped and shot him.

He did not see Grubb fall, for the mob's wrath downed

him. The last thing he heard as he went down under the deluge was the sound he wanted to hear: the bar falling shut inside the cabin door.

10

The rabble. The rabble. The first emotion he felt was contempt. Fear would come later. But no; fear had come. His mouth was cotton-dry.

He was bruised and battered, had been unconscious. He could not see the men he heard and despised. He lay face down on dirty boards and could see the ground through a crack. On a platform? No, his legs were bent and cramped. He was in a cart. He could not move his arms. They were bound to his body with rope.

The rabble shouted and jeered, but not all the jeering was for him—they could not agree among themselves. He knew where he was; under the hanging tree.

A voice cried furiously, "A trial! You've got to give the man a trial!"

Another shout mounted: "Sure, try him—he shot the preacher!"

This is the place and this is the tree, Joe Frail understood, and the rope must be almost ready. Grubb was the man, and I hardly knew he existed.

There was nothing that required doing. Someone else would do it all. There was something monstrous to be concerned about—but not for long.

And there was Elizabeth.

Joe Frail groaned and strained at the rope that bound him, and he heard Frenchy laugh.

"Let the boys see you, Doc," Frenchy urged. "Let 'em have a last good look!"

Someone heaved him to his feet and he blinked through his hair, fallen down over his eyes. The mob turned quiet, staring at a man who was as good as dead.

There was no need for dignity now, no need for anything. If he swayed, someone supported him. If he fell, they would stand him on his feet again. Everything that was to be done would be done by someone else. Joe Frail had no responsibilities any more. (Except—Elizabeth? Elizabeth?)

"Hell, that's no decent way to do it," someone argued with authority, not asking for justice but only for a proper execution. "The end of the cart will catch his feet that way. Put a plank across it. Then he'll get a good drop."

There was busy delay while men streamed down the hill to get planks

Joe Frail threw back his head with the old arrogant gesture and could see better with his hair tossed away from his eyes. He could see Skull Creek better than he wanted to, as clearly as when he first walked under the tree with Wonder Russell.

Elizabeth, Elizabeth. He was shaken with anger. When a man is at his own hanging, he should not have to think of anyone but himself.

And still, he understood, even now Joe Frail must fret helplessly about Elizabeth. Who ever really died at peace except those who had nothing to live for?

Men were coming with planks—four or five men, four or five planks. They busied themselves laying planks across the cart to make a platform so they could take satisfaction in having hanged him decently and with compassion. And from the side, Frenchy was bringing up a team of horses to pull the cart away.

Someone behind him slipped a noose down over his head, then took it off again, testing the length of the rope. Above, someone climbed along the out-thrust bough of the tree to tie it shorter. Joe Frail stood steady, not looking up, not glancing sideways at the horses being urged into position.

The crowd was quieter now, waiting.

Just as the team came into position in front of the cart, he saw movement down in the street of Skull Creek and strained forward.

Elizabeth's door had opened and Rune had come out of her cabin.

No! No! You damn young fool, stay in there and do what you can to save her! By tomorrow, they'll slink off like dogs and you can get her away safely. You fool! You utter fool!

What's he carrying? A red box.

No, Elizabeth! Oh, God, not Elizabeth! Stay in the cabin! Stay out of sight!

But the Lucky Lady had emerged from her refuge and was walking beside Rune. Walking fast, half running, with her head bent. Don't look, Elizabeth! My darling, don't look up! Turn back, turn back to the cabin. Tomorrow you can leave it.

A man behind Doc remarked, "Well, would you look at that!" but nobody else seemed to notice.

Doc said sharply, "What the hell are you waiting for?" Suddenly he was in a hurry. If they finished this fast enough, she would go back—Rune would see to it.

She was leaning forward against the wind of the desert that was thirty miles away. She was stumbling. But she did not fall. She had got past Flaunce's store.

The red box Rune is carrying? The box she keeps her gold in. Go back. Go back.

Someone slipped the noose down over his head again and he groaned and was ashamed.

She was struggling up the first slope of the barren hill, fighting the desert. Her right arm was across her eyes. But Doc could see Rune's face. Rune was carrying the heavy box and could not help the Lucky Lady, but the look on his face was one Doc had seen there seldom. It was pity.

The team was ready, the platform was prepared, the noose was around the condemned man's neck. The Lucky Lady stopped halfway up the hill.

There was almost no sound from the rabble except their breathing. Some of them were watching Elizabeth. She lifted her right hand and fired a shot from the derringer into the air.

Then they all watched her. The silence was complete and vast. The men stared and waited.

Rune put the red box on the ground and opened it, handed something to Elizabeth—a poke, Doc thought. She emptied it into her hand and threw nuggets toward the silent mob.

No one moved. No one spoke or even murmured.

Why, Rune has no gun, Doc saw. It is a long time since I have seen him with no holster on his hip. And

Elizabeth has fired into the air the one shot her pistol will hold. They are unarmed, helpless. As helpless as I am.

The voice he heard was his own, screaming, "Go back! Go back!"

A man behind him rested a hand on his shoulder without roughness, as if to say, Hush, hush, this is a time for silence.

Elizabeth stooped again to the box and took out something white—the sugar bowl. She flung the great, shining nuggets of her golden treasure, two and three at a time, toward the motionless men on the slope. Then they were not quite motionless, there was jerky movement among them, instantly ceasing, as they yearned toward the scattered treasure but would not yield.

Elizabeth stood for a while with her head bent and her hands hanging empty. Joe Frail saw her shoulders move as she gulped in great breaths of air. Rune stood watching her with that look of pity twisting his mouth.

She bent once more and took out a folded paper, held it high, and gave it to the wind. It sailed a little distance before it reached the ground. She waited with her head bowed, and the mob waited, stirring with the restless motion of puzzled men.

She tossed another paper and another. Someone asked the air a question: "Contracts? Grubstake contracts?"

And someone else said, "But which ones?"

Most of the contracts had no meaning any more, but a very few of them commanded for the Lucky Lady half the golden treasure that sifted out of paying mines.

Frenchy's voice roared with glee: "She's buying Doc Frail! The Lucky Lady is buying her man!"

Joe Frail quivered, thinking, This is the last indignity. She has gambled everything, and there will be nothing for her to remember except my shame.

All the contracts, one at a time, she offered to the mob, and the wind claimed each paper for a brief time. All the nuggets in the sugar bowl. All the pale dust in the little leather bags that made the red box heavy.

Elizabeth stood at last with her hands empty. She touched the box with her foot and Rune lifted it, turned it upside down to show that it held nothing more, and let it fall.

Frenchy's shout and Frenchy's forward rush broke the mob's indecision. He yelled, "Come and git it, boys! Git your share of the price she's paying for Doc Frail!"

Frenchy ran for the scattered papers, tossed away one after another, then held one up, roaring, and kissed it.

The rabble broke. Shouting and howling, the mob scattered, the men scrabbled for gold in the dust. They swarmed like vicious ants, fighting for the treasure.

A jeering voice behind Doc said, "Hell, if she wants you that bad!" and cut the rope that bound him. The knife slashed his wrist and he felt blood run.

The Lucky Lady was running up the slope to him, not stumbling, not hesitating, free of fear and treasure, up toward the hanging tree. Her face was pale, but her eyes were shining.

ABOUT DOROTHY M. JOHNSON

Dorothy M. Johnson was born in Iowa, and grew up in Whitefish, Montana, a little town lying along the Great Northern Railroad in the northwest corner of that state. Here she passed her childhood, absorbing the legends and stories of mountain men and Cheyenne, of miners and outlaws, of homesteaders and drifters, which she was later to draw upon in her stories.

After graduating from the University of Montana, she worked as a secretary in Washington and Wisconsin. For the next fifteen years she was a book and magazine editor in New York. Then in 1950 she returned to Whitefish for a vacation. She flew to New York to resign her position, and became news editor for the weekly Whitefish Pilot. In 1953, twenty-five years after leaving the MSU campus in Missoula, she returned to it as secretary-manager of the Montana State Press Association and is assistant professor in the School of Journalism.

The Western Writers of America have given Miss Johnson their highest honor: the 1957 Spur Award, which annually goes to the best short story of the West.